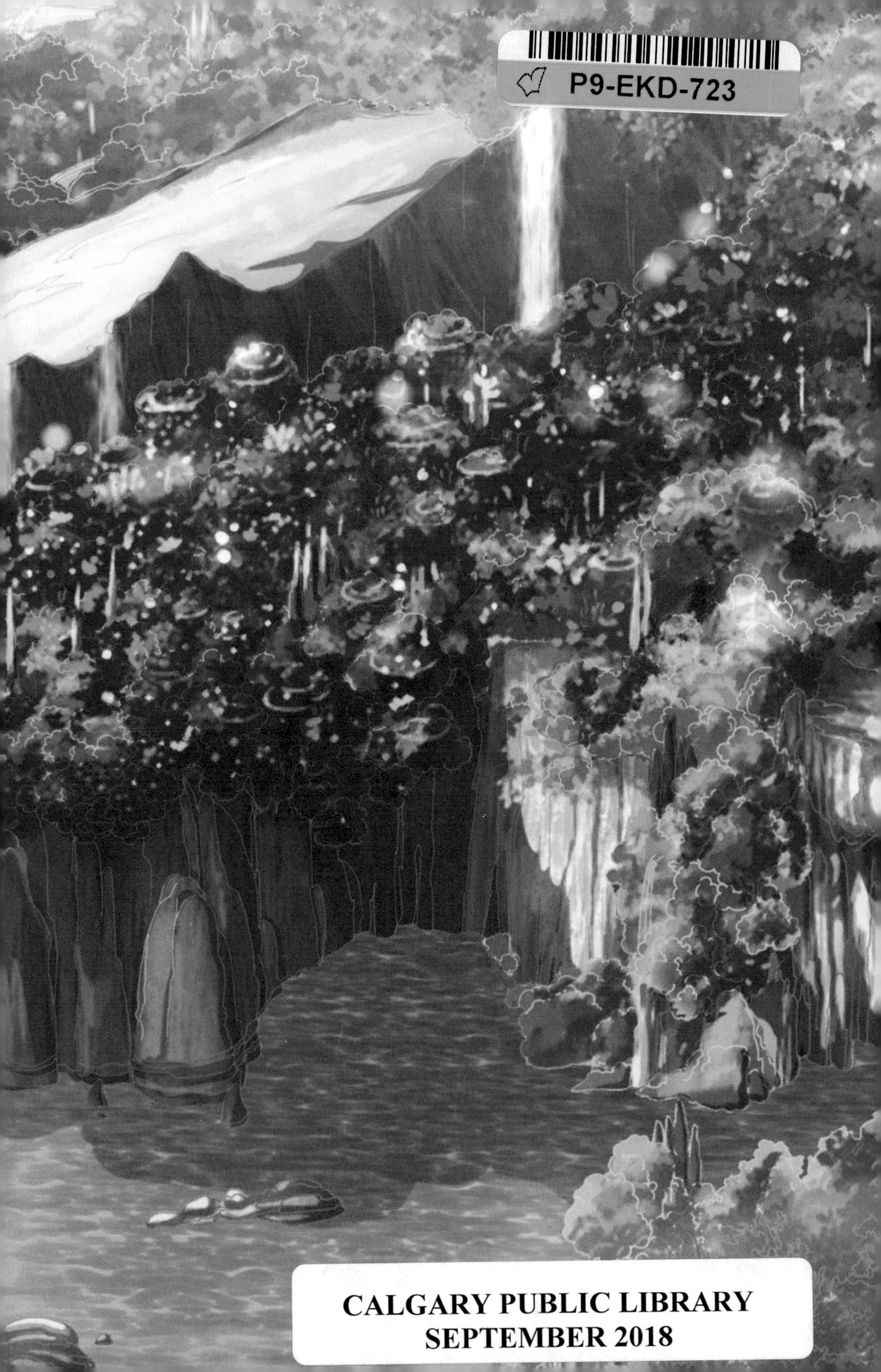

Regal Academy™

PAPERCUTZ™

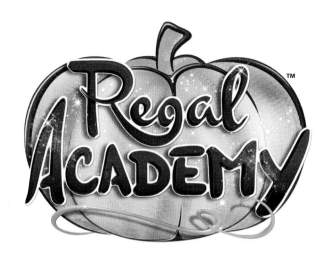

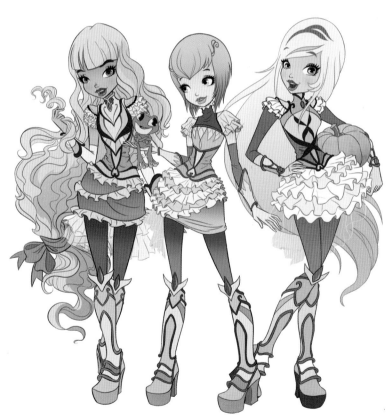

Use either the QR code or this link:

http://www.regalacademy.com/en/download/pap355

to download your exclusive digital REGAL ACADEMY booklet. Enjoy!

#2 "The First Ball"

Regal Academy™© 2018 Rainbow S.r.l. All rights reserved. Regal Academy™ names, characters and related indicia are copyright, trademark and exclusive license of Rainbow S.r.l. Series created and directed by Iginio Straffi. www.regalacademy.com

"The First Ball"
Script: Rainbow Srl/Luana Vergari
Comics: Rainbow Srl/Red Whale

"The Forge Dragon"
Script: Rainbow Srl/Luana Vergari
Comics: Rainbow Srl/Red Whale

"The Croaky Queen"
Script: Rainbow Srl/Luana Vergari
Comics: Rainbow Srl/Red Whale

"Behind the Canvas"
Script: Rainbow Srl/Luana Vergari
Comics: Rainbow Srl/Red Whale

Papercutz books may be purchased for business or promotional use. For information on bulk purchases please contact Macmillan Corporate and Premium Sales Department at (800) 221-7945 x5442

Lettering and Production – Manosaur Martin
Editorial Intern – Spenser Nellis
Editor – Jeff Whitman
Jim Salicrup
Editor-in-Chief

PB ISBN: 978-1-62991-885-3
HC ISBN: 978-1-62991-886-0

Printed in China
January 2018

Distributed by Macmillan
First Papercutz Printing

Regal Academy™

#2 "The First Ball"

Table of Contents

PAPERCUTZ™
New York

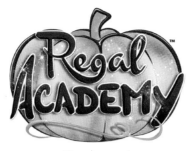

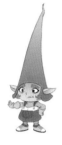

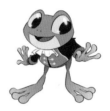

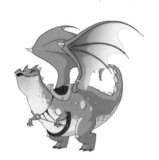

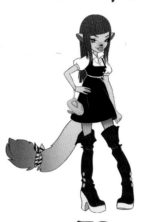

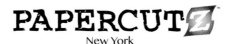

Get to know Regal Academy!

ROSE CINDERELLA

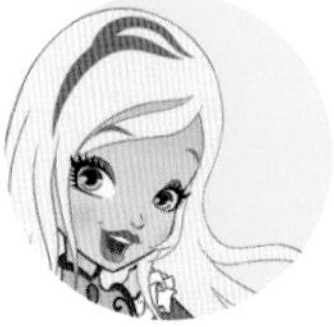

Rose is a modern teenager who never lost her love of fairy tales. Having grown up on Earth, she constantly experiences a "culture shock" between her modern, shoe-filled life on Earth and the magical Fairy Tale Land. She is a very positive girl who thinks everything is great all the time. She is happy even if she gets the worst grades in her class! She is never sad or disappointed but always full of sunshine, acting as a ray of hope for the team.

TRAVIS BEAST

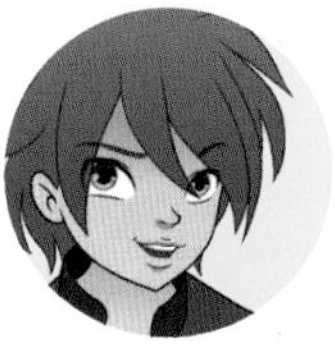

Travis is a frail, artsy sort of boy, but when he gets angry he becomes a real Beast! When it comes to getting physical though, he would much rather focus on his artistic skills. He is a true artist thanks to the talent inherited from Beauty, his grandmother, but he is totally underrated. Since he comes from Earth, Travis manages to recreate very beautiful paintings and sculptures inspired by earthly masterpieces. He aims to control his beastly strength and become a true artist.

ASTORIA RAPUNZEL

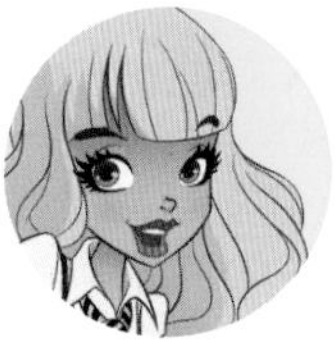

Regal Academy's resident bookworm and perfect, poised, princess... just as long as everything goes her way. Her perfectionist streak has her snapping from being absorbed in a book to up in arms, to back to studying quietly in an instant! She aims to be the best student, always the first to reply to the teachers' questions, always asking for more hours at school, more homework, or for more complicated exams.

JOY LeFROG

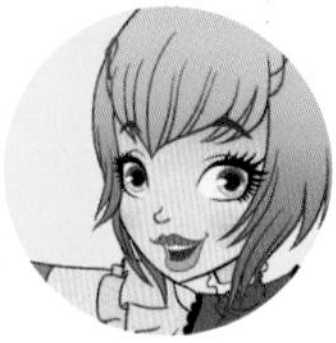

Joy loves creepy-crawlies and sometimes forgets that not everyone else does! She loves to cheer on her friends, but she's as likely to encourage their BAD ideas as well as their good ones! Because of her curse, she accidentally turns into a frog – and can't turn back unless someone is available to kiss her. Most of the times, Hawk or Travis have to save her... even if they'd rather do anything else than kiss a frog.

HAWK SNOWWHITE

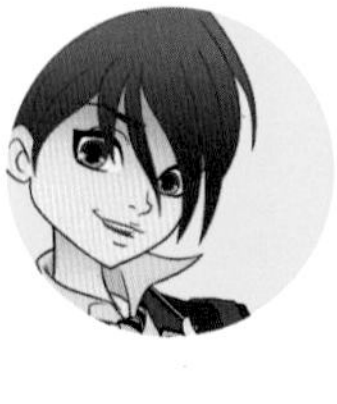

Hawk thinks he's the perfect fairy tale hero, but to his level-headed friends and the teachers, his habit of leaping head-first into trouble makes him a regal pain, because he puts himself and his team in danger! His love of apples and the ladies of Regal Academy is second only to his love of proving himself. He wants to be the best fairy tale in all of history but he's got a long way to go if he's ever going to make it.

PROFESSOR SNOWWHITE

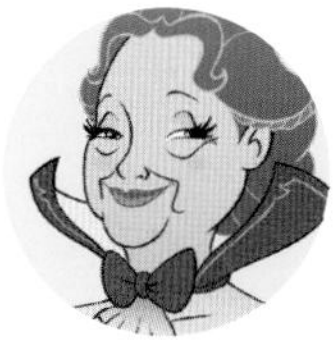

Professor SnowWhite is a stickler for the school rules and often ends up butting heads with our heroes on their adventures. This puts her at odds with her rebellious grandson Hawk, wanting him to become the most proper prince he can be. Despite her strictness, her mind is still "pure as snow" so she is very trusting. Our heroes (and the villains as well) can often get by her with a bit of cleverness.

HEADMISTRESS CINDERELLA

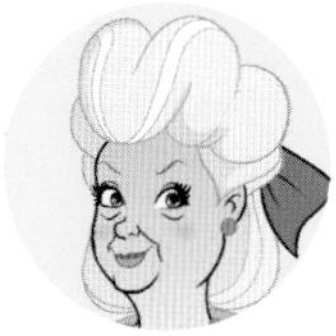

Headmistress Cinderella was able to hold her own against her mean stepmother and stepsisters when she was a teenager, so she sure isn't afraid to speak her mind now that she's a grandmother. She often sticks up for the heroes against the strict Professor Snow White. She's a kindly mentor who has watched over Rose her entire life.

COACH BEAST

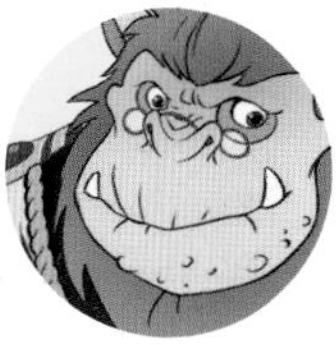

The Beast is a brash teacher, always yelling at the students to run a thousand laps or do a thousand pushups. When the Headmistress has a problem with someone breaking the rules, he scoops them up and carries them off to detention. He's always pushing his grandson Travis to give up art and become a real warrior with his beastly strength. Underneath it all, he has a heart of gold that occasionally pops up and compels him to help our heroes out of a jam.

MAGISTER RAPUNZEL

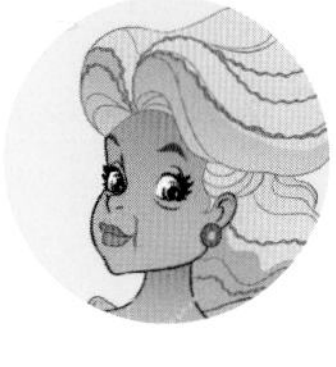

Magister Rapunzel has spent way too much time locked in her tower and has a carefree attitude on life. She excitedly wants to chat or show off her books to anyone who will listen, but often accidentally forgets herself and starts talking to statues or paintings instead of real people. She tries to get her perfectionist granddaughter, Astoria, to relax and let loose at times.

DOCTOR LeFROG

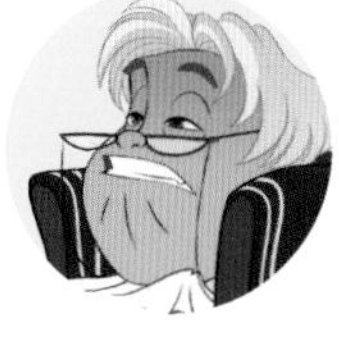

Doctor LeFrog is an old-fashioned professor at Regal Academy. He tends to be absent-minded at times, even if his classroom was exploding he would keep on teaching. He is also very blind without his glasses. He always embarrasses his number-one granddaughter, Joy, by introducing frogs to her as possible dates but wants only the best for her.

VICKY BROOMSTICK

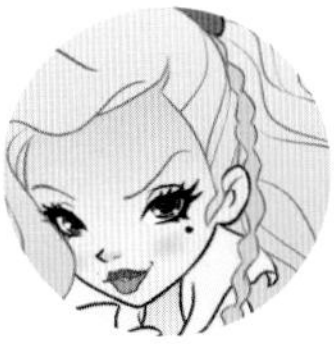

Vicky is Regal Academy's resident Mean Girl, leading her pack of villainous grandkids to accomplish her goals by any means necessary! Vicky is the intelligent and powerful granddaughter of the Broomstick Witch, but every time she tries to carry out her evil plans something goes wrong and she's thwarted by Rose and her friends. Rose and her friends are all that's preventing Vicky from opening up the Gate and releasing the old Fairytale Villains on Earth!

RUBY STEPSISTER

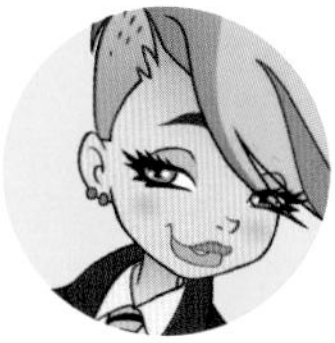

Ruby is one of Vicky's loyal henchmen in the Mean Team and not the sharpest tool in the shed. Utterly in love with Hawk SnowWhite, she helps Vicky in all of her evil plans just so she can get a chance to see her beloved. She's more than happy to do whatever dirty work Vicky couldn't be bothered with if it means being near Hawk.

CYRUS BROOMSTICK

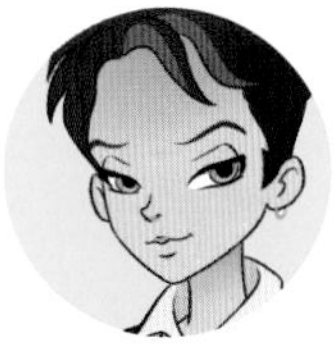

Cyrus is the lazy and cowardly grandson of the Broomstick Witch, as well as Vicky's cousin and reluctant member of the Mean Team. He is so lazy that he must be bribed by Vicky to help with her evil plans. He'd much rather be sleeping than plotting world domination.

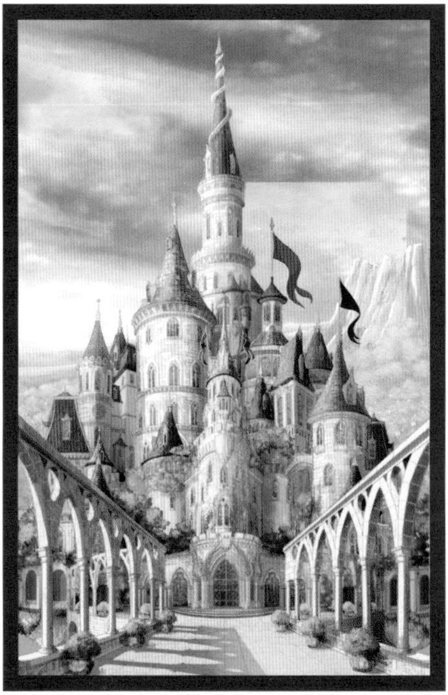

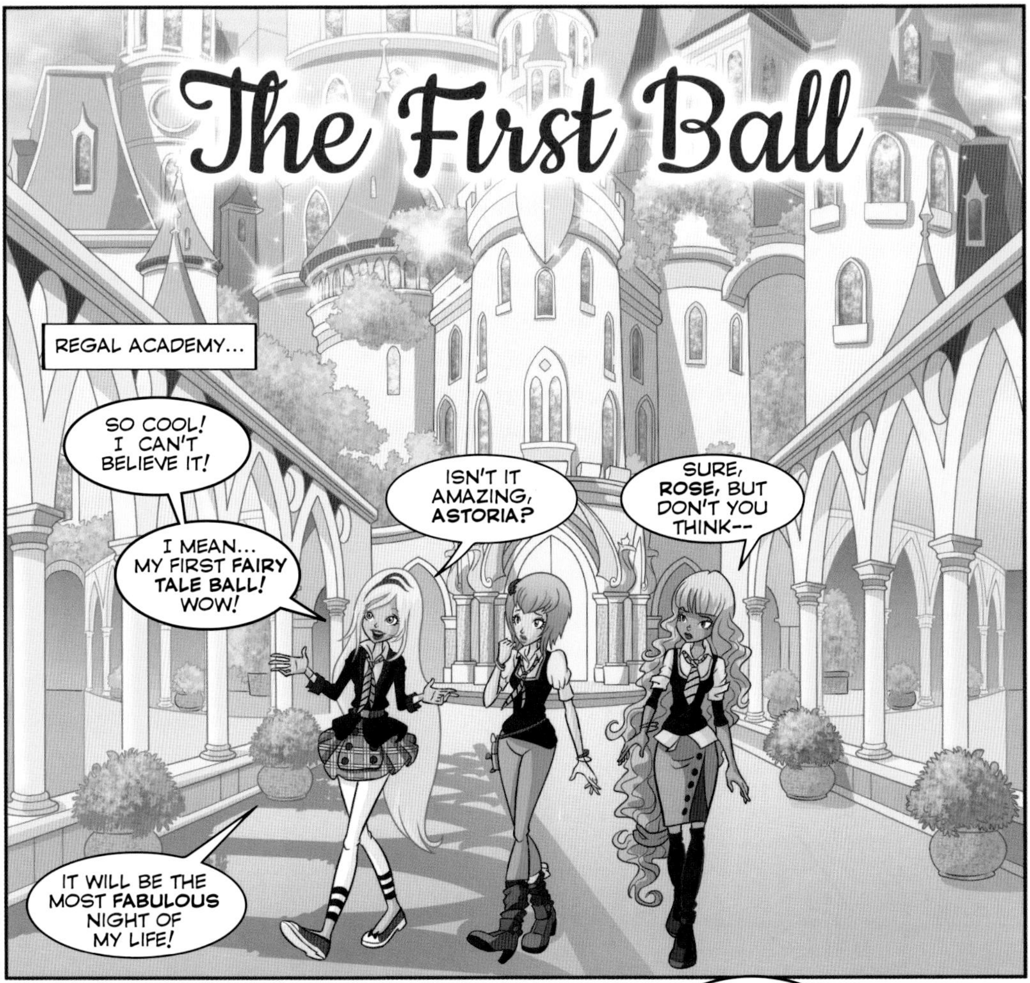
The First Ball
REGAL ACADEMY...
SO COOL! I CAN'T BELIEVE IT!
I MEAN... MY FIRST FAIRY TALE BALL! WOW!
IT WILL BE THE MOST FABULOUS NIGHT OF MY LIFE!
ISN'T IT AMAZING, ASTORIA?
SURE, ROSE, BUT DON'T YOU THINK--

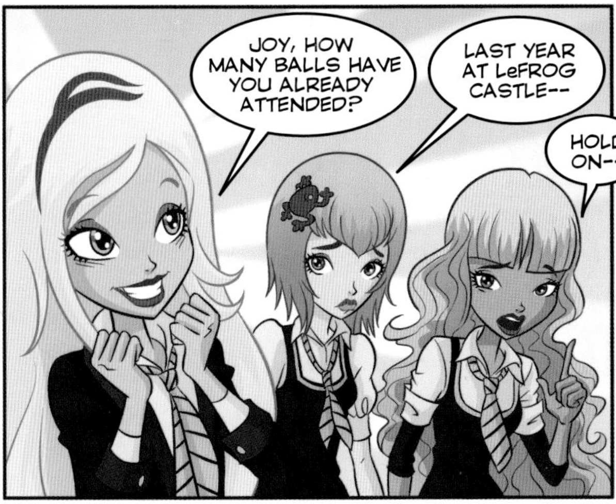
JOY, HOW MANY BALLS HAVE YOU ALREADY ATTENDED?
LAST YEAR AT LeFROG CASTLE--
HOLD ON--

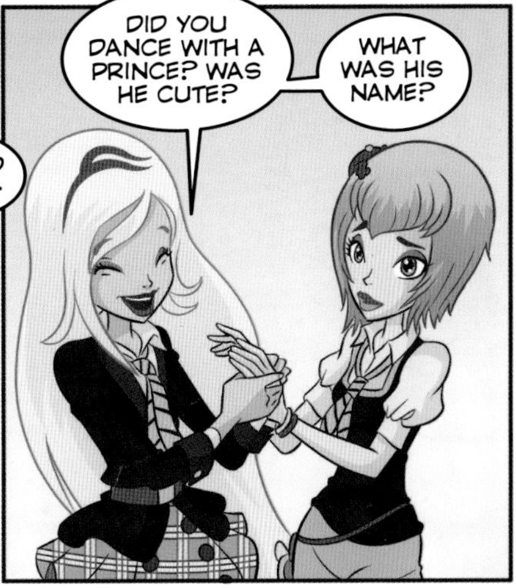
DID YOU DANCE WITH A PRINCE? WAS HE CUTE?
WHAT WAS HIS NAME?

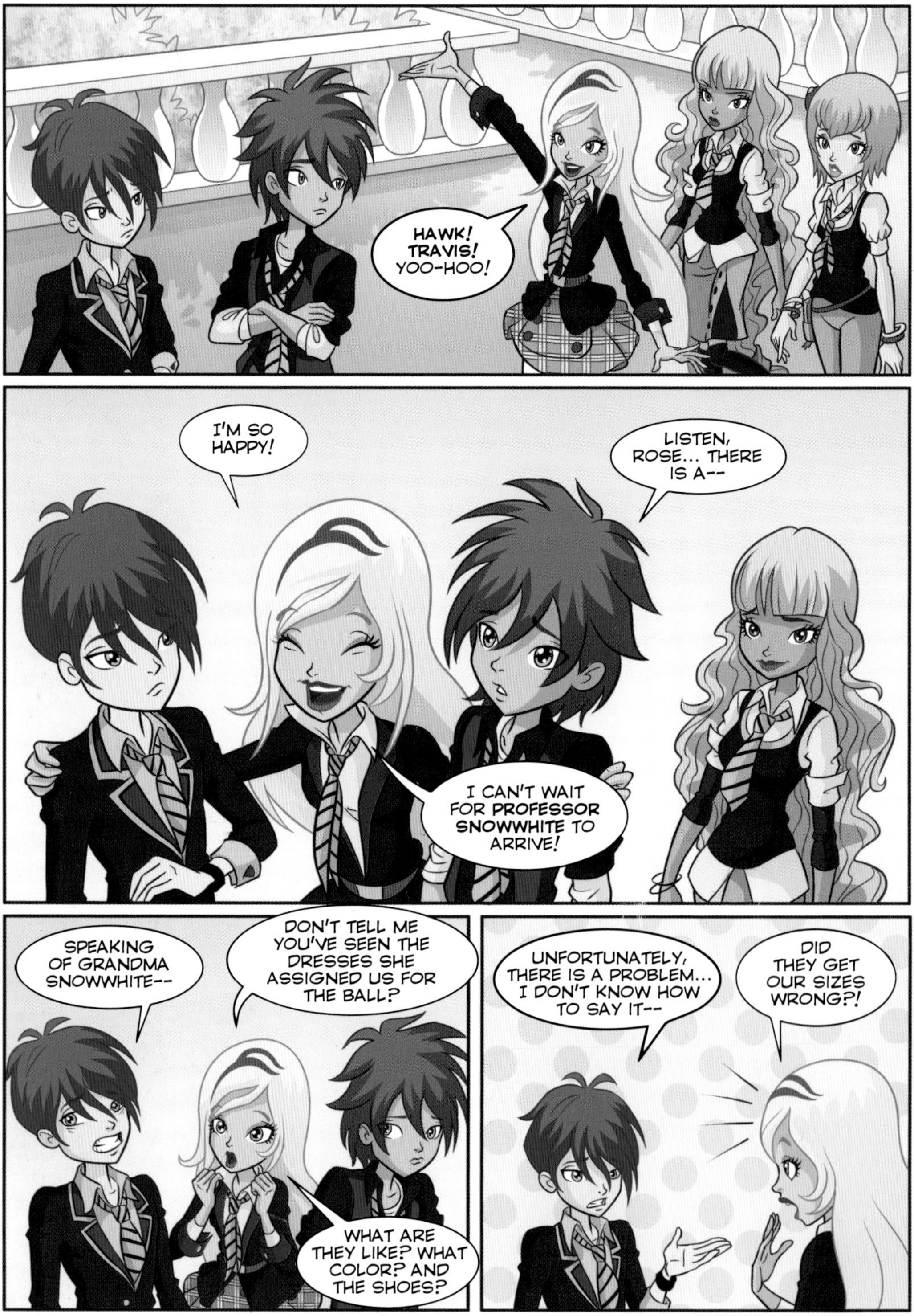
HAWK! TRAVIS! YOO-HOO!
I'M SO HAPPY!
LISTEN, ROSE... THERE IS A--
I CAN'T WAIT FOR PROFESSOR SNOWWHITE TO ARRIVE!
SPEAKING OF GRANDMA SNOWWHITE--
DON'T TELL ME YOU'VE SEEN THE DRESSES SHE ASSIGNED US FOR THE BALL?
WHAT ARE THEY LIKE? WHAT COLOR? AND THE SHOES?
UNFORTUNATELY, THERE IS A PROBLEM... I DON'T KNOW HOW TO SAY IT--
DID THEY GET OUR SIZES WRONG?!

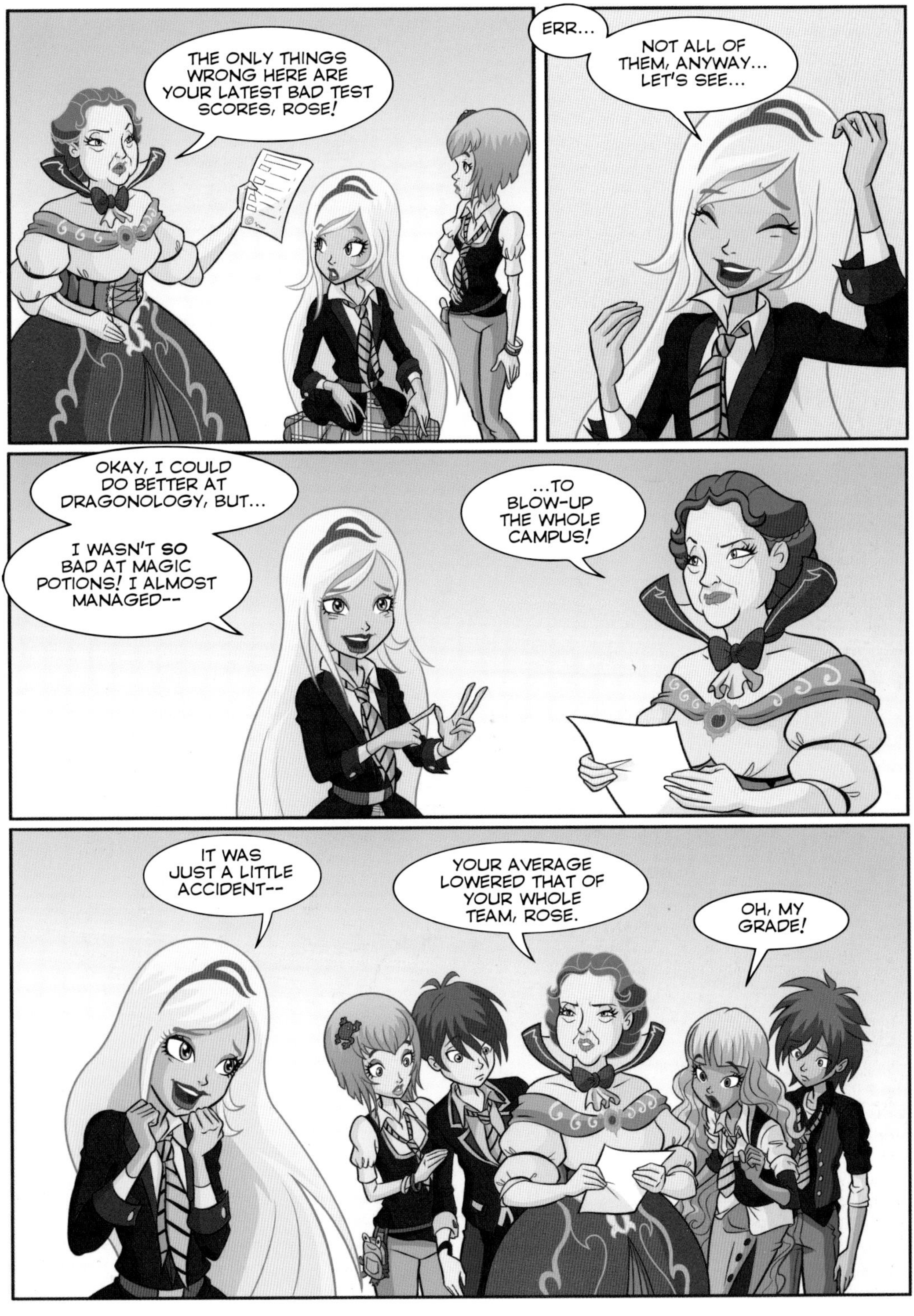
THE ONLY THINGS WRONG HERE ARE YOUR LATEST BAD TEST SCORES, ROSE!
ERR...
NOT ALL OF THEM, ANYWAY... LET'S SEE...
OKAY, I COULD DO BETTER AT DRAGONOLOGY, BUT...
I WASN'T SO BAD AT MAGIC POTIONS! I ALMOST MANAGED--
...TO BLOW-UP THE WHOLE CAMPUS!
IT WAS JUST A LITTLE ACCIDENT--
YOUR AVERAGE LOWERED THAT OF YOUR WHOLE TEAM, ROSE.
OH, MY GRADE!

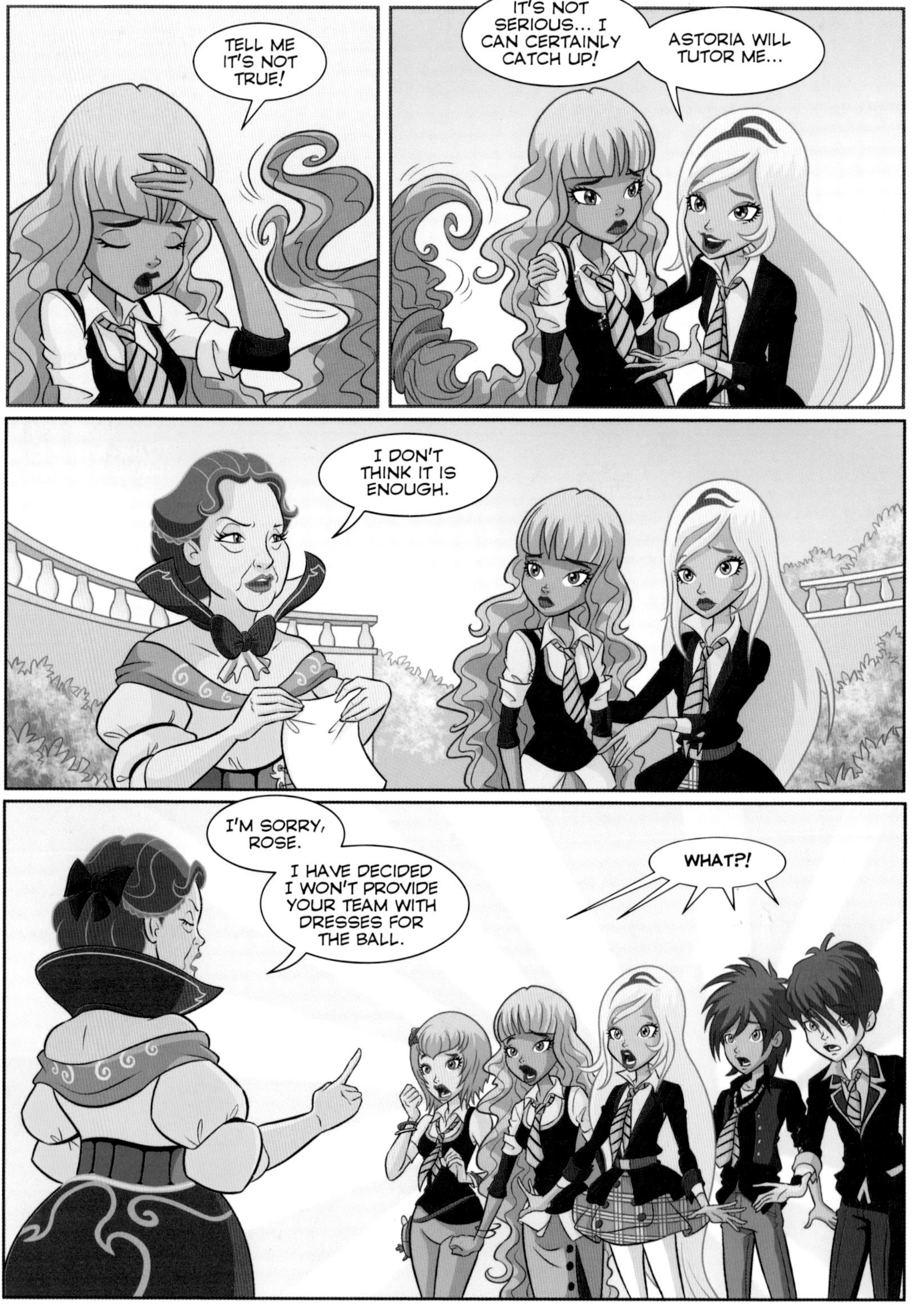

TELL ME IT'S NOT TRUE!
IT'S NOT SERIOUS... I CAN CERTAINLY CATCH UP!
ASTORIA WILL TUTOR ME...
I DON'T THINK IT IS ENOUGH.
I'M SORRY, ROSE.
I HAVE DECIDED I WON'T PROVIDE YOUR TEAM WITH DRESSES FOR THE BALL.
WHAT?!

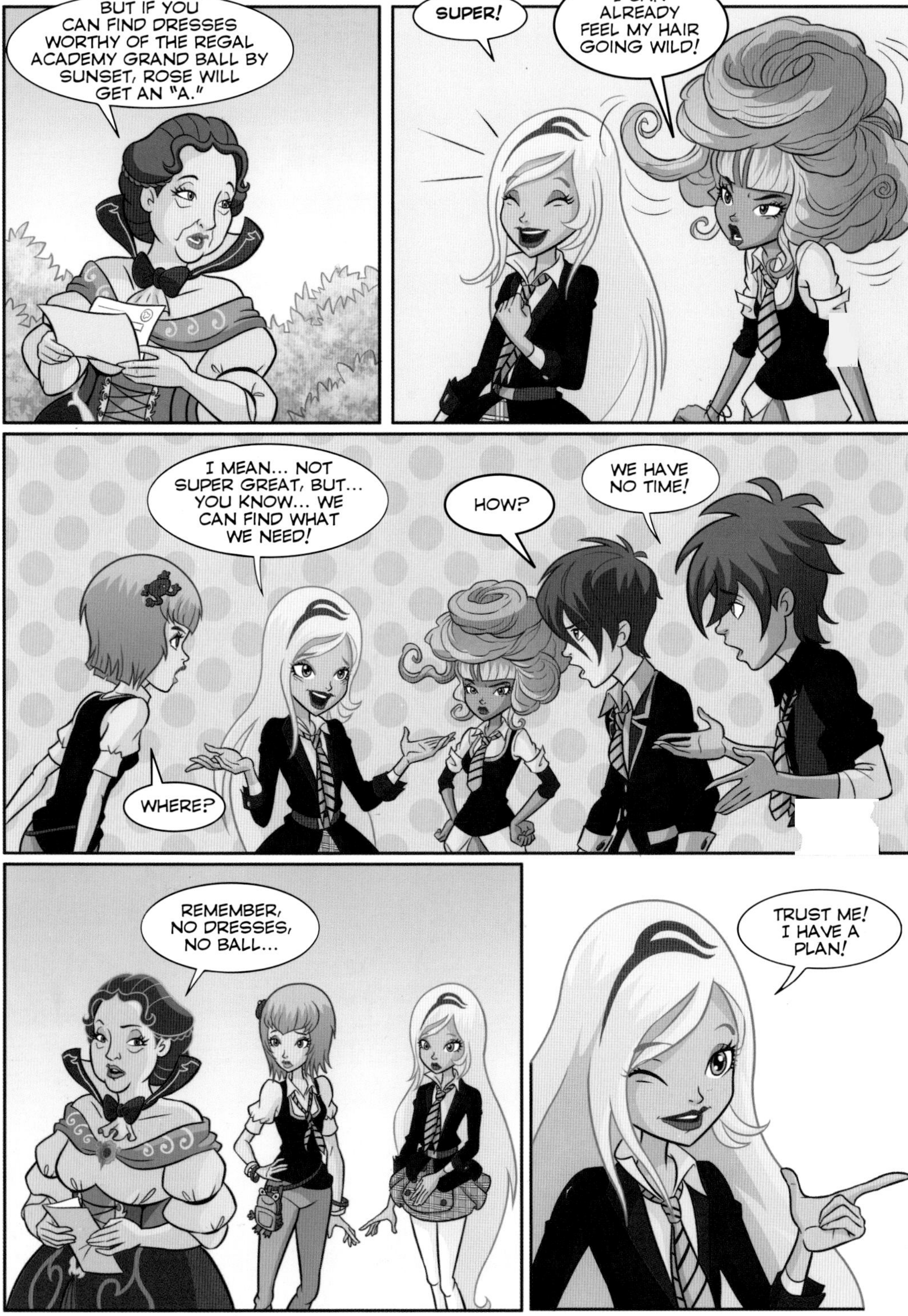
BUT IF YOU CAN FIND DRESSES WORTHY OF THE REGAL ACADEMY GRAND BALL BY SUNSET, ROSE WILL GET AN "A."
SUPER!
I CAN ALREADY FEEL MY HAIR GOING WILD!
I MEAN... NOT SUPER GREAT, BUT... YOU KNOW... WE CAN FIND WHAT WE NEED!
HOW?
WE HAVE NO TIME!
WHERE?
REMEMBER, NO DRESSES, NO BALL...
TRUST ME! I HAVE A PLAN!

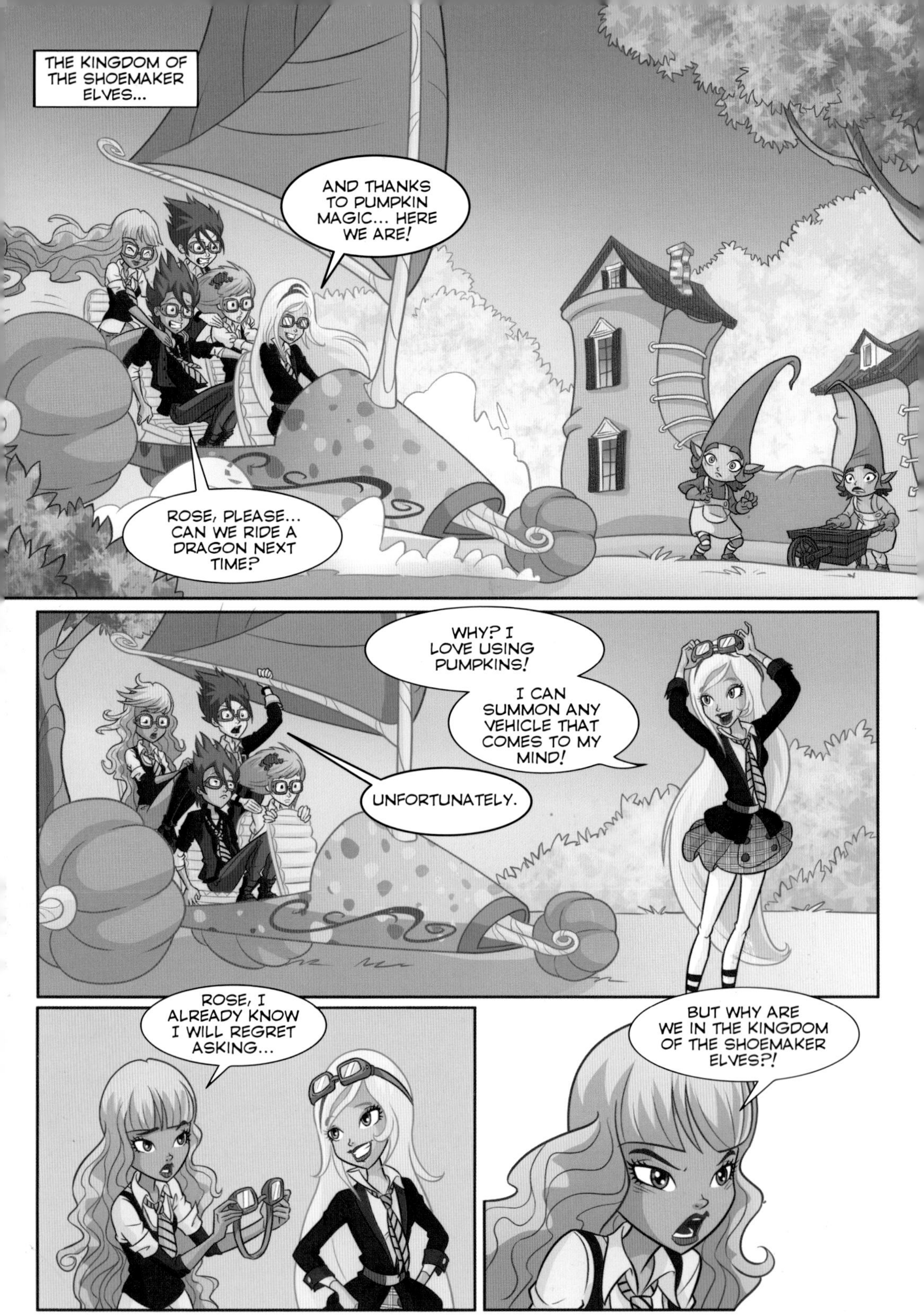
THE KINGDOM OF THE SHOEMAKER ELVES...
AND THANKS TO PUMPKIN MAGIC... HERE WE ARE!
ROSE, PLEASE... CAN WE RIDE A DRAGON NEXT TIME?
WHY? I LOVE USING PUMPKINS!
I CAN SUMMON ANY VEHICLE THAT COMES TO MY MIND!
UNFORTUNATELY.
ROSE, I ALREADY KNOW I WILL REGRET ASKING...
BUT WHY ARE WE IN THE KINGDOM OF THE SHOEMAKER ELVES?!

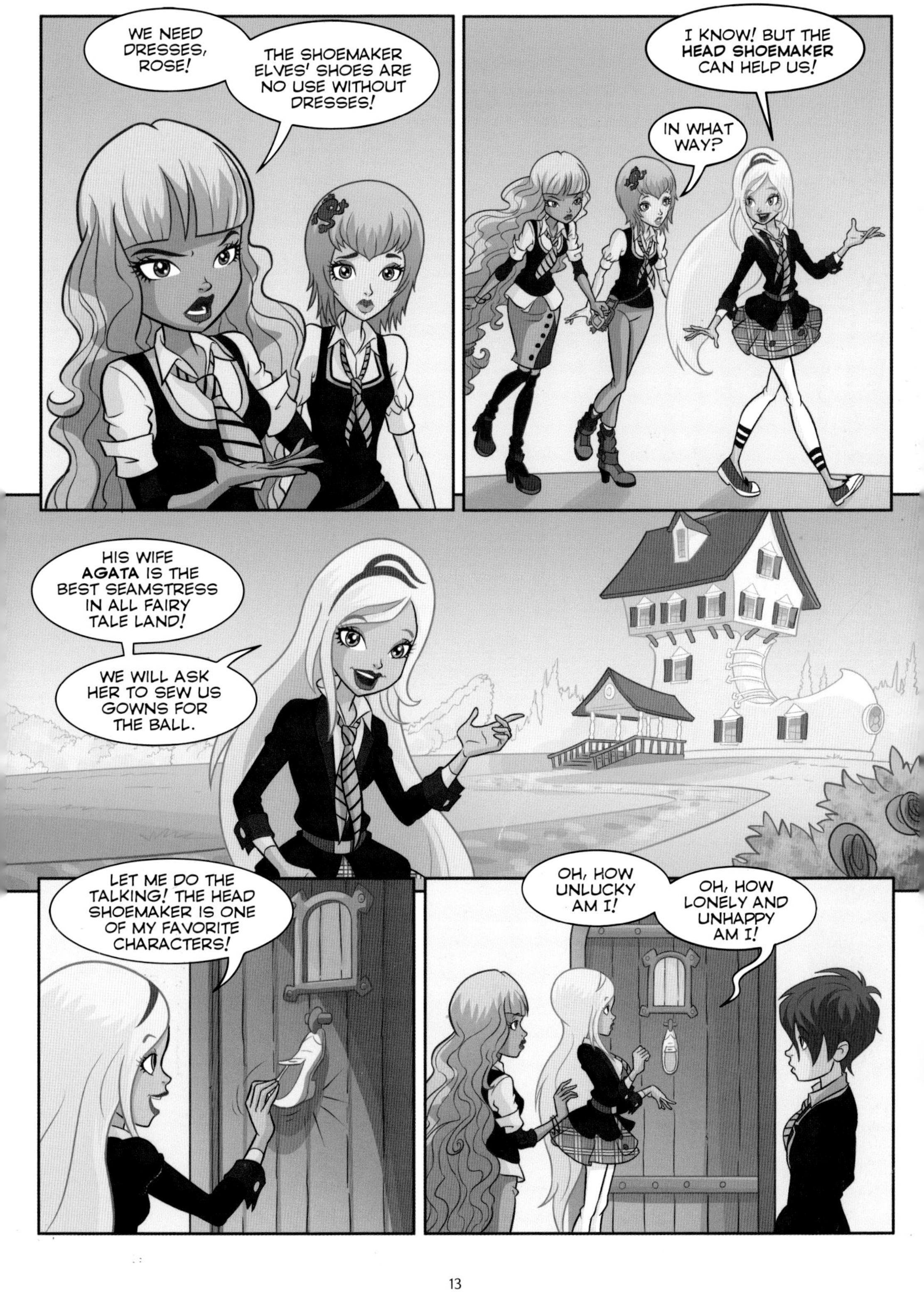
WE NEED DRESSES, ROSE!
THE SHOEMAKER ELVES' SHOES ARE NO USE WITHOUT DRESSES!
I KNOW! BUT THE HEAD SHOEMAKER CAN HELP US!
IN WHAT WAY?
HIS WIFE AGATA IS THE BEST SEAMSTRESS IN ALL FAIRY TALE LAND!
WE WILL ASK HER TO SEW US GOWNS FOR THE BALL.
LET ME DO THE TALKING! THE HEAD SHOEMAKER IS ONE OF MY FAVORITE CHARACTERS!
OH, HOW UNLUCKY AM I!
OH, HOW LONELY AND UNHAPPY AM I!

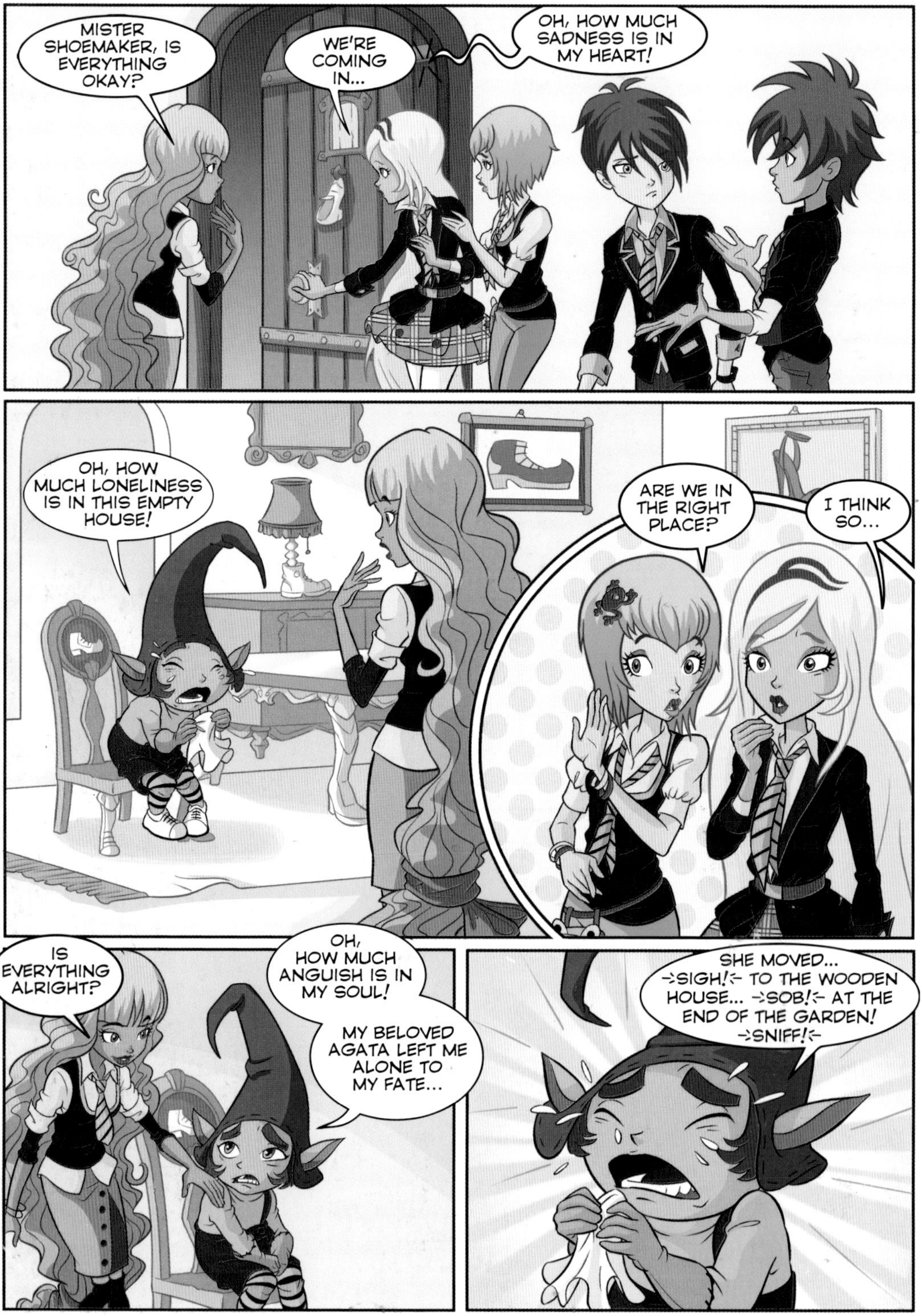
MISTER SHOEMAKER, IS EVERYTHING OKAY?
WE'RE COMING IN...
OH, HOW MUCH SADNESS IS IN MY HEART!
OH, HOW MUCH LONELINESS IS IN THIS EMPTY HOUSE!
ARE WE IN THE RIGHT PLACE?
I THINK SO...
IS EVERYTHING ALRIGHT?
OH, HOW MUCH ANGUISH IS IN MY SOUL!
MY BELOVED AGATA LEFT ME ALONE TO MY FATE...
SHE MOVED... -SIGH!- TO THE WOODEN HOUSE... -SOB!- AT THE END OF THE GARDEN! -SNIFF!-

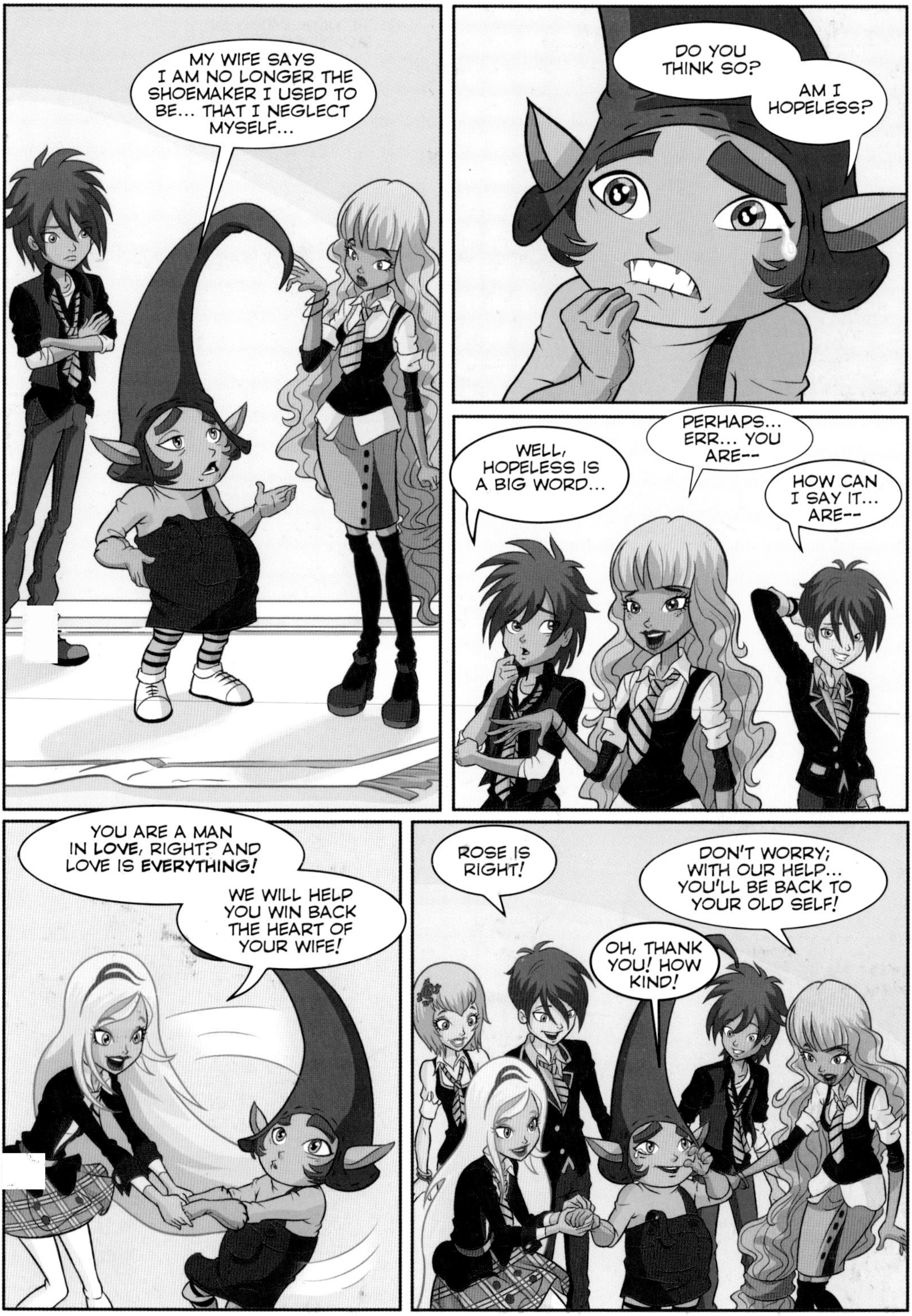
MY WIFE SAYS I AM NO LONGER THE SHOEMAKER I USED TO BE... THAT I NEGLECT MYSELF...
DO YOU THINK SO?
AM I HOPELESS?
WELL, HOPELESS IS A BIG WORD...
PERHAPS... ERR... YOU ARE--
HOW CAN I SAY IT... ARE--
YOU ARE A MAN IN LOVE, RIGHT? AND LOVE IS EVERYTHING!
WE WILL HELP YOU WIN BACK THE HEART OF YOUR WIFE!
ROSE IS RIGHT!
DON'T WORRY; WITH OUR HELP... YOU'LL BE BACK TO YOUR OLD SELF!
OH, THANK YOU! HOW KIND!

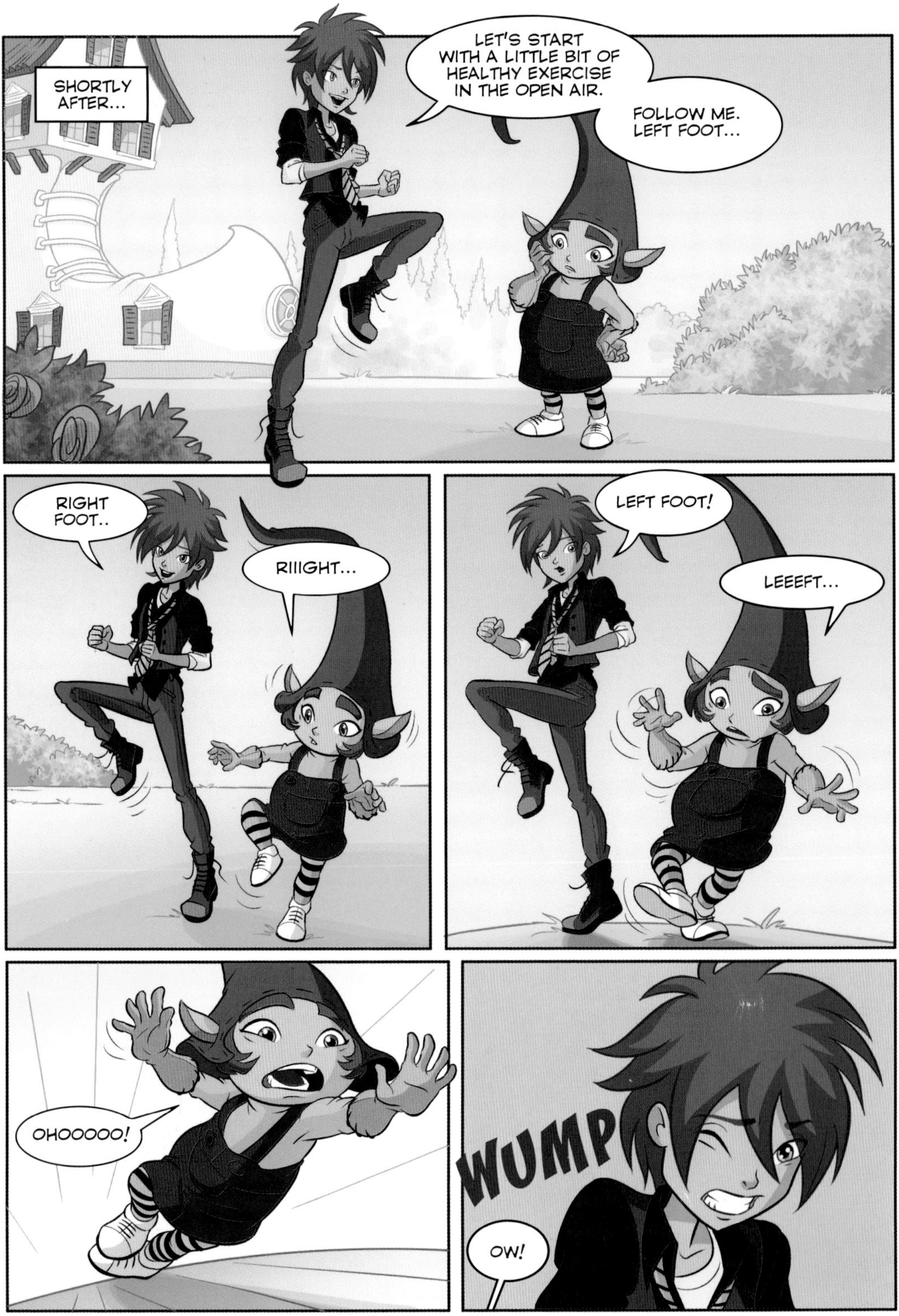
SHORTLY AFTER...
LET'S START WITH A LITTLE BIT OF HEALTHY EXERCISE IN THE OPEN AIR.
FOLLOW ME. LEFT FOOT...
RIGHT FOOT..
RIIIGHT...
LEFT FOOT!
LEEEFT...
OHOOOOO!
WUMP
OW!

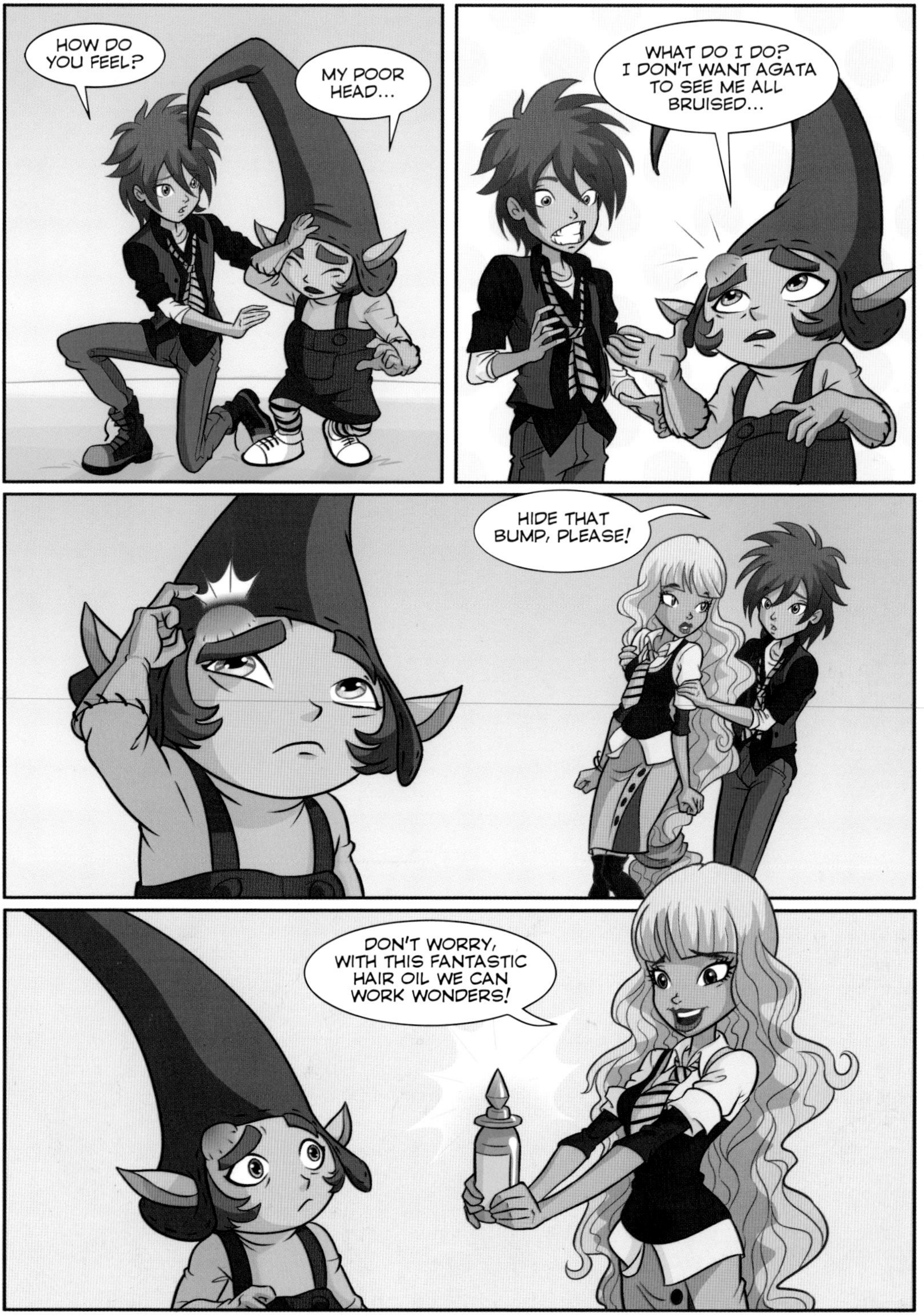
HOW DO YOU FEEL?
MY POOR HEAD...
WHAT DO I DO? I DON'T WANT AGATA TO SEE ME ALL BRUISED...
HIDE THAT BUMP, PLEASE!
DON'T WORRY, WITH THIS FANTASTIC HAIR OIL WE CAN WORK WONDERS!

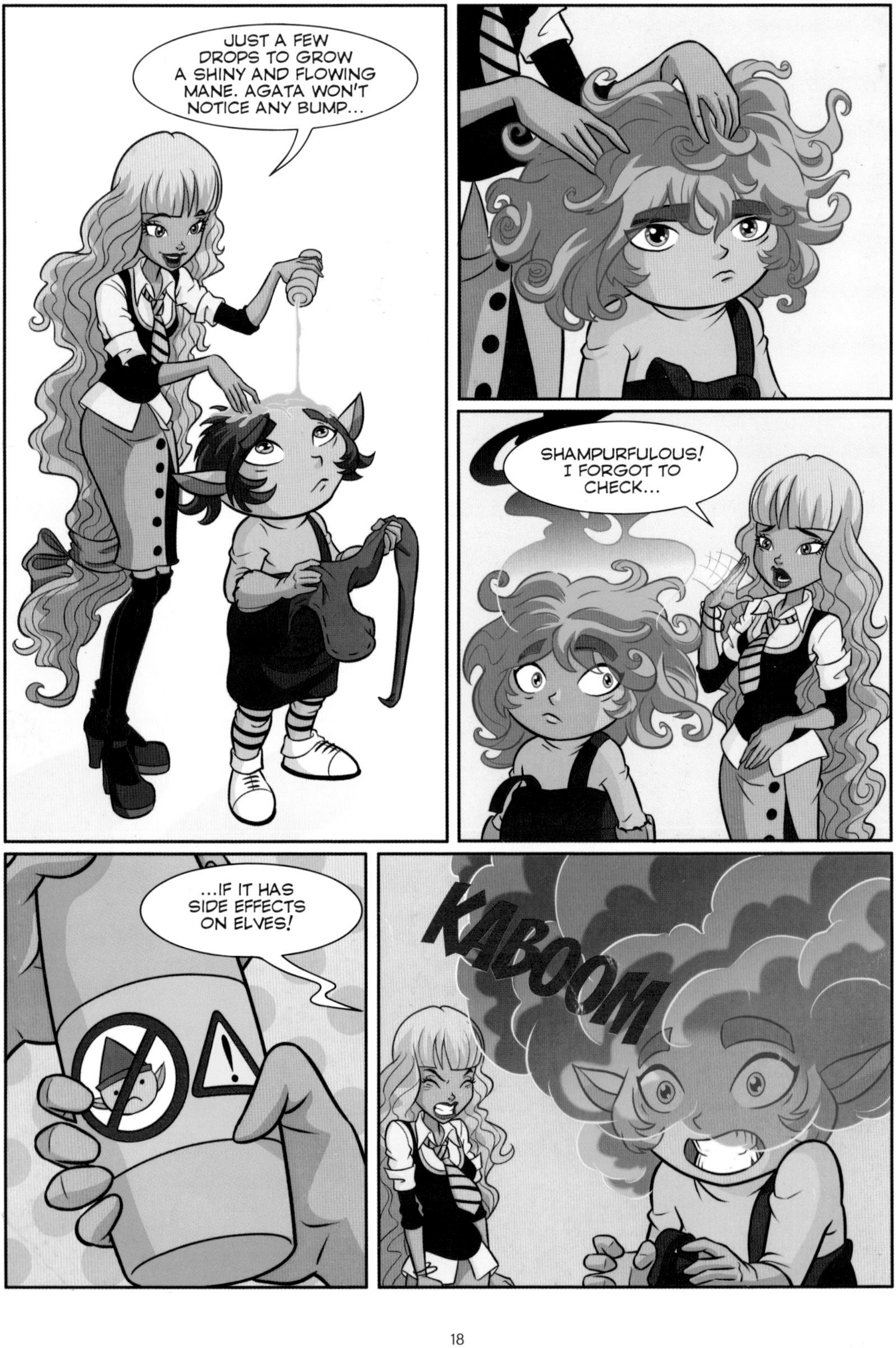
JUST A FEW DROPS TO GROW A SHINY AND FLOWING MANE. AGATA WON'T NOTICE ANY BUMP...
SHAMPURFULOUS! I FORGOT TO CHECK...
...IF IT HAS SIDE EFFECTS ON ELVES!
KABOOM

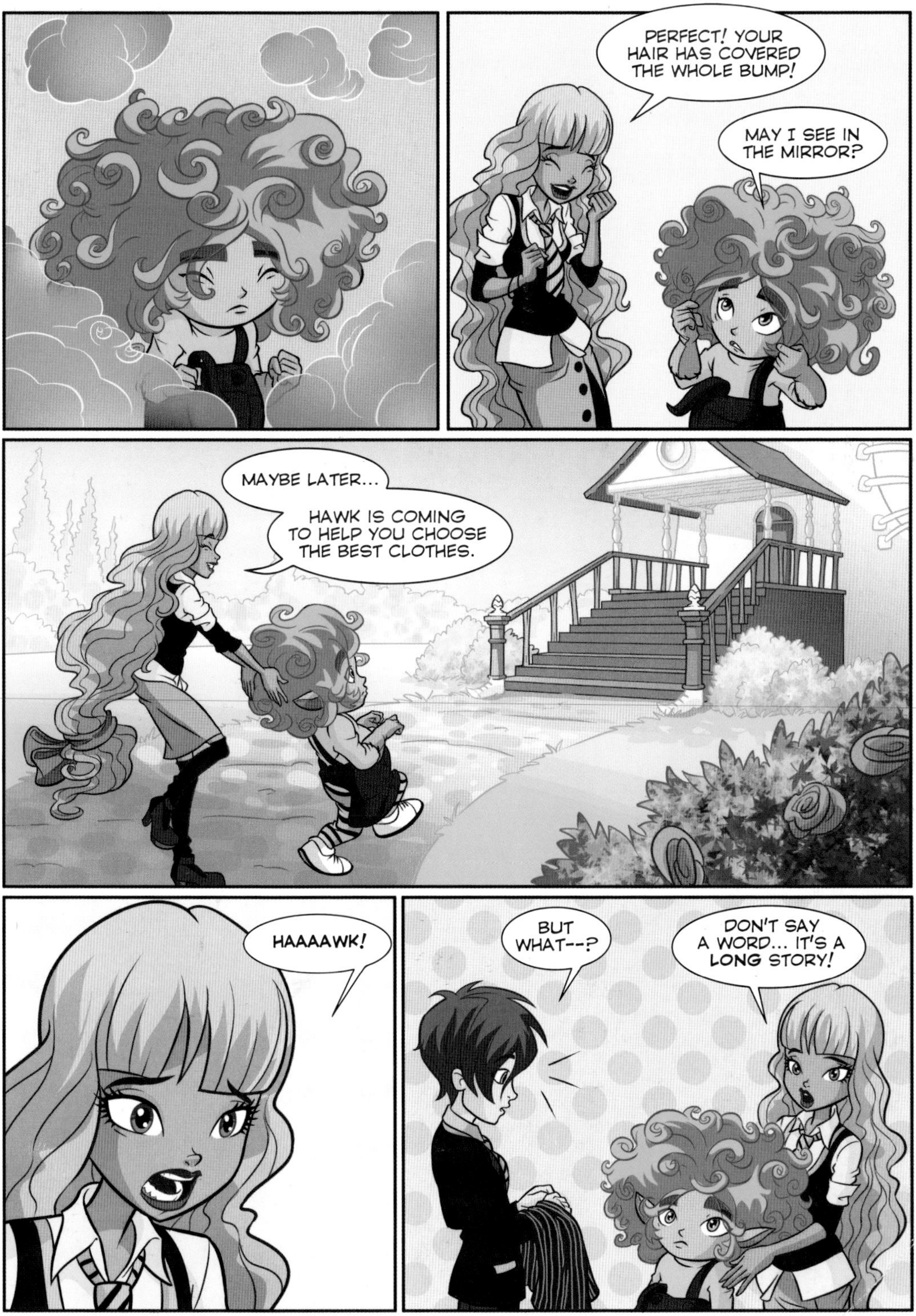
PERFECT! YOUR HAIR HAS COVERED THE WHOLE BUMP!
MAY I SEE IN THE MIRROR?
MAYBE LATER...
HAWK IS COMING TO HELP YOU CHOOSE THE BEST CLOTHES.
HAAAAWK!
BUT WHAT--?
DON'T SAY A WORD... IT'S A LONG STORY!

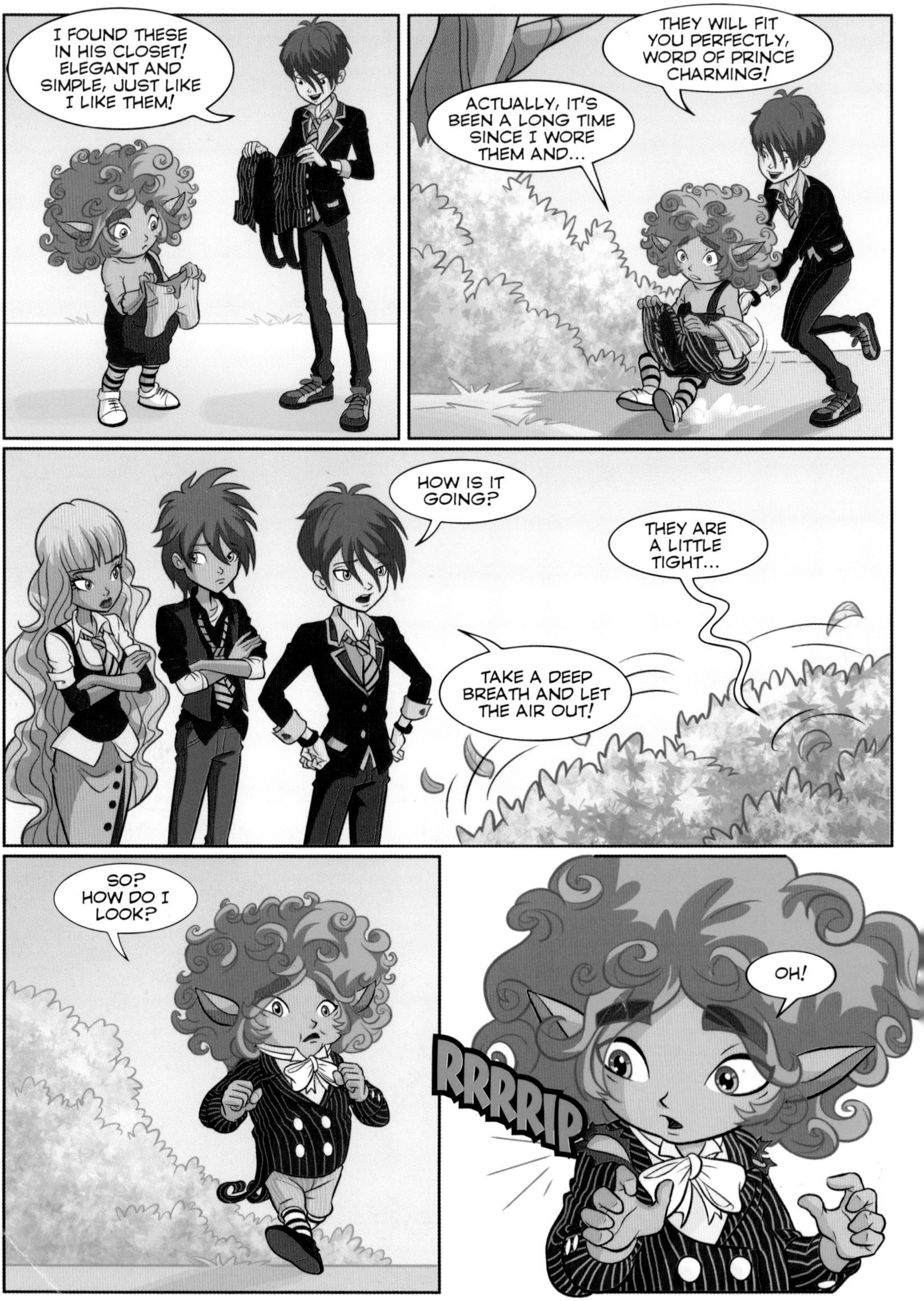
I FOUND THESE IN HIS CLOSET! ELEGANT AND SIMPLE, JUST LIKE I LIKE THEM!
THEY WILL FIT YOU PERFECTLY, WORD OF PRINCE CHARMING!
ACTUALLY, IT'S BEEN A LONG TIME SINCE I WORE THEM AND...
HOW IS IT GOING?
THEY ARE A LITTLE TIGHT...
TAKE A DEEP BREATH AND LET THE AIR OUT!
SO? HOW DO I LOOK?
RRRRRIP
OH!

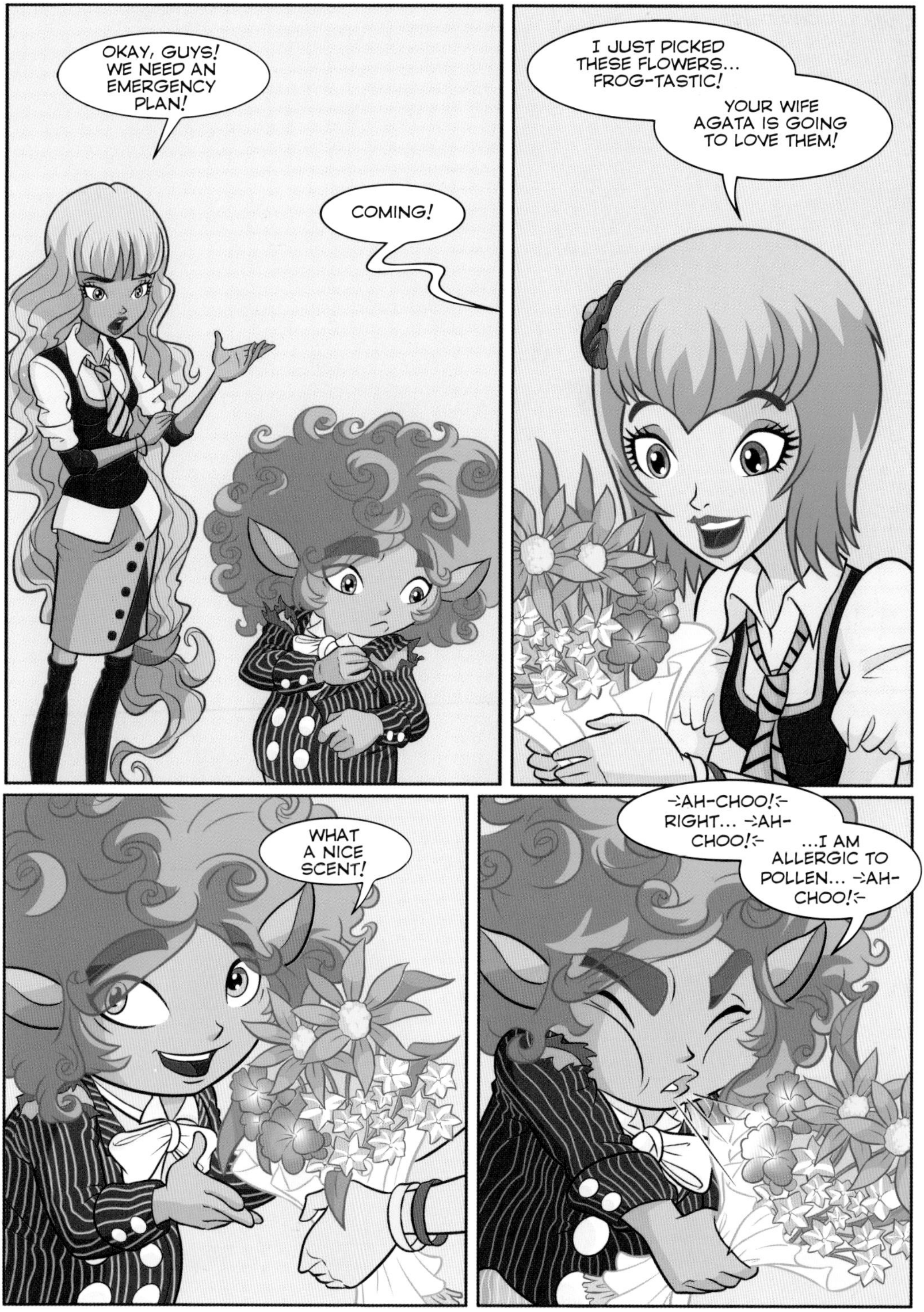
OKAY, GUYS! WE NEED AN EMERGENCY PLAN!
COMING!
I JUST PICKED THESE FLOWERS... FROG-TASTIC!
YOUR WIFE AGATA IS GOING TO LOVE THEM!
WHAT A NICE SCENT!
-AH-CHOO!- RIGHT... -AH-CHOO!- ...I AM ALLERGIC TO POLLEN... -AH-CHOO!-

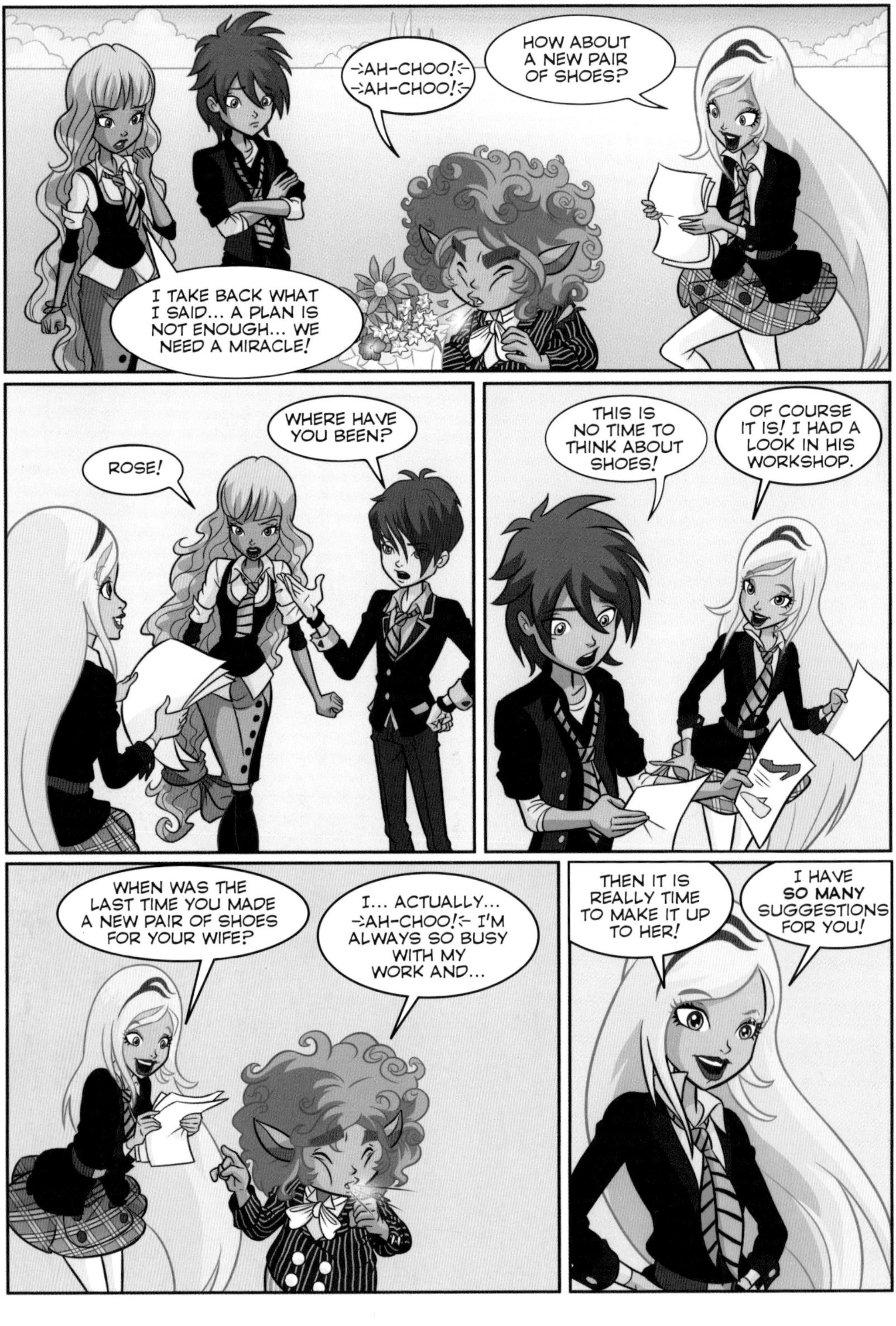
HOW ABOUT A NEW PAIR OF SHOES?
-AH-CHOO!- -AH-CHOO!-
I TAKE BACK WHAT I SAID... A PLAN IS NOT ENOUGH... WE NEED A MIRACLE!
ROSE!
WHERE HAVE YOU BEEN?
THIS IS NO TIME TO THINK ABOUT SHOES!
OF COURSE IT IS! I HAD A LOOK IN HIS WORKSHOP.
WHEN WAS THE LAST TIME YOU MADE A NEW PAIR OF SHOES FOR YOUR WIFE?
I... ACTUALLY... -AH-CHOO!- I'M ALWAYS SO BUSY WITH MY WORK AND...
THEN IT IS REALLY TIME TO MAKE IT UP TO HER!
I HAVE SO MANY SUGGESTIONS FOR YOU!

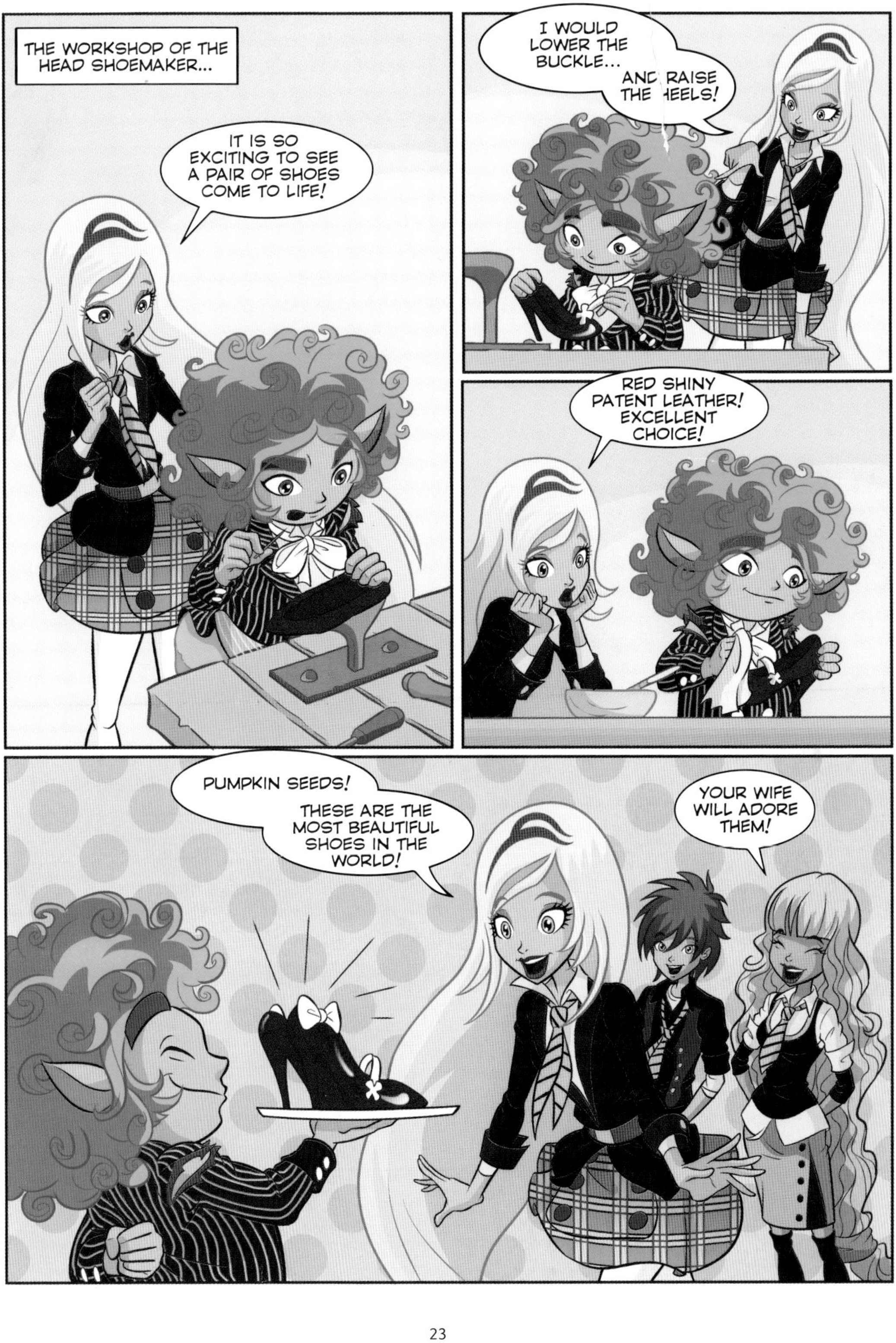
THE WORKSHOP OF THE HEAD SHOEMAKER...
IT IS SO EXCITING TO SEE A PAIR OF SHOES COME TO LIFE!
I WOULD LOWER THE BUCKLE...
AND RAISE THE HEELS!
RED SHINY PATENT LEATHER! EXCELLENT CHOICE!
PUMPKIN SEEDS!
THESE ARE THE MOST BEAUTIFUL SHOES IN THE WORLD!
YOUR WIFE WILL ADORE THEM!

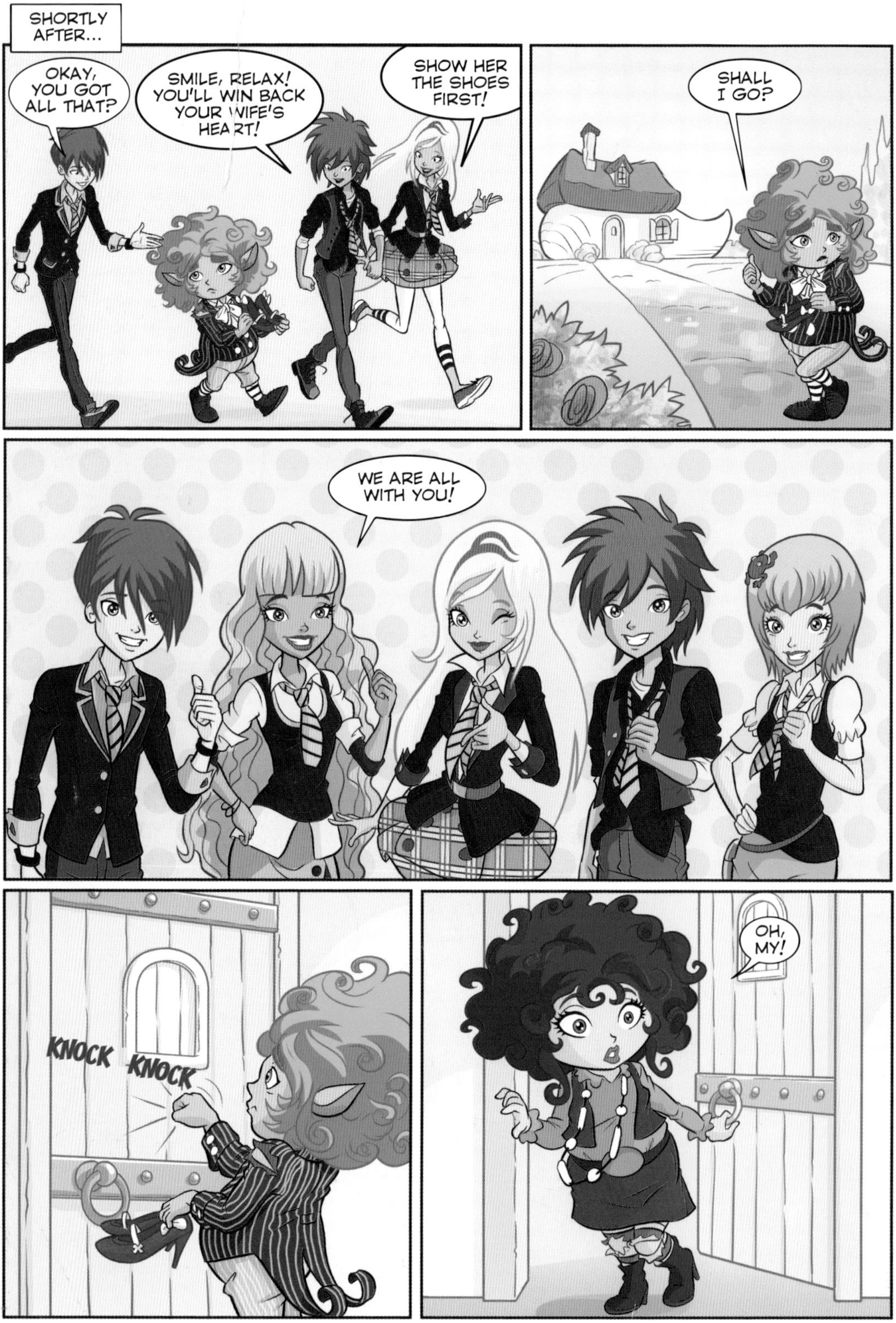
SHORTLY AFTER...
OKAY, YOU GOT ALL THAT?
SMILE, RELAX! YOU'LL WIN BACK YOUR WIFE'S HEART!
SHOW HER THE SHOES FIRST!
SHALL I GO?
WE ARE ALL WITH YOU!
KNOCK KNOCK
OH, MY!

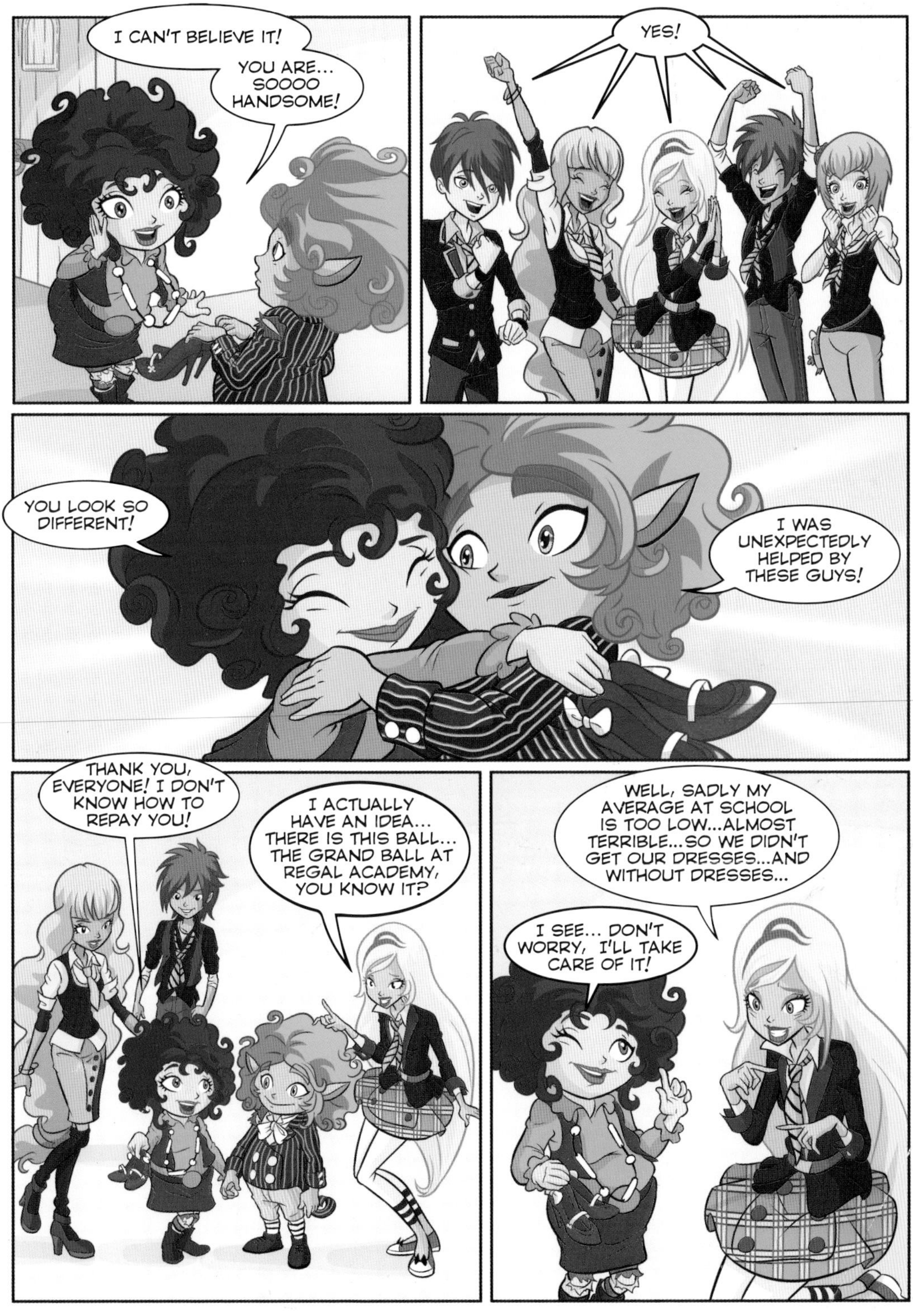
I CAN'T BELIEVE IT!
YOU ARE... SOOOO HANDSOME!
YES!
YOU LOOK SO DIFFERENT!
I WAS UNEXPECTEDLY HELPED BY THESE GUYS!
THANK YOU, EVERYONE! I DON'T KNOW HOW TO REPAY YOU!
I ACTUALLY HAVE AN IDEA... THERE IS THIS BALL... THE GRAND BALL AT REGAL ACADEMY, YOU KNOW IT?
WELL, SADLY MY AVERAGE AT SCHOOL IS TOO LOW...ALMOST TERRIBLE...SO WE DIDN'T GET OUR DRESSES...AND WITHOUT DRESSES...
I SEE... DON'T WORRY, I'LL TAKE CARE OF IT!

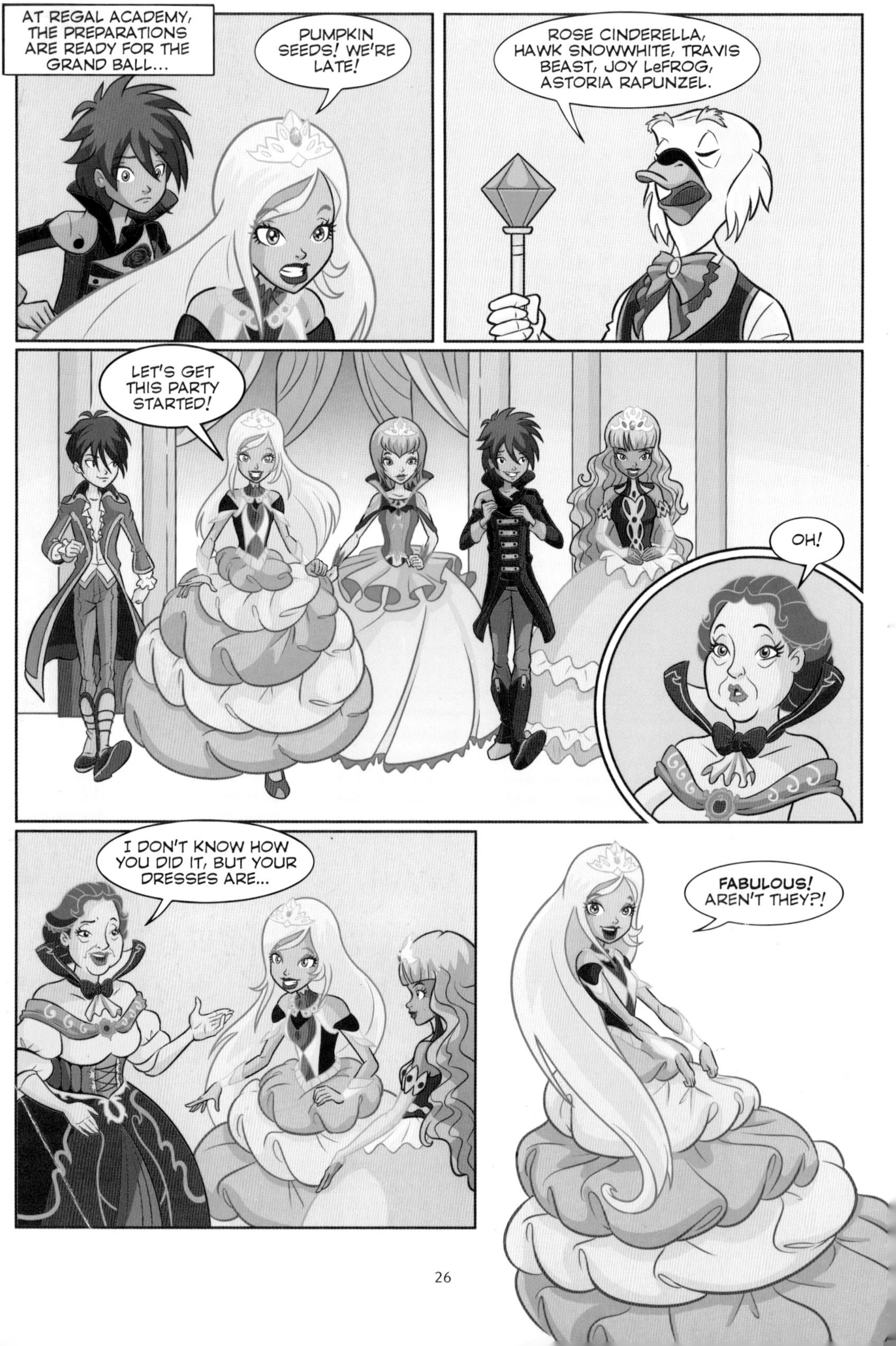
AT REGAL ACADEMY, THE PREPARATIONS ARE READY FOR THE GRAND BALL...
PUMPKIN SEEDS! WE'RE LATE!
ROSE CINDERELLA, HAWK SNOWWHITE, TRAVIS BEAST, JOY LeFROG, ASTORIA RAPUNZEL.
LET'S GET THIS PARTY STARTED!
OH!
I DON'T KNOW HOW YOU DID IT, BUT YOUR DRESSES ARE...
FABULOUS! AREN'T THEY?!

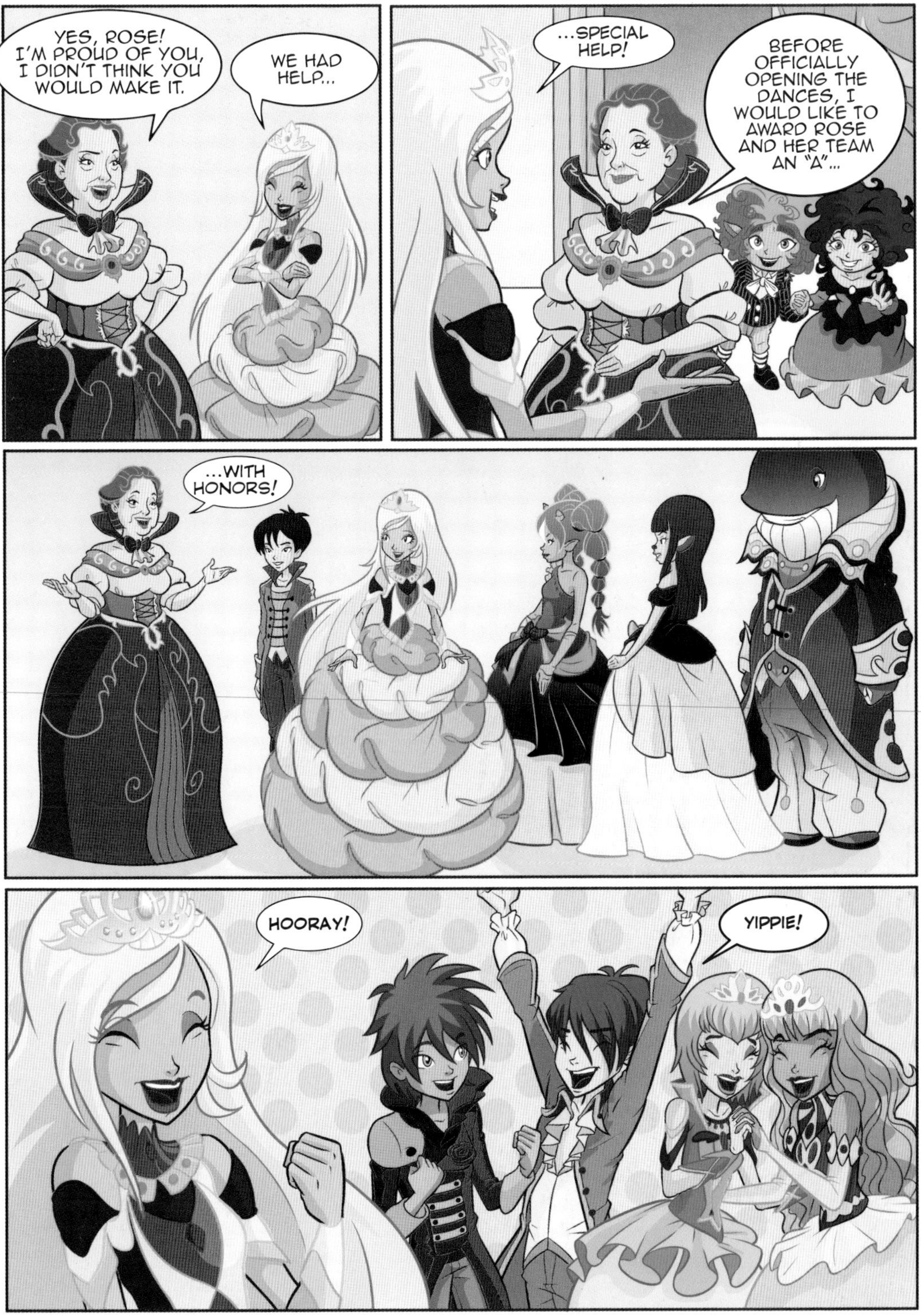
YES, ROSE! I'M PROUD OF YOU, I DIDN'T THINK YOU WOULD MAKE IT.
WE HAD HELP...
...SPECIAL HELP!
BEFORE OFFICIALLY OPENING THE DANCES, I WOULD LIKE TO AWARD ROSE AND HER TEAM AN "A"...
...WITH HONORS!
HOORAY!
YIPPIE!

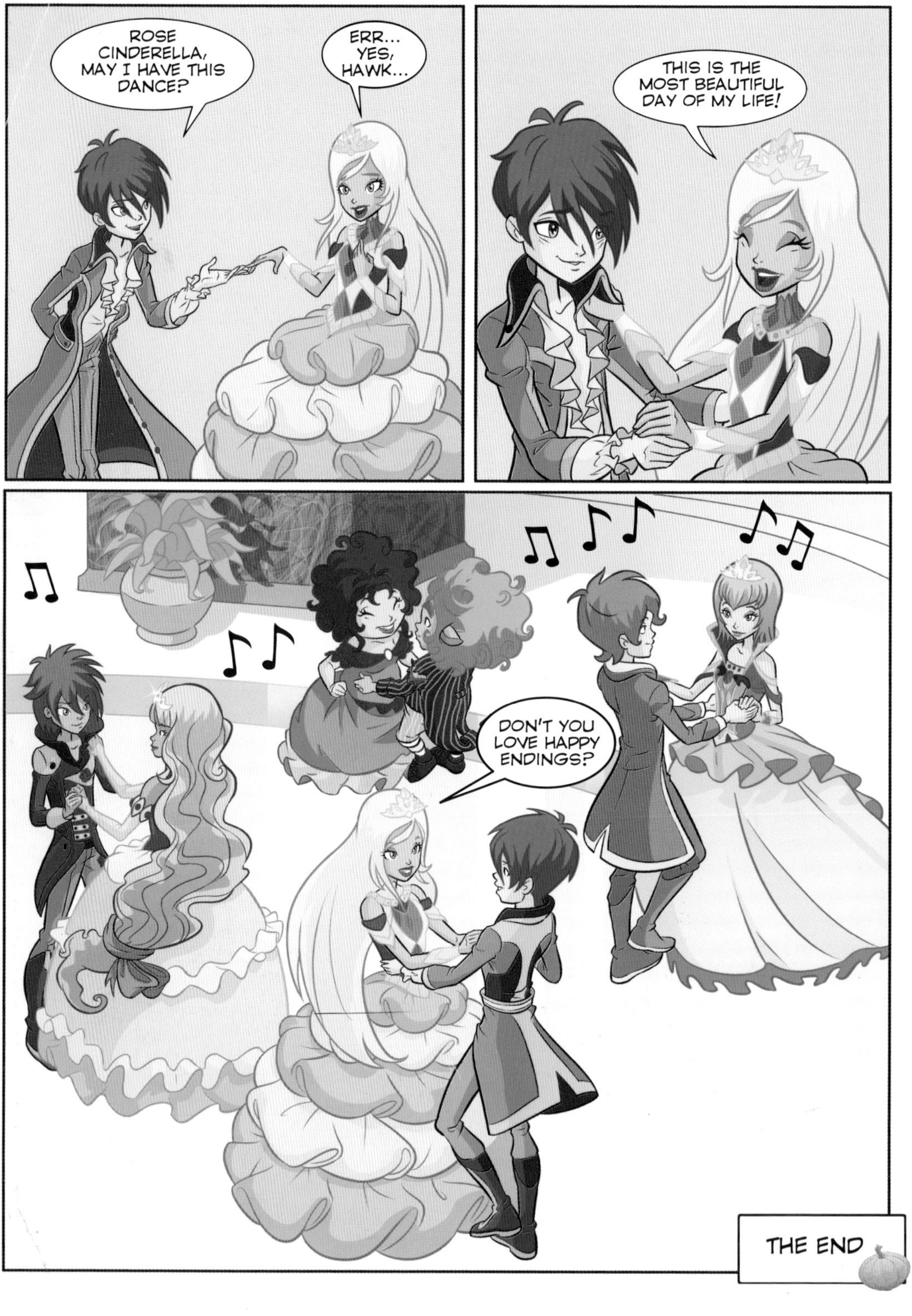
ROSE CINDERELLA, MAY I HAVE THIS DANCE?
ERR... YES, HAWK...
THIS IS THE MOST BEAUTIFUL DAY OF MY LIFE!
DON'T YOU LOVE HAPPY ENDINGS?
THE END

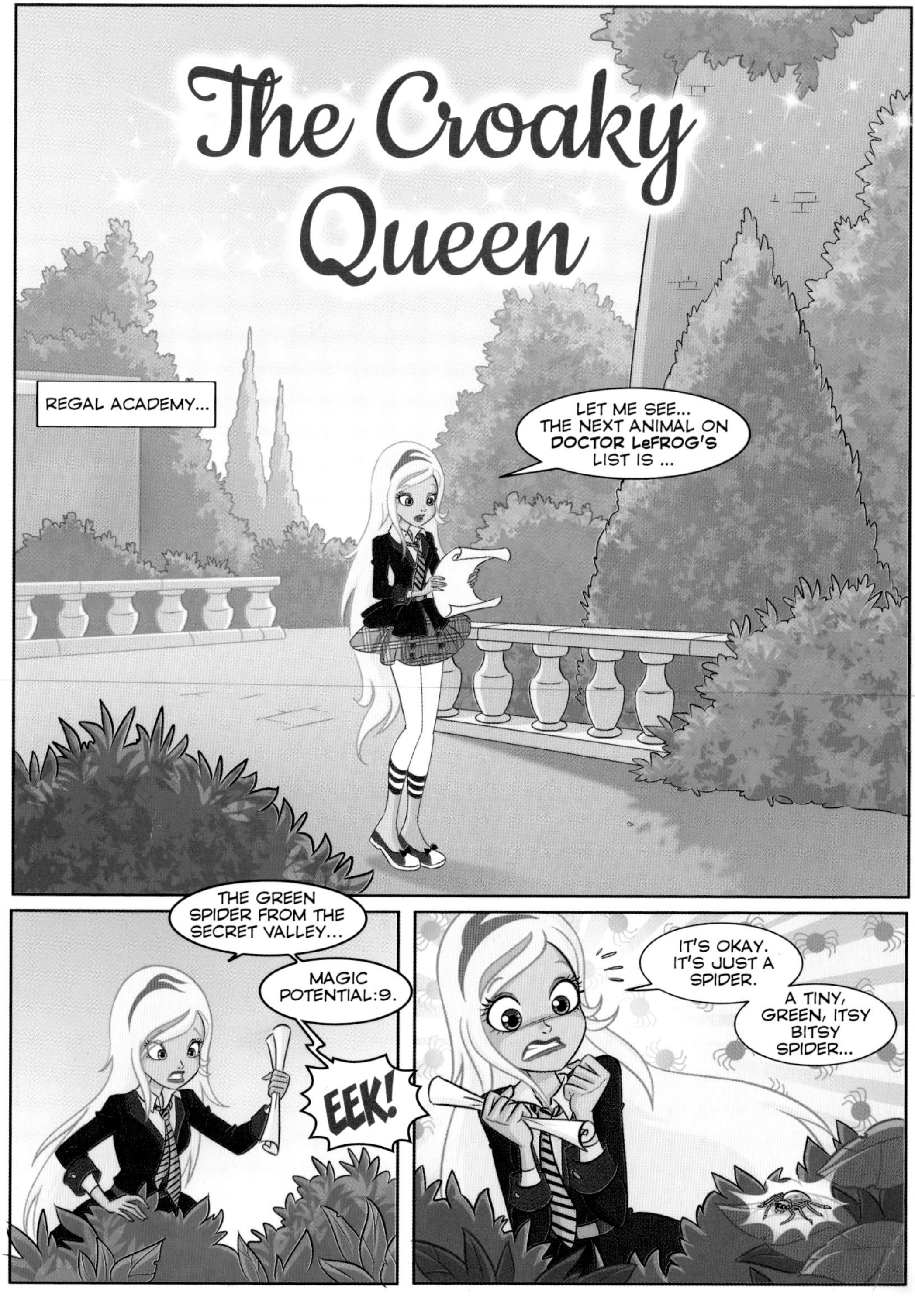
The Croaky Queen
REGAL ACADEMY...
LET ME SEE... THE NEXT ANIMAL ON DOCTOR LeFROG'S LIST IS ...
THE GREEN SPIDER FROM THE SECRET VALLEY...
MAGIC POTENTIAL:9.
EEK!
IT'S OKAY. IT'S JUST A SPIDER.
A TINY, GREEN, ITSY BITSY SPIDER...

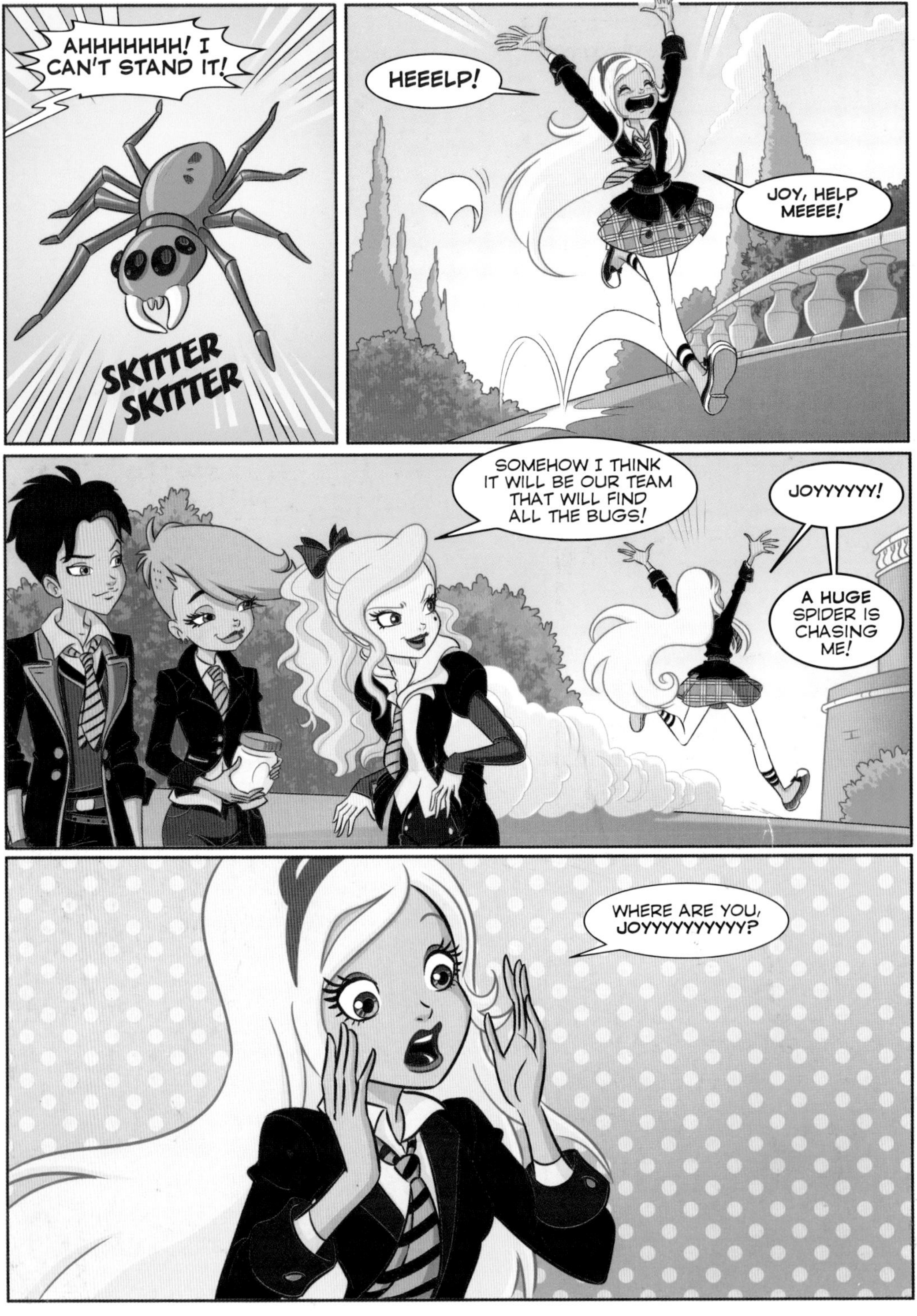
AHHHHHHH! I CAN'T STAND IT!
SKITTER SKITTER
HEEELP!
JOY, HELP MEEEE!
SOMEHOW I THINK IT WILL BE OUR TEAM THAT WILL FIND ALL THE BUGS!
JOYYYYYY!
A HUGE SPIDER IS CHASING ME!
WHERE ARE YOU, JOYYYYYYYYYY?

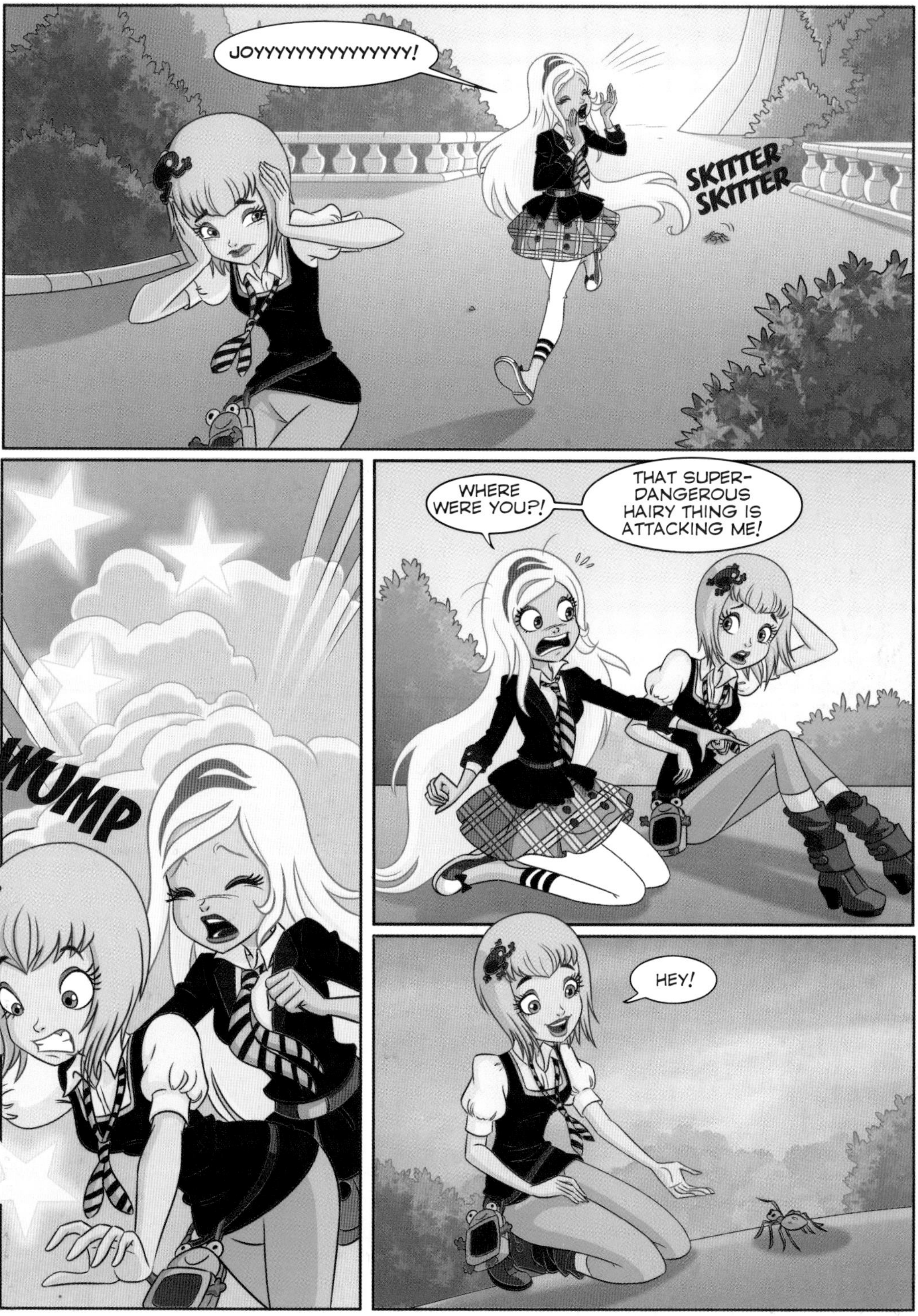
JOYYYYYYYYYYYYYYY!
SKITTER SKITTER
WUMP
WHERE WERE YOU?!
THAT SUPER-DANGEROUS HAIRY THING IS ATTACKING ME!
HEY!

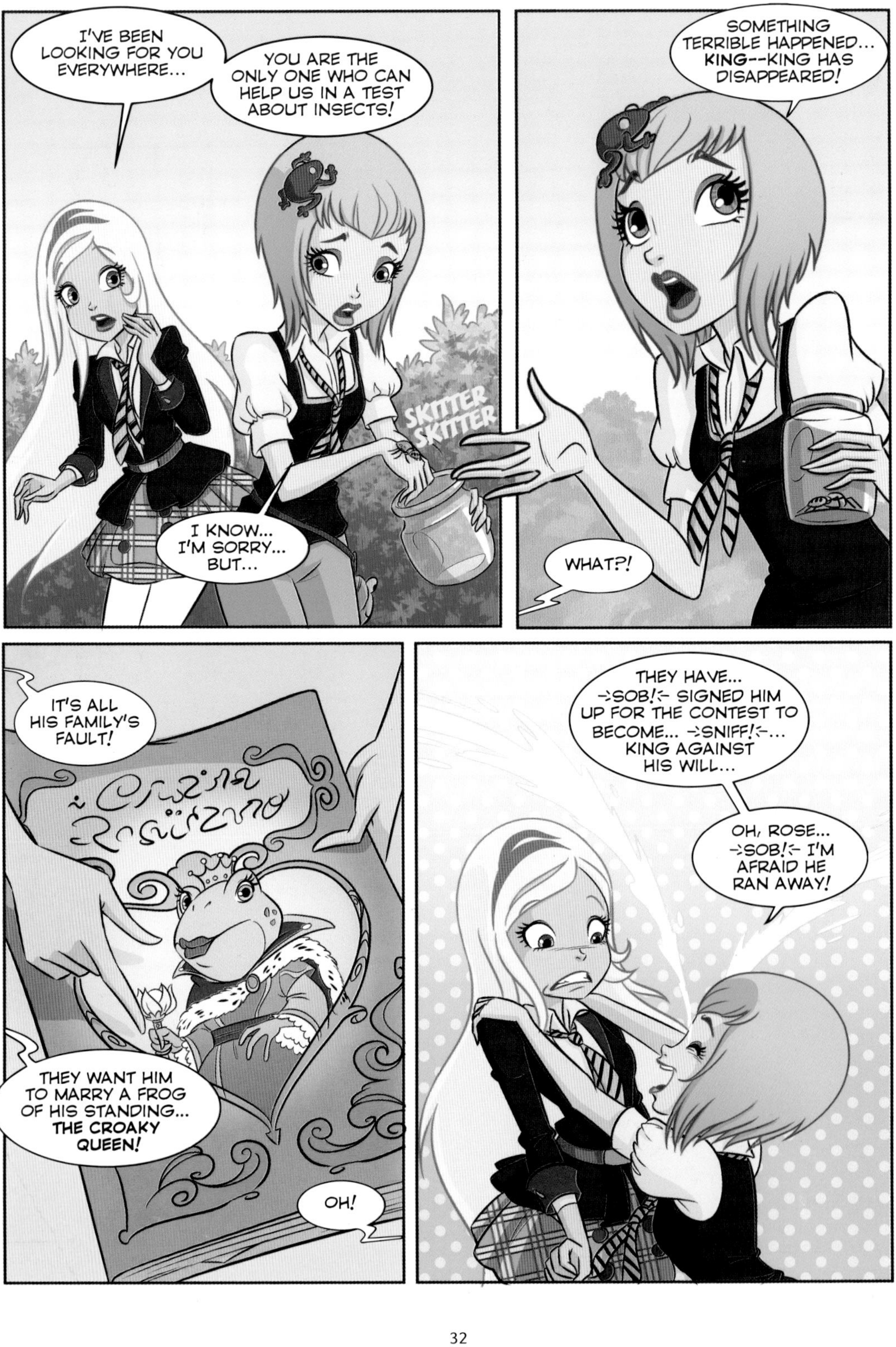
I'VE BEEN LOOKING FOR YOU EVERYWHERE...
YOU ARE THE ONLY ONE WHO CAN HELP US IN A TEST ABOUT INSECTS!
SKITTER SKITTER
I KNOW... I'M SORRY... BUT...
SOMETHING TERRIBLE HAPPENED... KING--KING HAS DISAPPEARED!
WHAT?!
IT'S ALL HIS FAMILY'S FAULT!
THEY WANT HIM TO MARRY A FROG OF HIS STANDING... THE CROAKY QUEEN!
OH!
THEY HAVE... SOB! SIGNED HIM UP FOR THE CONTEST TO BECOME... SNIFF!... KING AGAINST HIS WILL...
OH, ROSE... SOB! I'M AFRAID HE RAN AWAY!

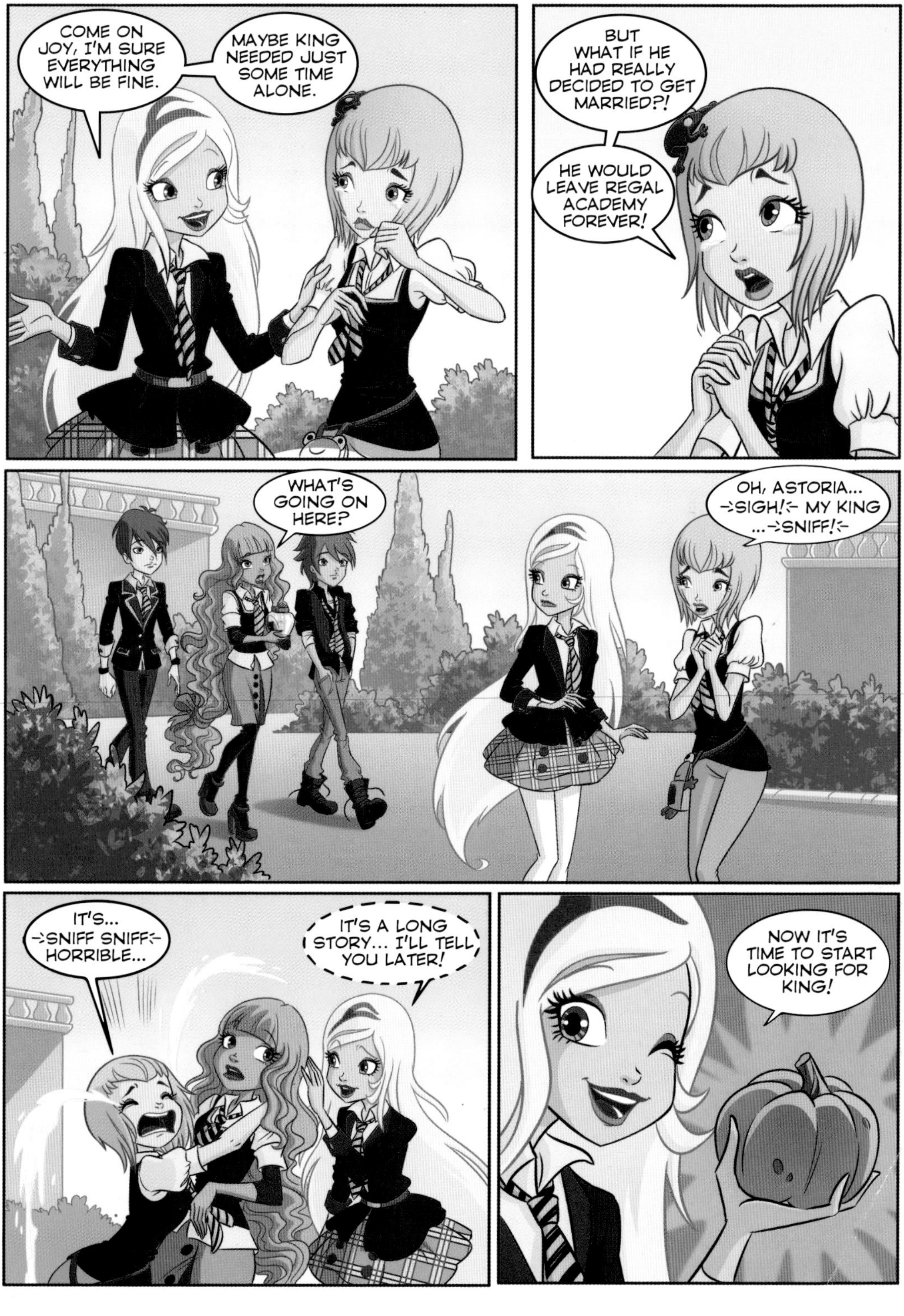
COME ON JOY, I'M SURE EVERYTHING WILL BE FINE.
MAYBE KING NEEDED JUST SOME TIME ALONE.
BUT WHAT IF HE HAD REALLY DECIDED TO GET MARRIED?!
HE WOULD LEAVE REGAL ACADEMY FOREVER!
WHAT'S GOING ON HERE?
OH, ASTORIA... -SIGH!- MY KING ...-SNIFF!-
IT'S... -SNIFF SNIFF- HORRIBLE...
IT'S A LONG STORY... I'LL TELL YOU LATER!
NOW IT'S TIME TO START LOOKING FOR KING!

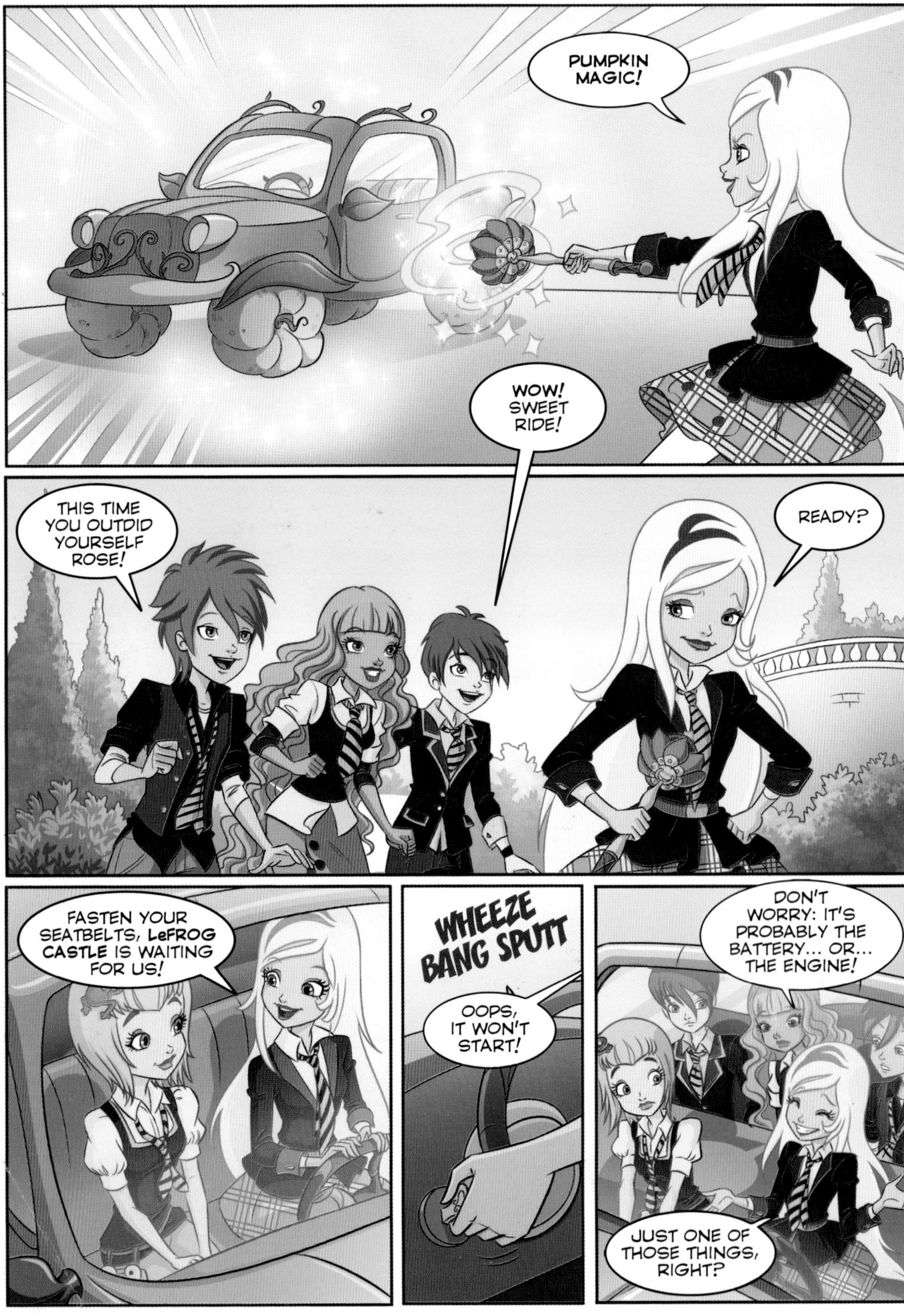
PUMPKIN MAGIC!
WOW! SWEET RIDE!
THIS TIME YOU OUTDID YOURSELF ROSE!
READY?
FASTEN YOUR SEATBELTS, **LeFROG CASTLE** IS WAITING FOR US!
WHEEZE BANG SPUTT
OOPS, IT WON'T START!
DON'T WORRY: IT'S PROBABLY THE BATTERY... OR... THE ENGINE!
JUST ONE OF THOSE THINGS, RIGHT?

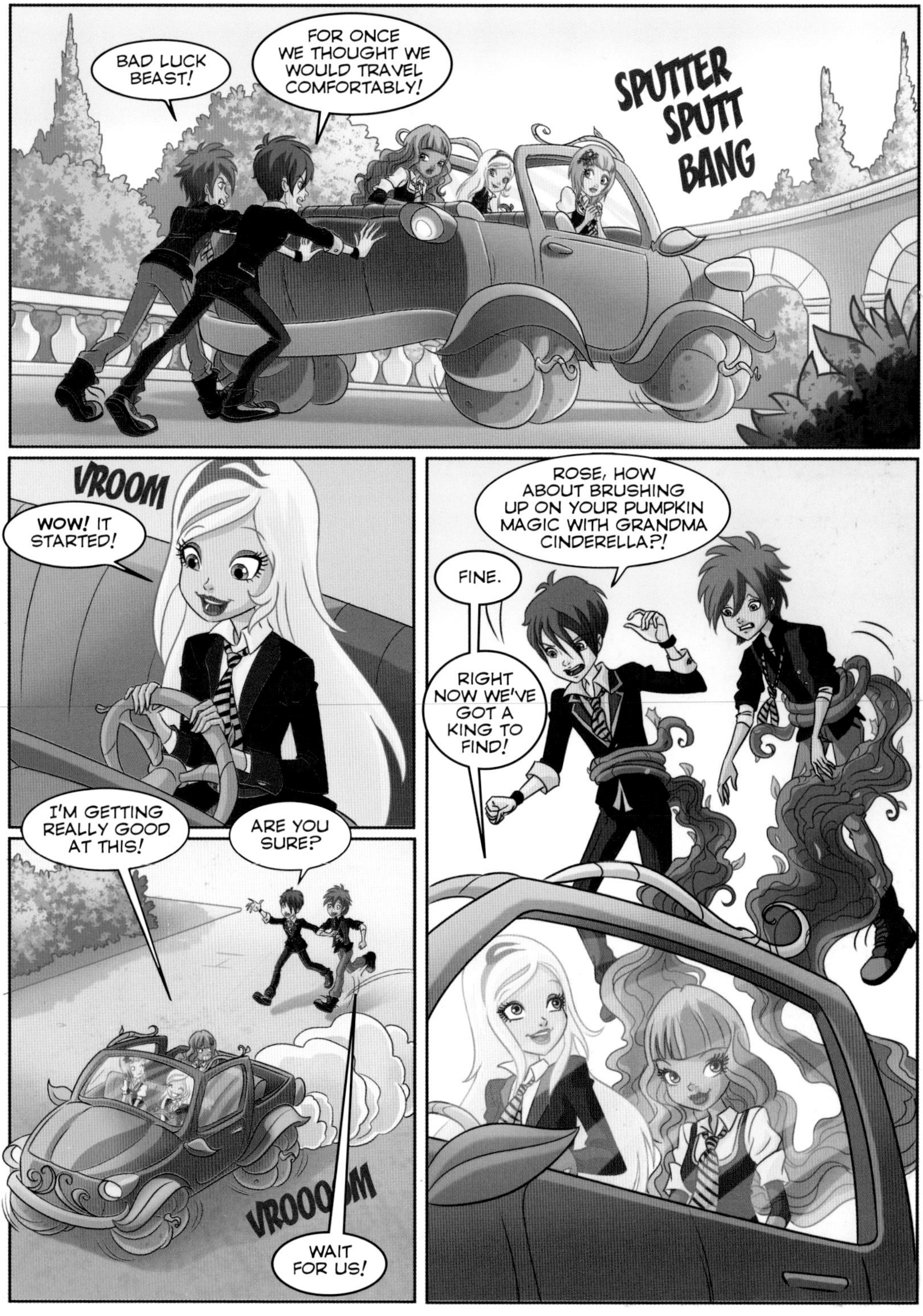

BAD LUCK BEAST!
FOR ONCE WE THOUGHT WE WOULD TRAVEL COMFORTABLY!
SPUTTER SPUTT BANG
VROOM
WOW! IT STARTED!
I'M GETTING REALLY GOOD AT THIS!
ARE YOU SURE?
VROOOOM
WAIT FOR US!
ROSE, HOW ABOUT BRUSHING UP ON YOUR PUMPKIN MAGIC WITH GRANDMA CINDERELLA?!
FINE.
RIGHT NOW WE'VE GOT A KING TO FIND!

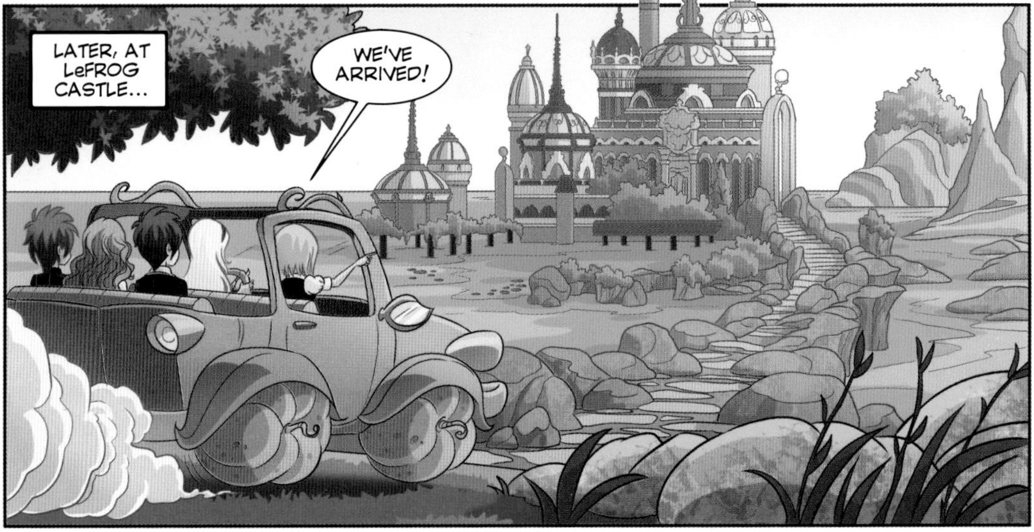
LATER, AT LeFROG CASTLE...
WE'VE ARRIVED!

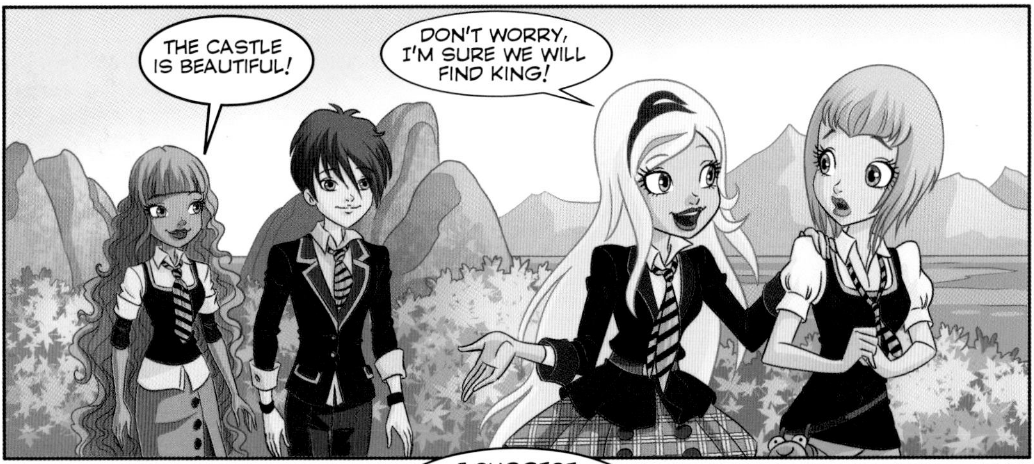
THE CASTLE IS BEAUTIFUL!
DON'T WORRY, I'M SURE WE WILL FIND KING!

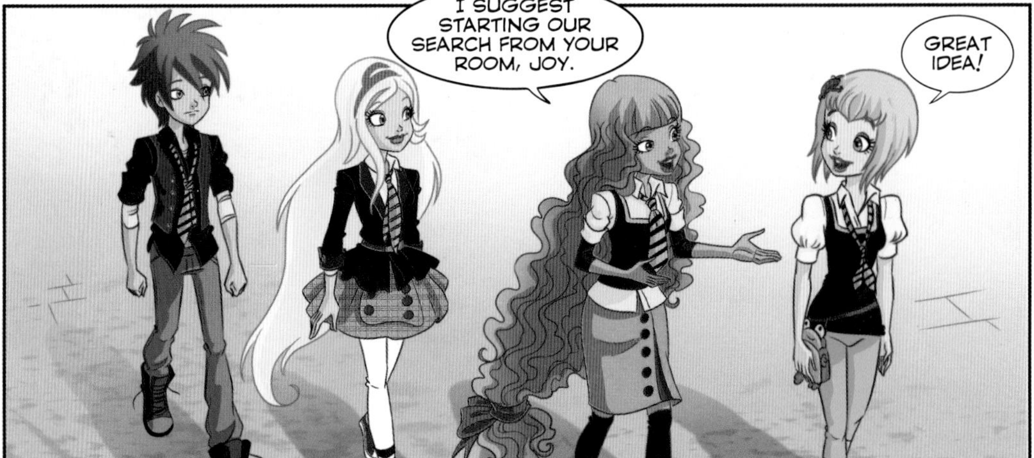
I SUGGEST STARTING OUR SEARCH FROM YOUR ROOM, JOY.
GREAT IDEA!

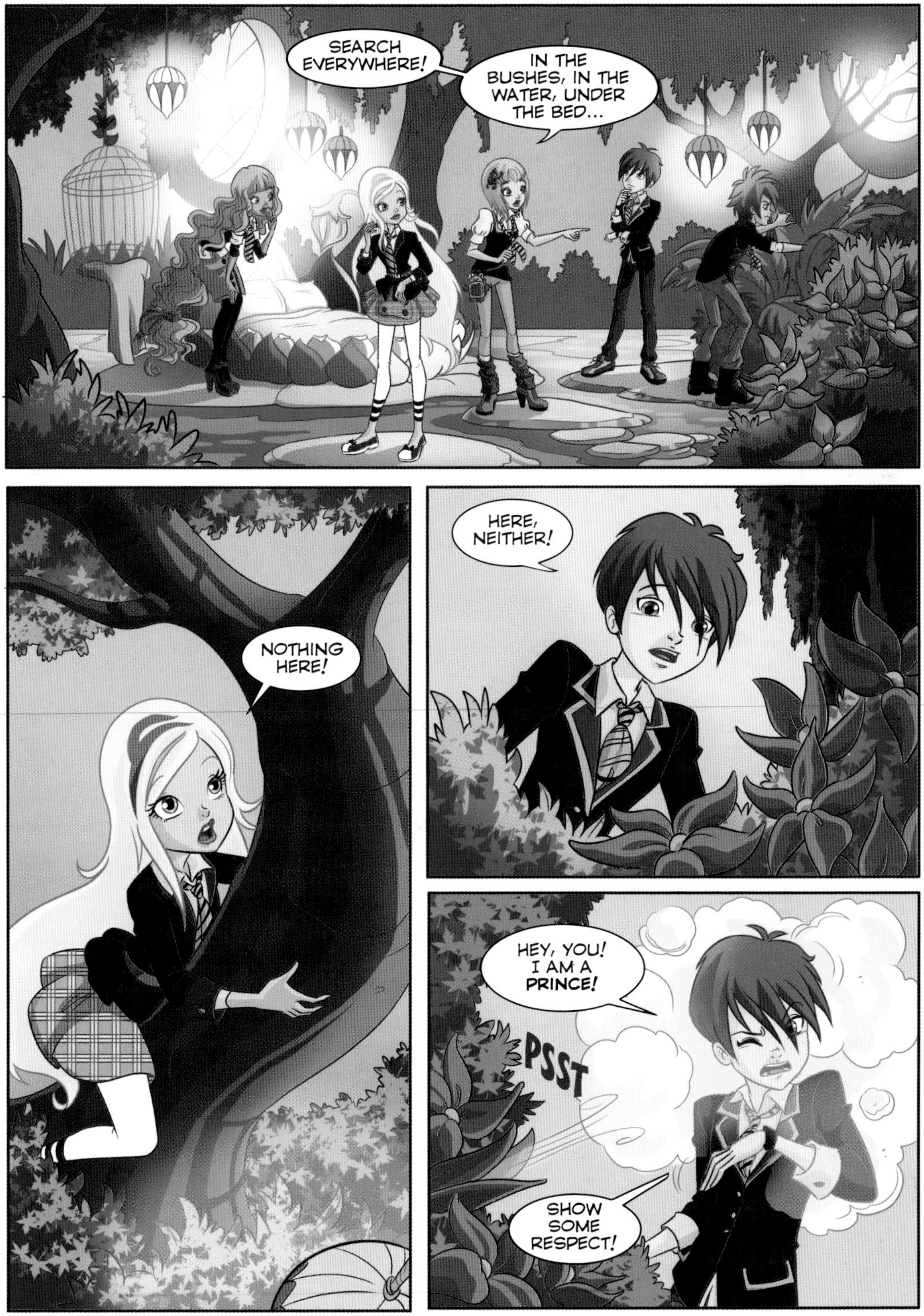
SEARCH EVERYWHERE!
IN THE BUSHES, IN THE WATER, UNDER THE BED...
NOTHING HERE!
HERE, NEITHER!
HEY, YOU! I AM A **PRINCE**!
PSST
SHOW SOME RESPECT!

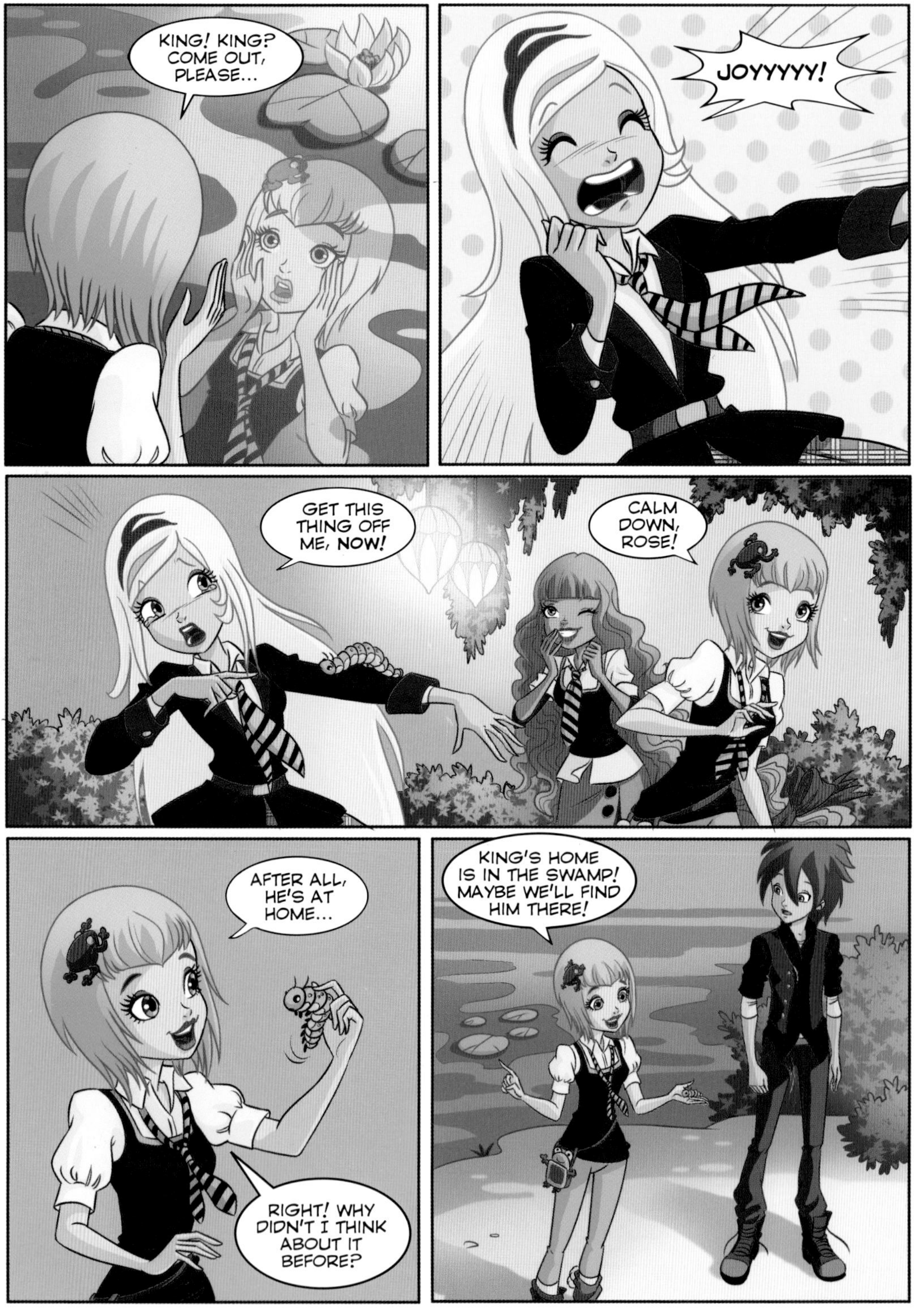
KING! KING? COME OUT, PLEASE...
JOYYYYY!
GET THIS THING OFF ME, NOW!
CALM DOWN, ROSE!
AFTER ALL, HE'S AT HOME...
RIGHT! WHY DIDN'T I THINK ABOUT IT BEFORE?
KING'S HOME IS IN THE SWAMP! MAYBE WE'LL FIND HIM THERE!

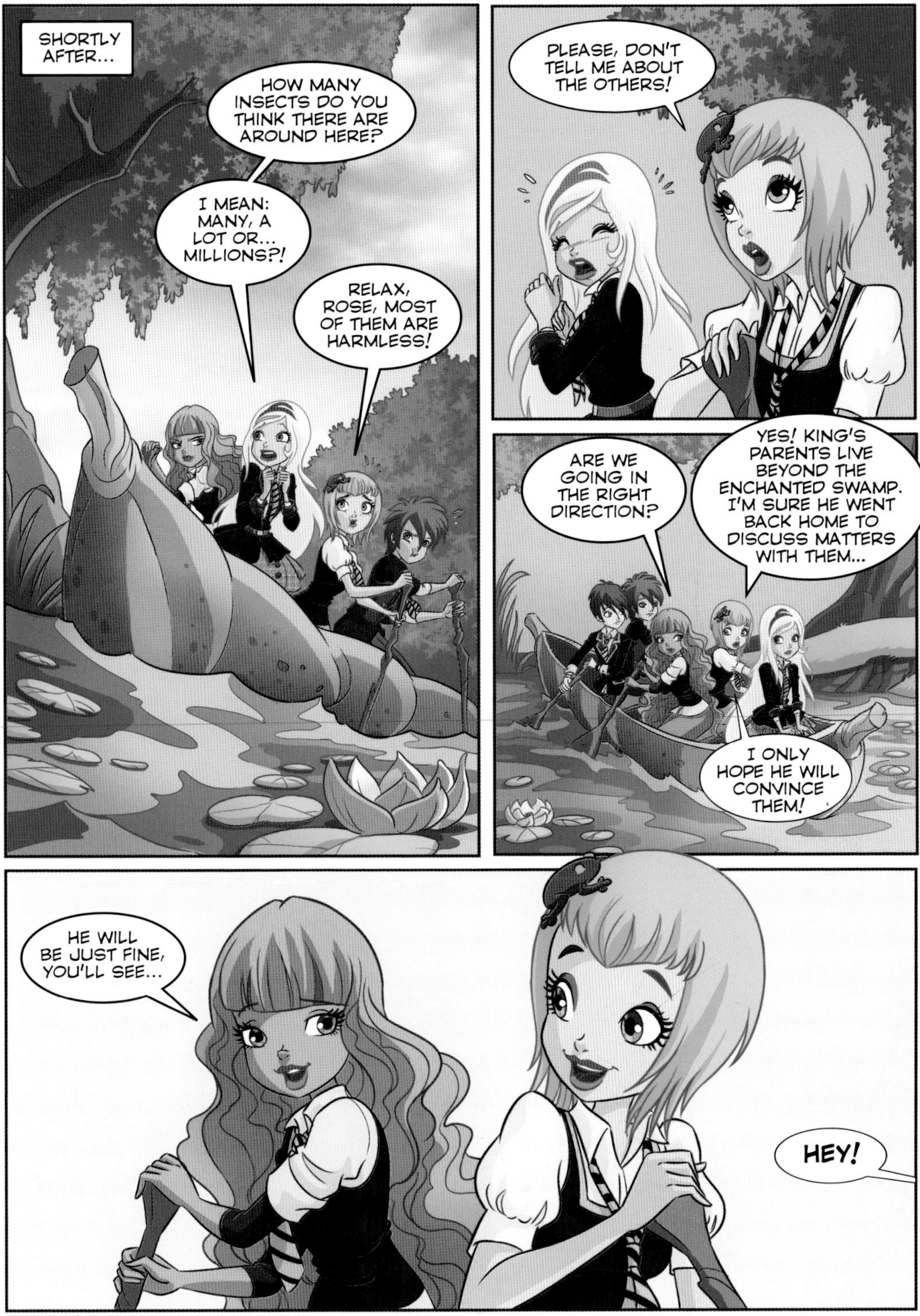
SHORTLY AFTER...
HOW MANY INSECTS DO YOU THINK THERE ARE AROUND HERE?
I MEAN: MANY, A LOT OR... MILLIONS?!
RELAX, ROSE, MOST OF THEM ARE HARMLESS!
PLEASE, DON'T TELL ME ABOUT THE OTHERS!
ARE WE GOING IN THE RIGHT DIRECTION?
YES! KING'S PARENTS LIVE BEYOND THE ENCHANTED SWAMP. I'M SURE HE WENT BACK HOME TO DISCUSS MATTERS WITH THEM...
I ONLY HOPE HE WILL CONVINCE THEM!
HE WILL BE JUST FINE, YOU'LL SEE...
HEY!

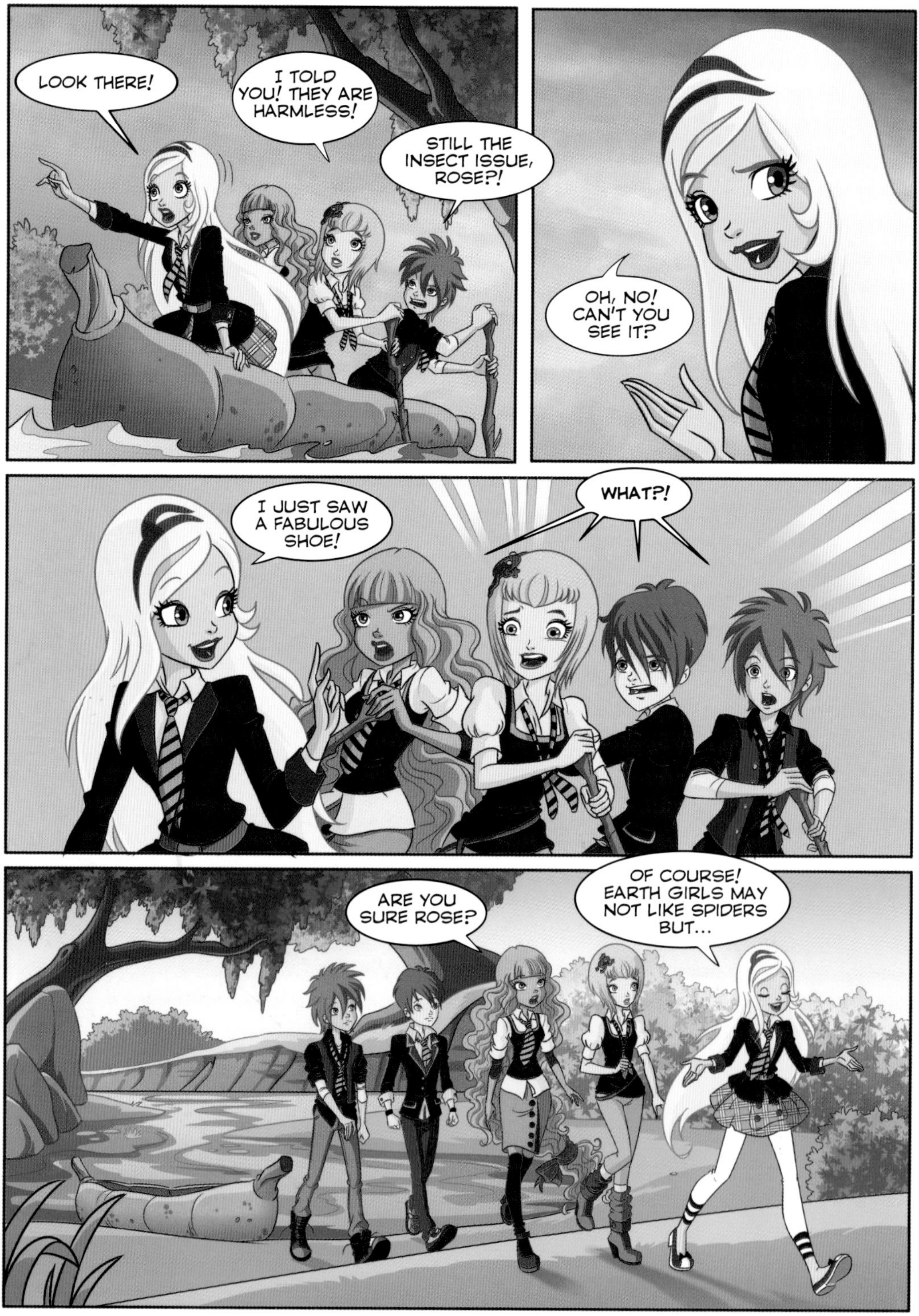
LOOK THERE!
I TOLD YOU! THEY ARE HARMLESS!
STILL THE INSECT ISSUE, ROSE?!
OH, NO! CAN'T YOU SEE IT?
I JUST SAW A FABULOUS SHOE!
WHAT?!
ARE YOU SURE ROSE?
OF COURSE! EARTH GIRLS MAY NOT LIKE SPIDERS BUT...

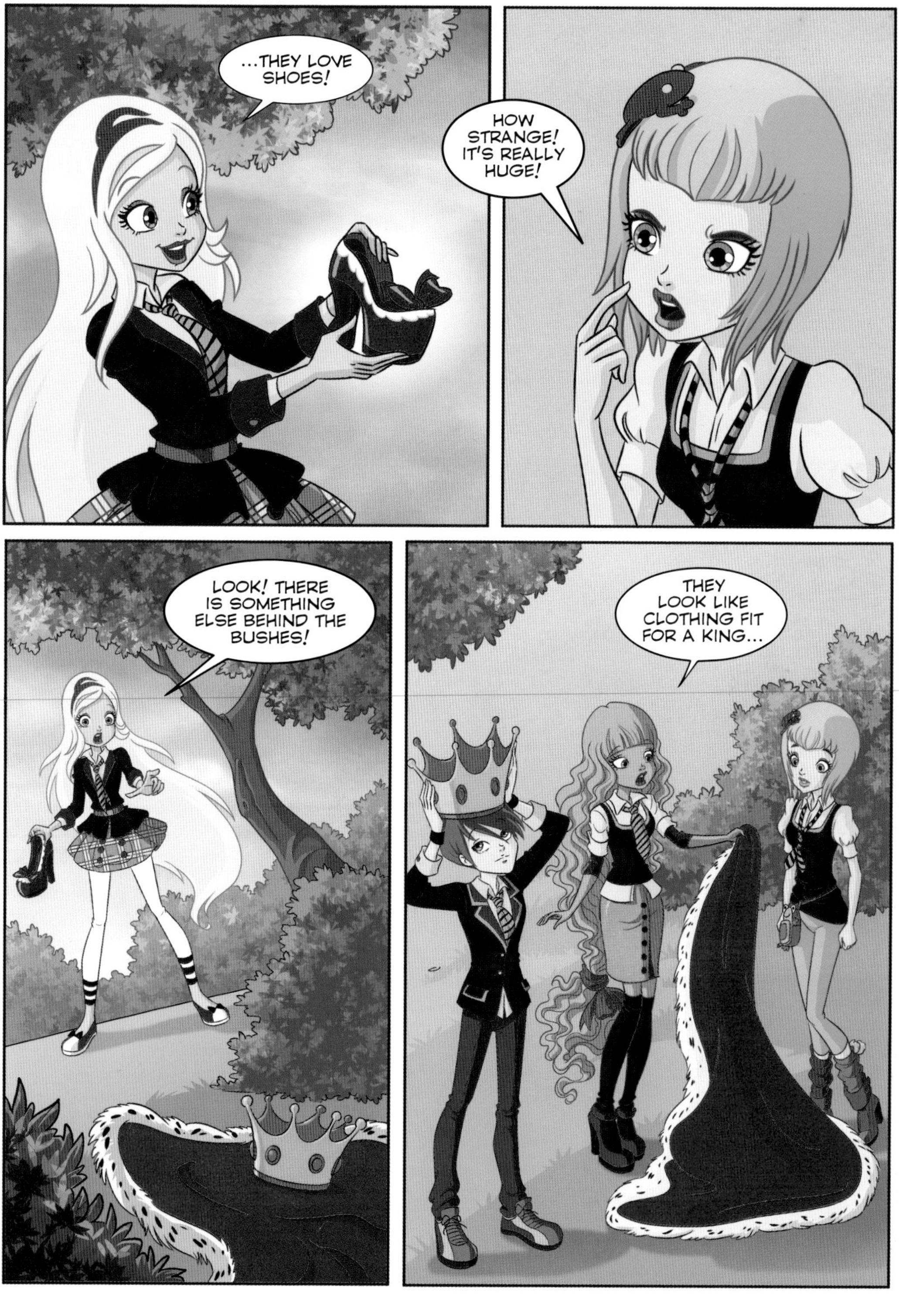
...THEY LOVE SHOES!
HOW STRANGE! IT'S REALLY HUGE!
LOOK! THERE IS SOMETHING ELSE BEHIND THE BUSHES!
THEY LOOK LIKE CLOTHING FIT FOR A KING...

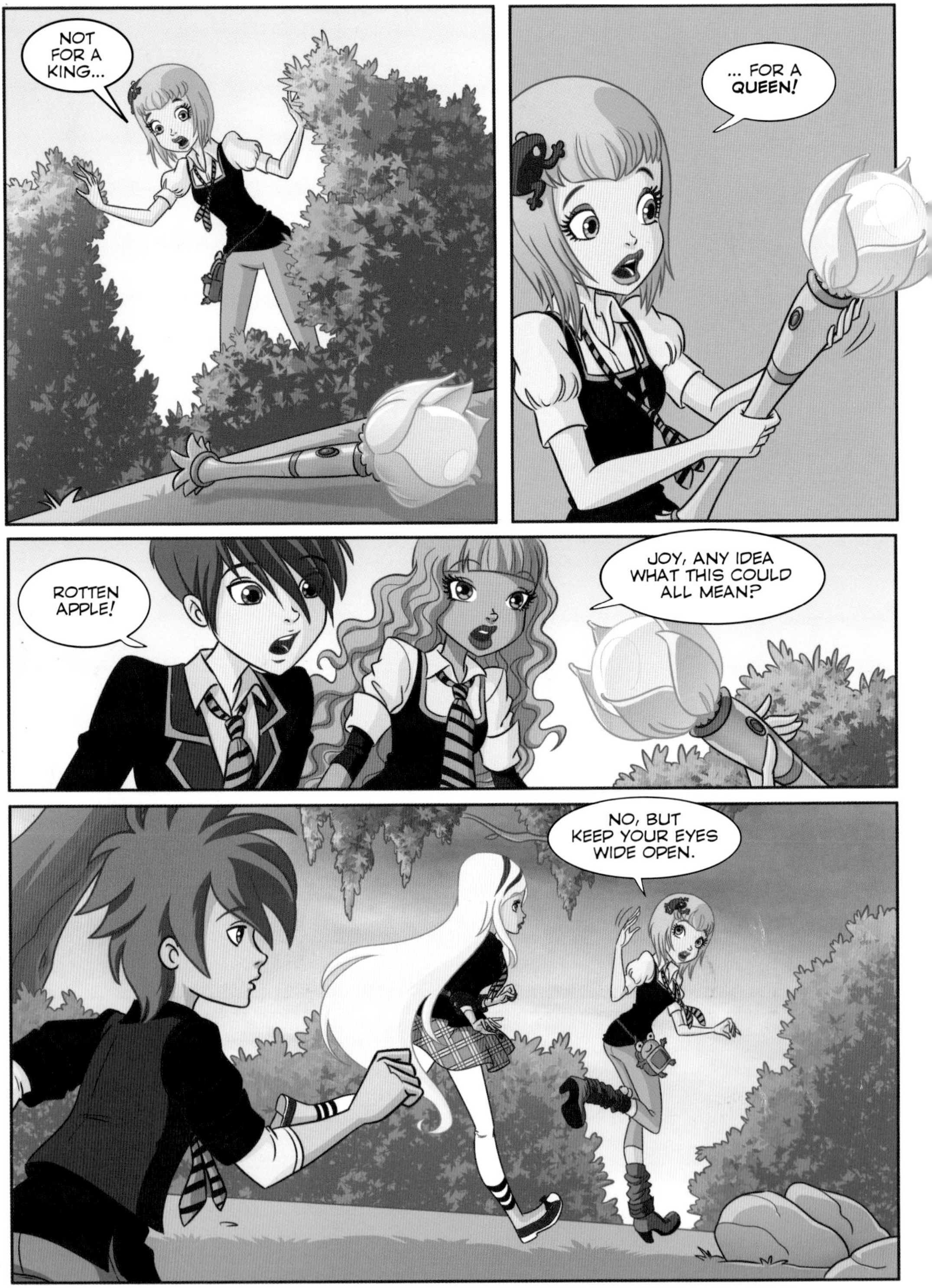
NOT FOR A KING...
... FOR A QUEEN!
ROTTEN APPLE!
JOY, ANY IDEA WHAT THIS COULD ALL MEAN?
NO, BUT KEEP YOUR EYES WIDE OPEN.

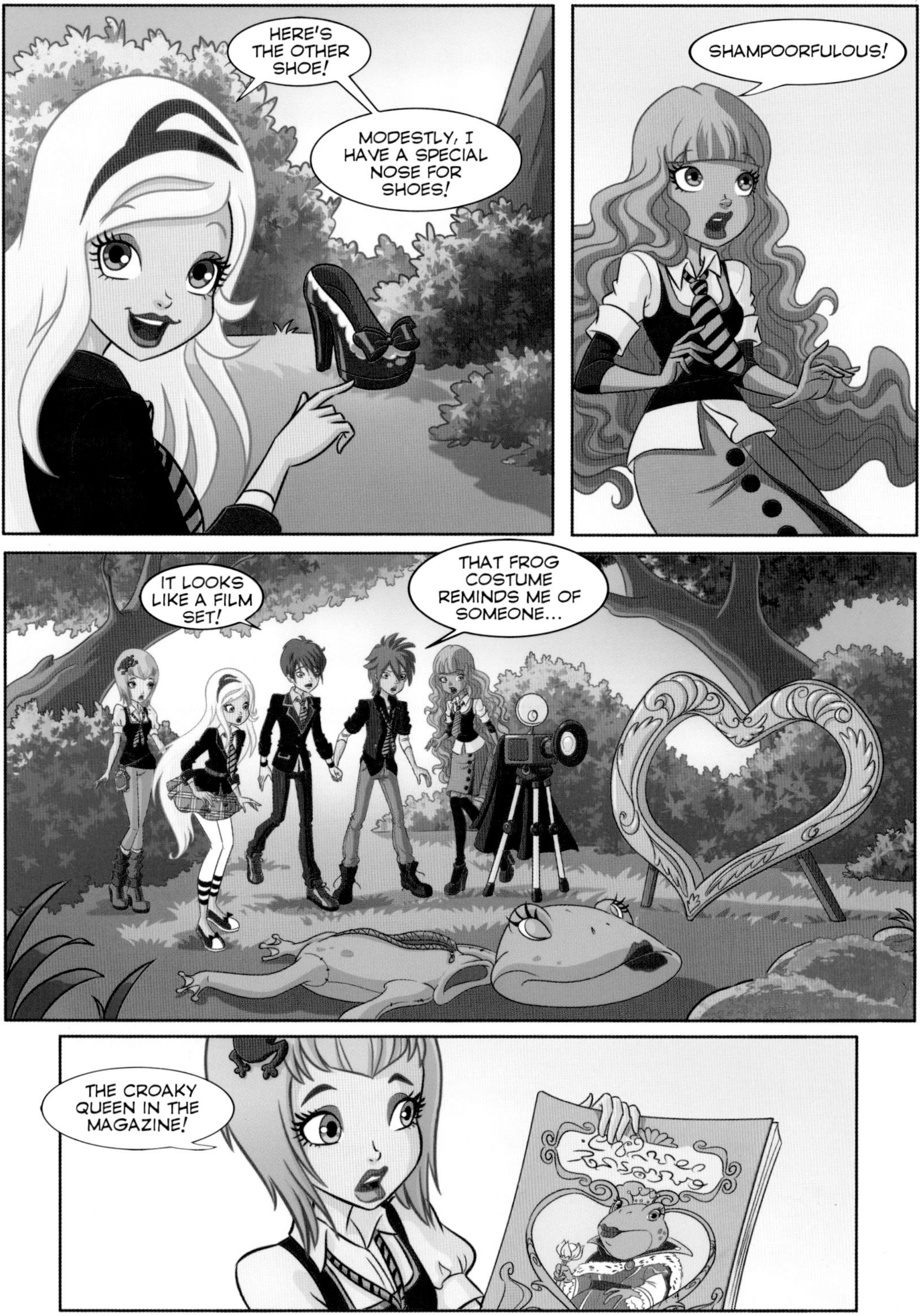
HERE'S THE OTHER SHOE!
MODESTLY, I HAVE A SPECIAL NOSE FOR SHOES!
SHAMPOORFULOUS!
IT LOOKS LIKE A FILM SET!
THAT FROG COSTUME REMINDS ME OF SOMEONE...
THE CROAKY QUEEN IN THE MAGAZINE!

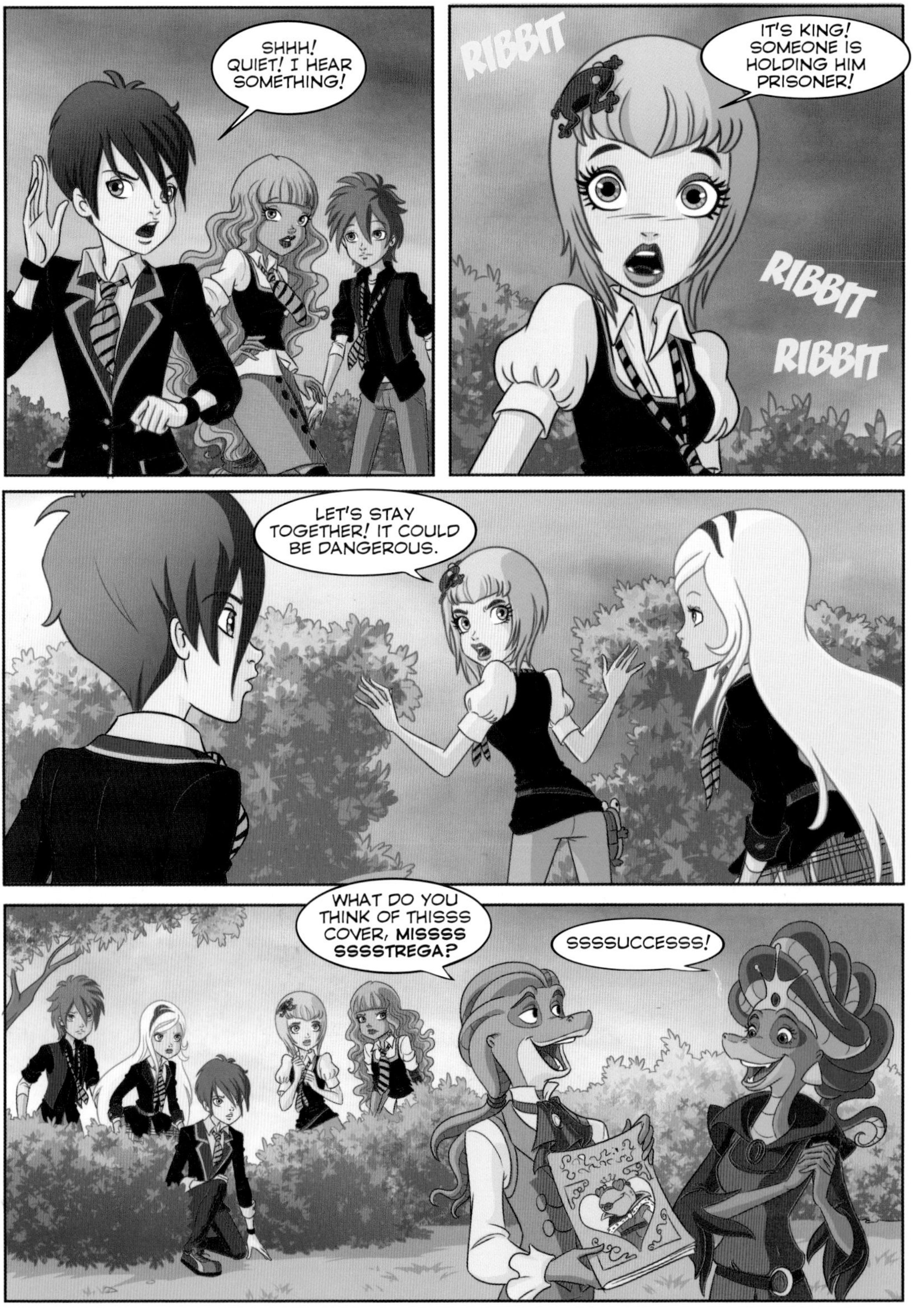
SHHH! QUIET! I HEAR SOMETHING!
RIBBIT
IT'S KING! SOMEONE IS HOLDING HIM PRISONER!
RIBBIT
RIBBIT
LET'S STAY TOGETHER! IT COULD BE DANGEROUS.
WHAT DO YOU THINK OF THISSS COVER, MISSSS SSSSTREGA?
SSSSUCCESSS!

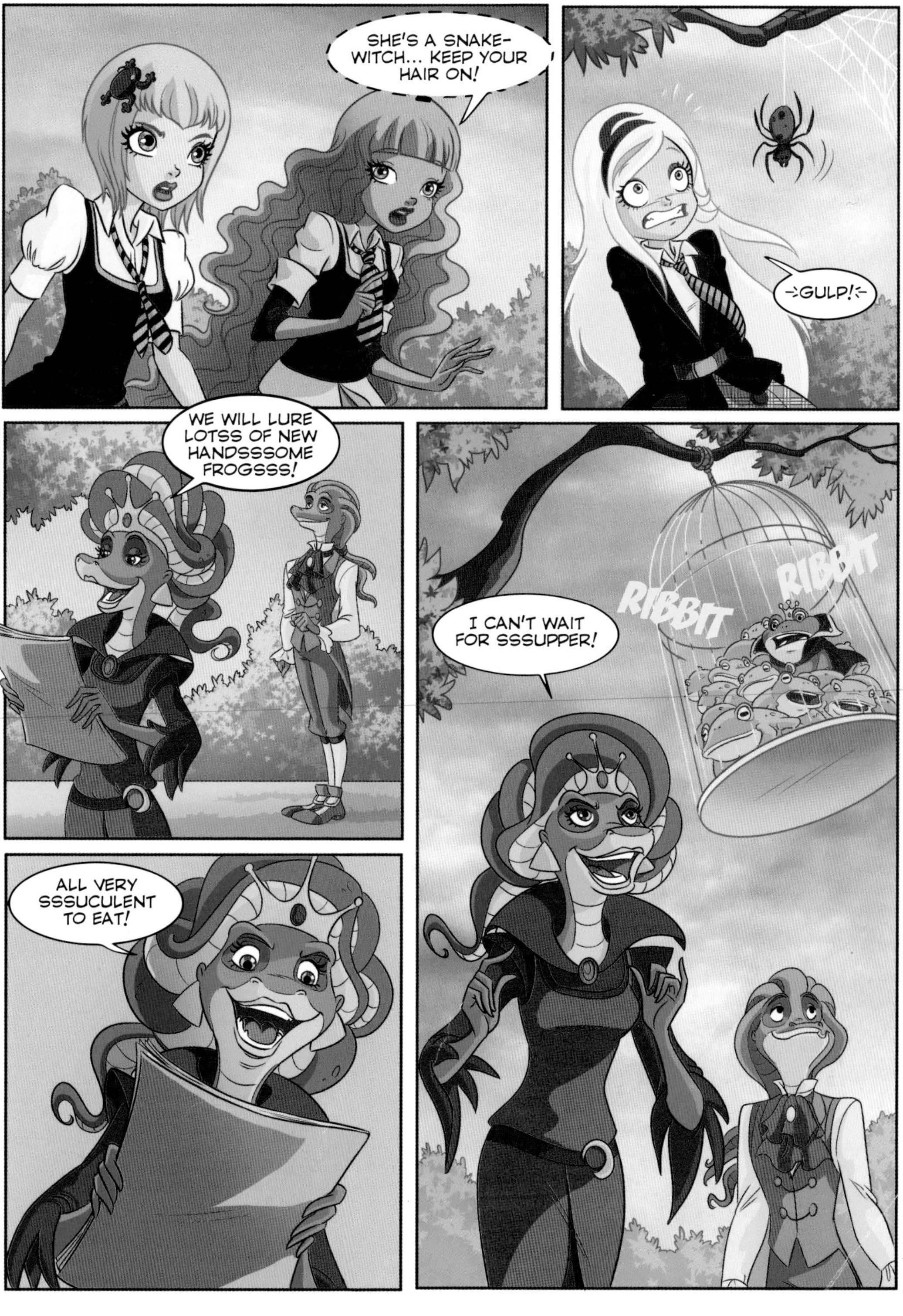
SHE'S A SNAKE-WITCH... KEEP YOUR HAIR ON!
GULP!
WE WILL LURE LOTSS OF NEW HANDSSSOME FROGSSS!
RIBBIT
RIBBIT
I CAN'T WAIT FOR SSSUPPER!
ALL VERY SSSUCULENT TO EAT!

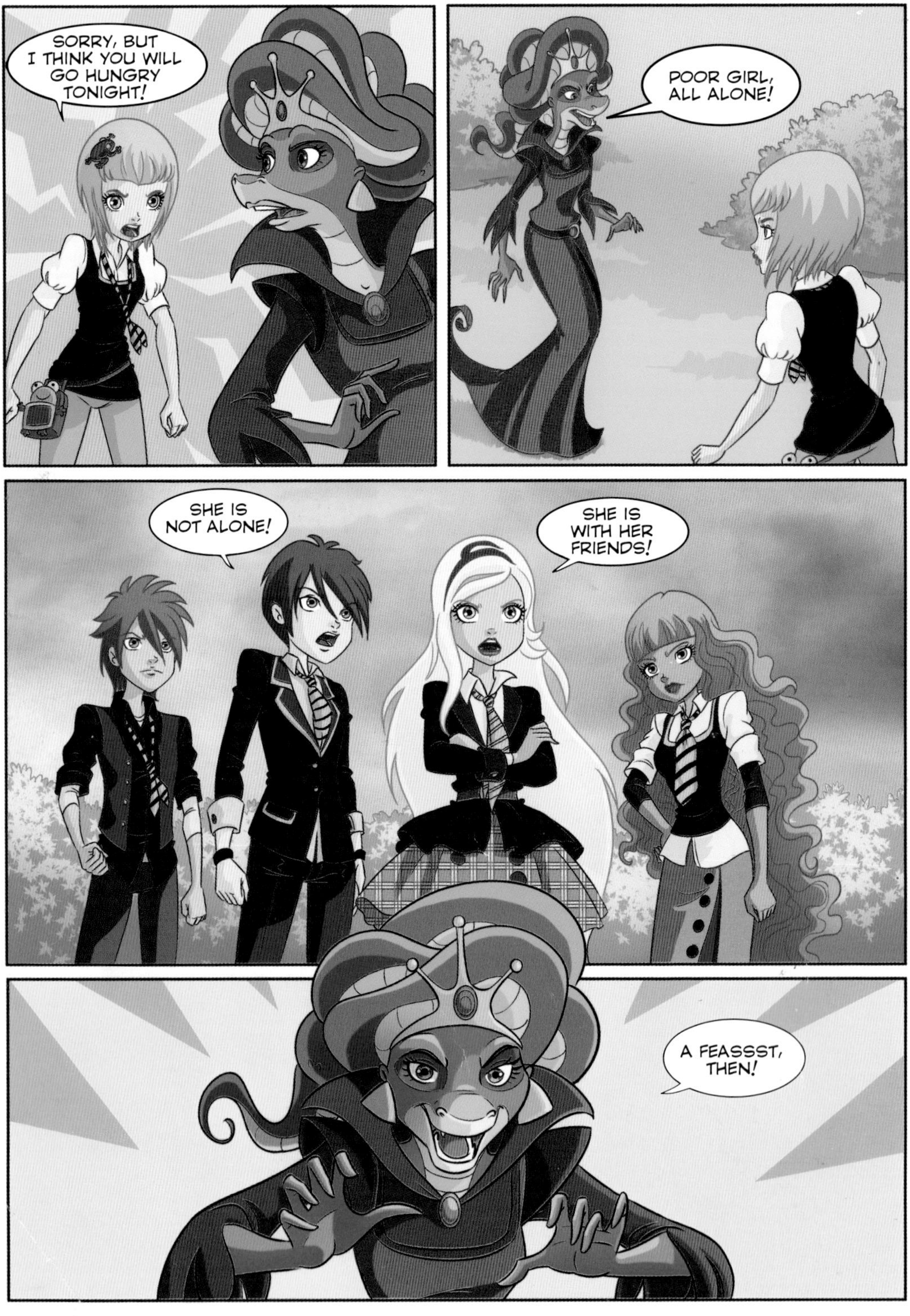
SORRY, BUT I THINK YOU WILL GO HUNGRY TONIGHT!
POOR GIRL, ALL ALONE!
SHE IS NOT ALONE!
SHE IS WITH HER FRIENDS!
A FEASSST, THEN!

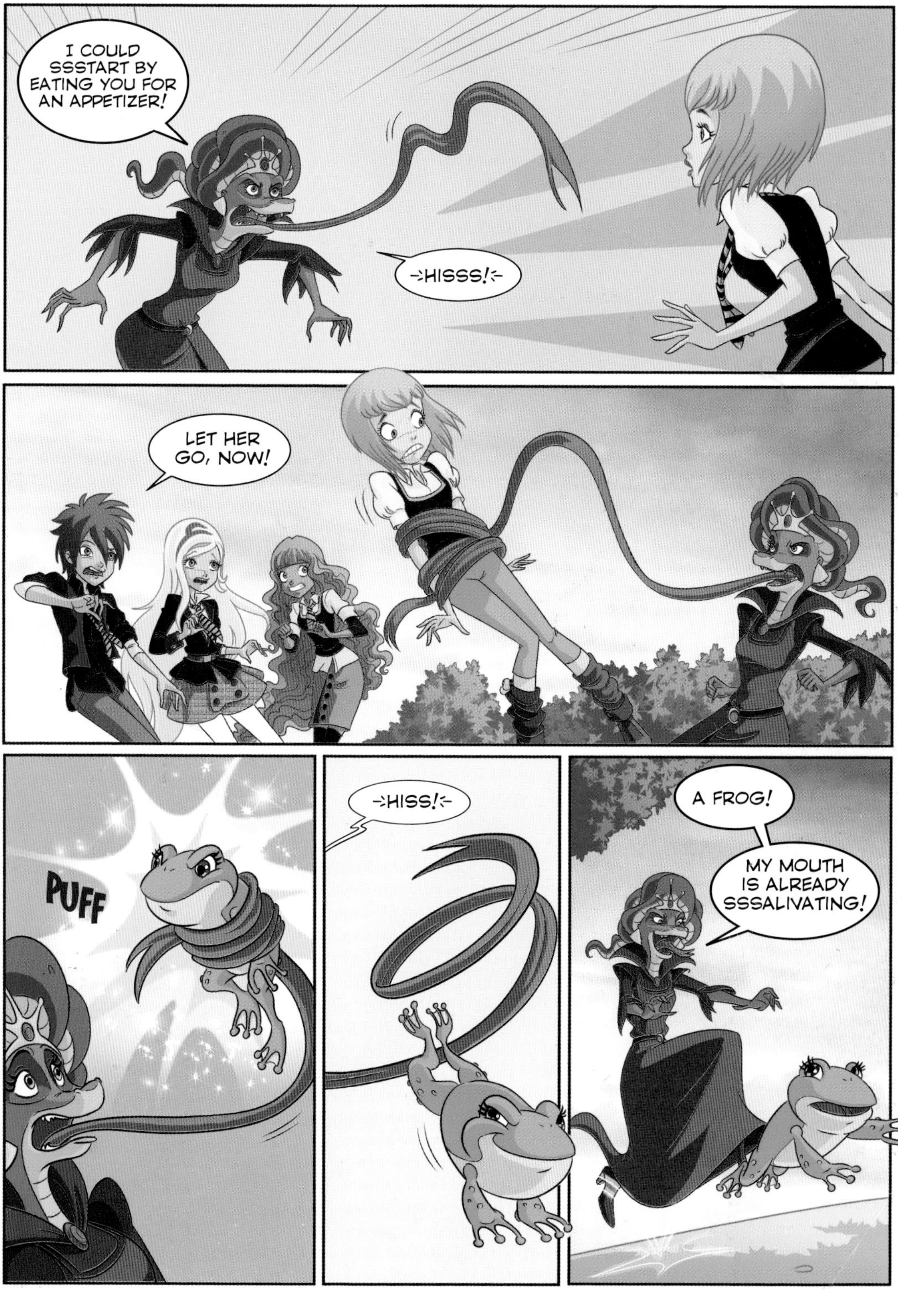
I COULD SSSTART BY EATING YOU FOR AN APPETIZER!
-HISSS!-
LET HER GO, NOW!
PUFF
-HISS!-
A FROG!
MY MOUTH IS ALREADY SSSALIVATING!

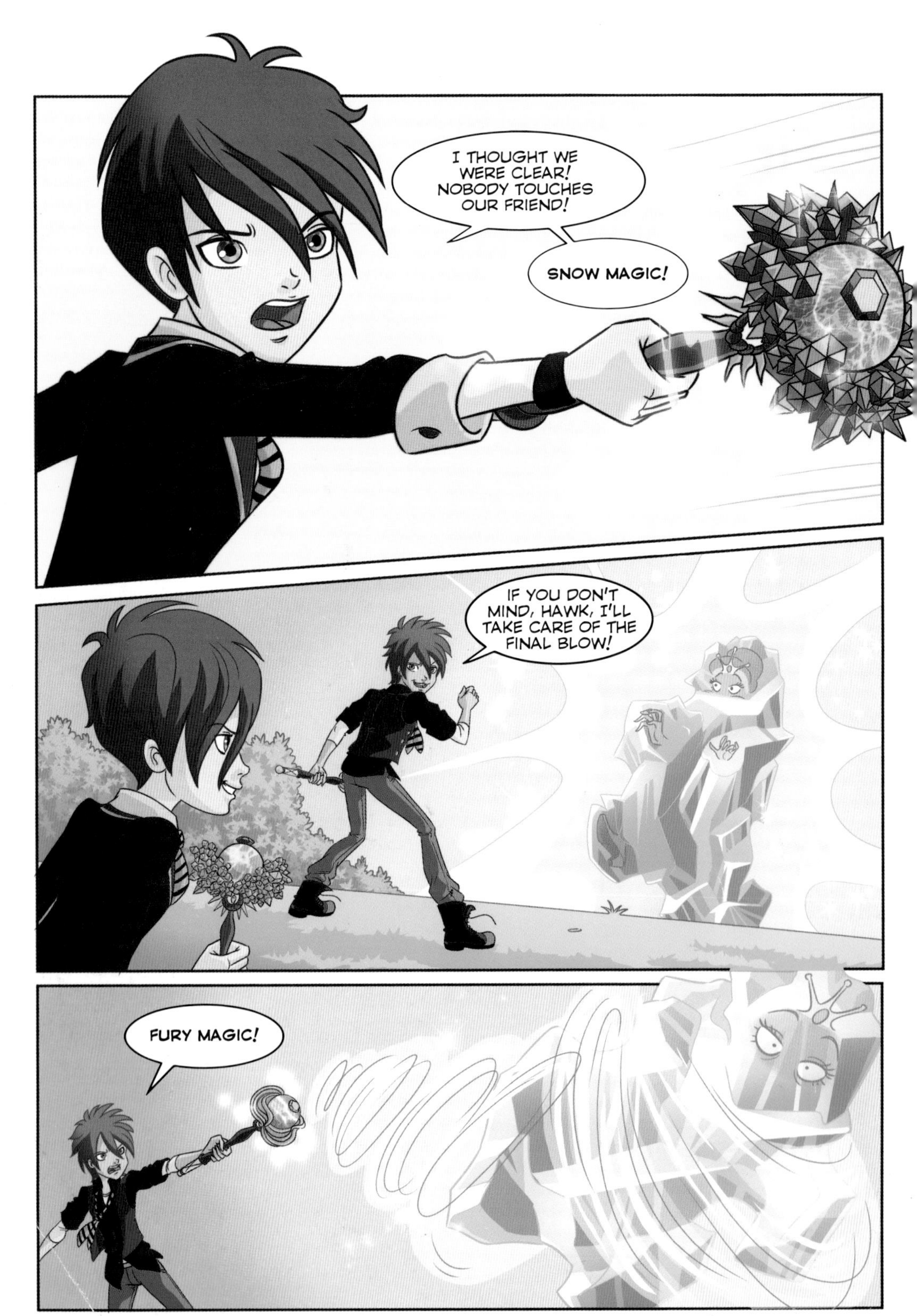
I THOUGHT WE WERE CLEAR! NOBODY TOUCHES OUR FRIEND!
SNOW MAGIC!
IF YOU DON'T MIND, HAWK, I'LL TAKE CARE OF THE FINAL BLOW!
FURY MAGIC!

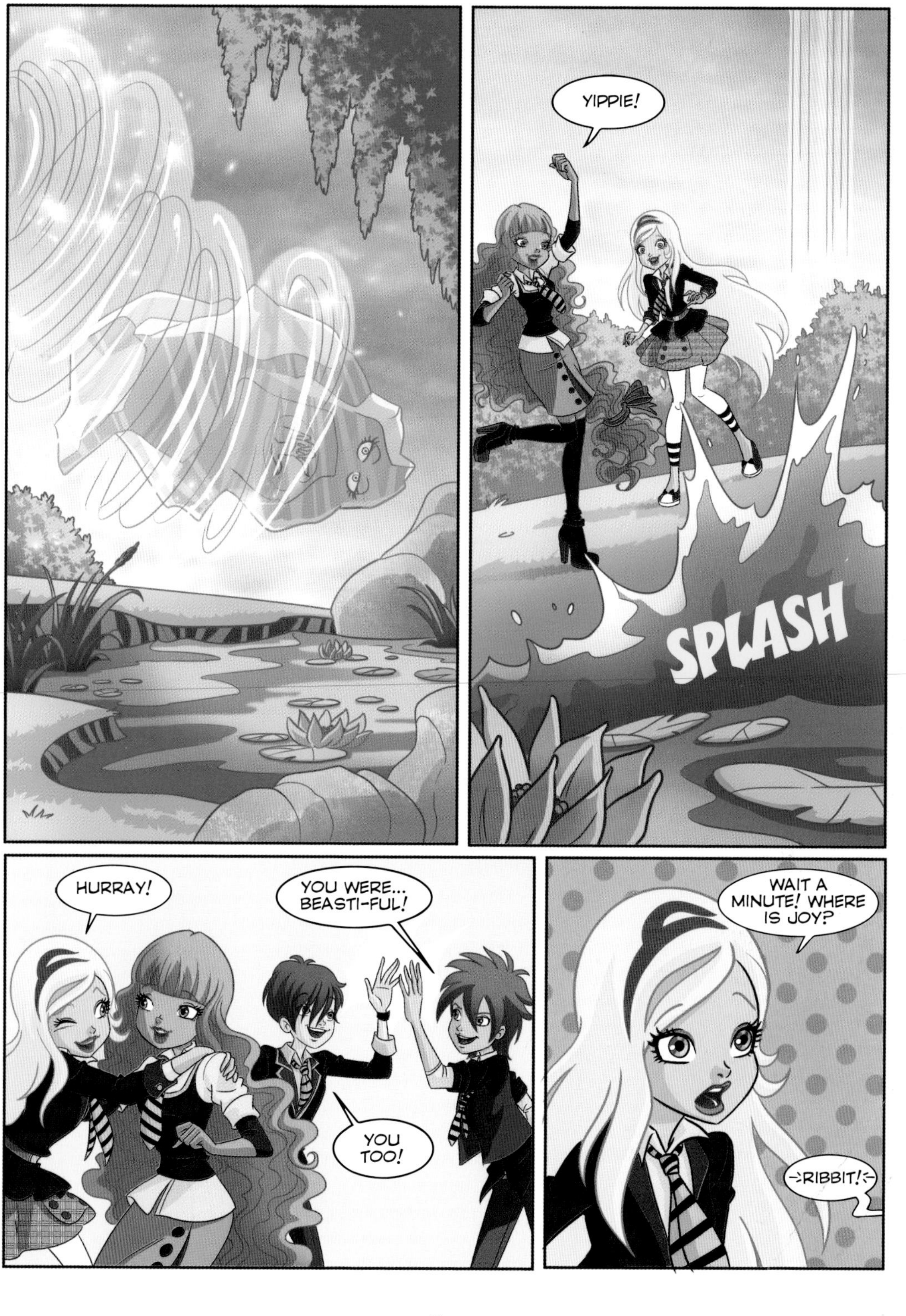
YIPPIE!
SPLASH
HURRAY!
YOU WERE... BEASTI-FUL!
YOU TOO!
WAIT A MINUTE! WHERE IS JOY?
RIBBIT!

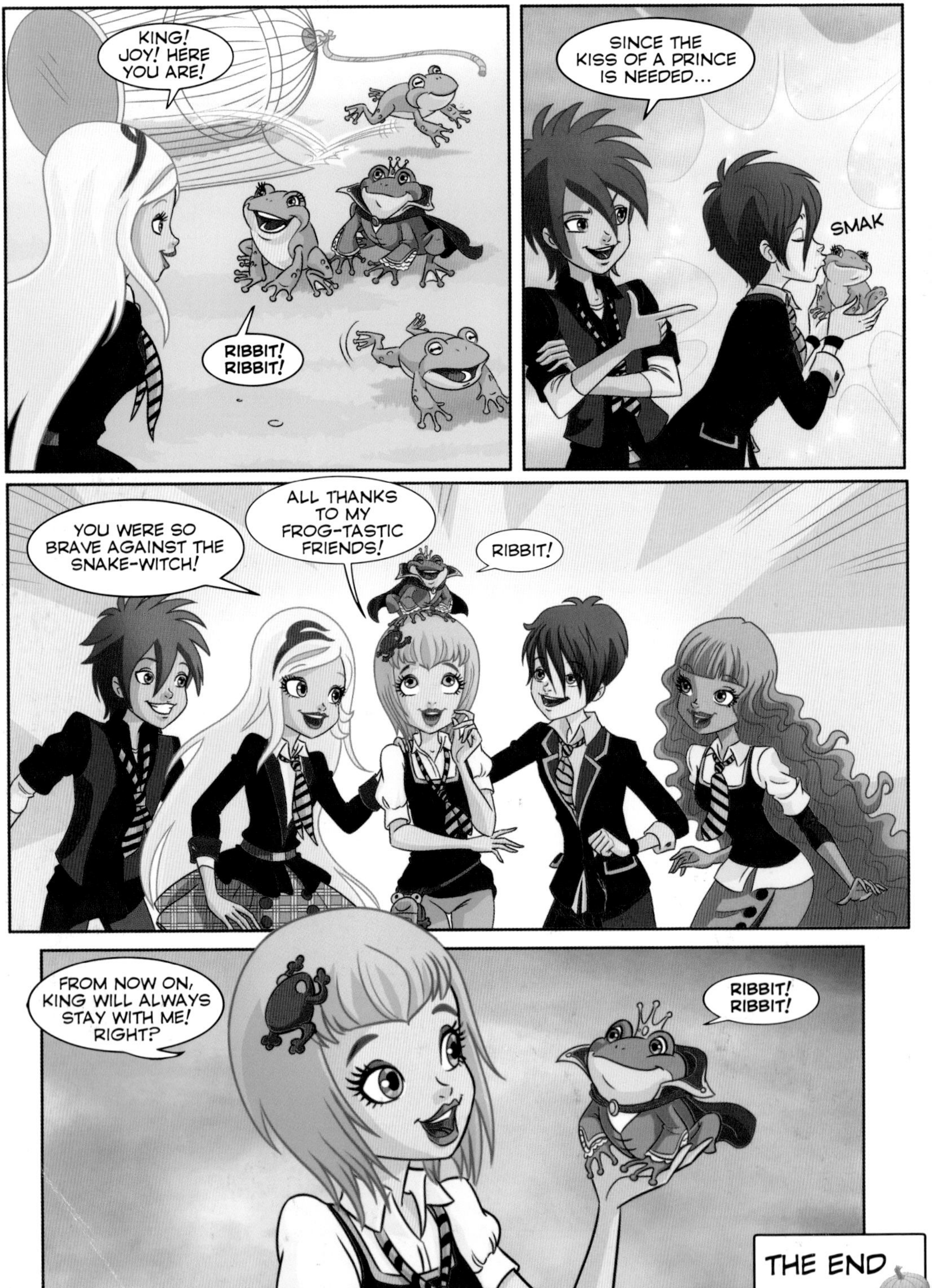
KING! JOY! HERE YOU ARE!
RIBBIT! RIBBIT!
SINCE THE KISS OF A PRINCE IS NEEDED...
SMAK
YOU WERE SO BRAVE AGAINST THE SNAKE-WITCH!
ALL THANKS TO MY FROG-TASTIC FRIENDS!
RIBBIT!
FROM NOW ON, KING WILL ALWAYS STAY WITH ME! RIGHT?
RIBBIT! RIBBIT!
THE END

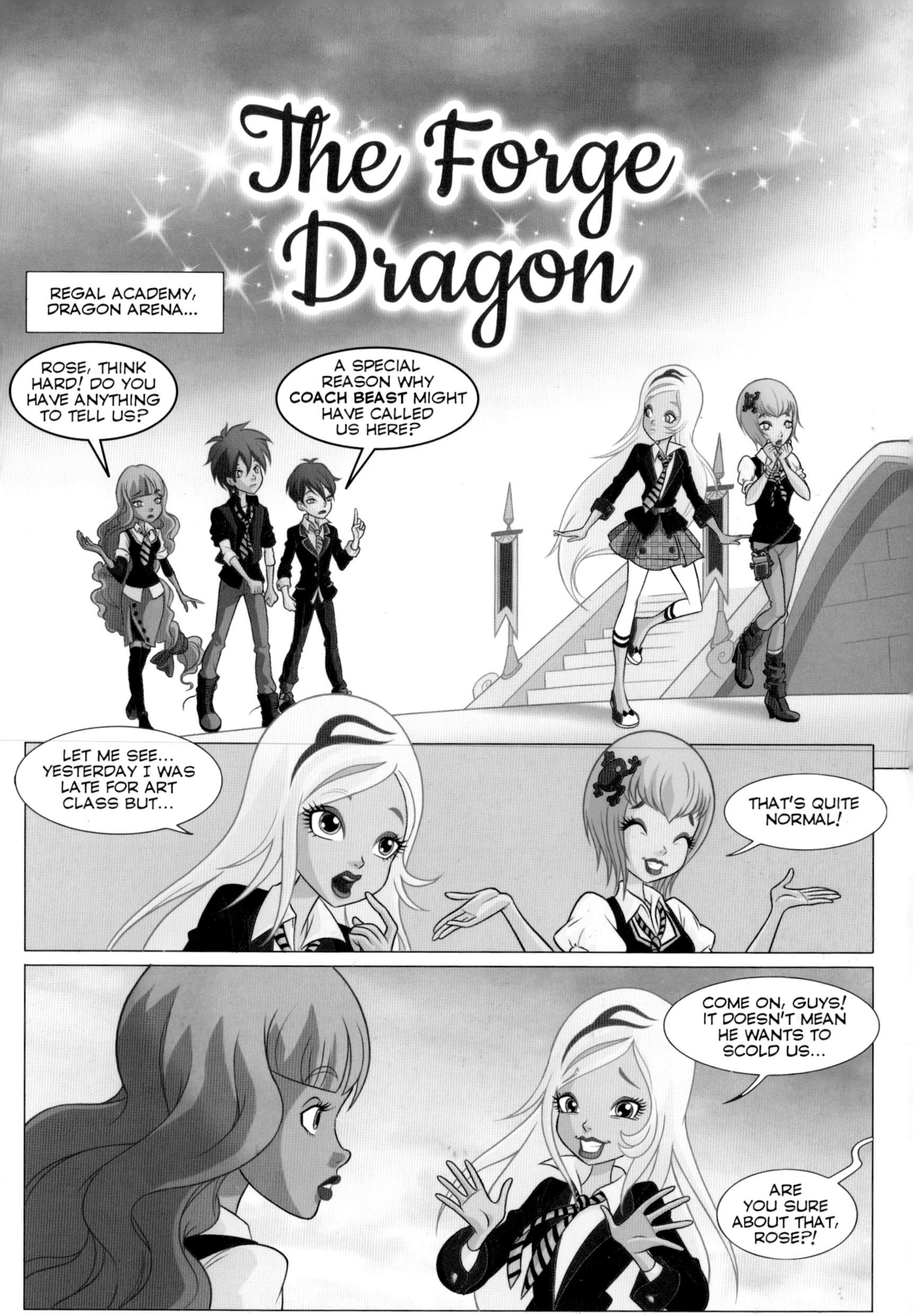
The Forge Dragon
REGAL ACADEMY, DRAGON ARENA...
ROSE, THINK HARD! DO YOU HAVE ANYTHING TO TELL US?
A SPECIAL REASON WHY COACH BEAST MIGHT HAVE CALLED US HERE?
LET ME SEE... YESTERDAY I WAS LATE FOR ART CLASS BUT...
THAT'S QUITE NORMAL!
COME ON, GUYS! IT DOESN'T MEAN HE WANTS TO SCOLD US...
ARE YOU SURE ABOUT THAT, ROSE?!

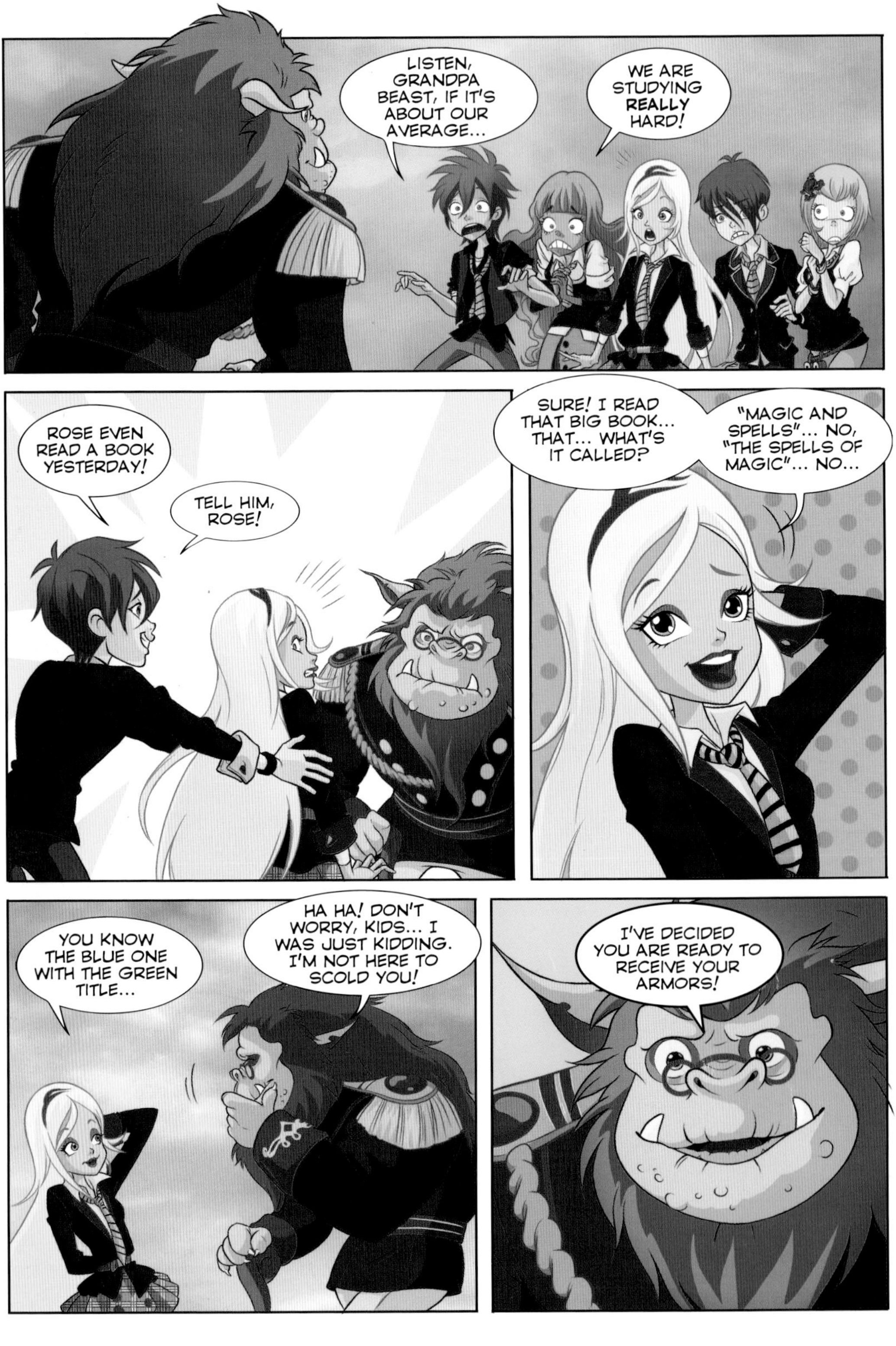
LISTEN, GRANDPA BEAST, IF IT'S ABOUT OUR AVERAGE...
WE ARE STUDYING **REALLY** HARD!
ROSE EVEN READ A BOOK YESTERDAY!
TELL HIM, ROSE!
SURE! I READ THAT BIG BOOK... THAT... WHAT'S IT CALLED?
"MAGIC AND SPELLS"... NO, "THE SPELLS OF MAGIC"... NO...
YOU KNOW THE BLUE ONE WITH THE GREEN TITLE...
HA HA! DON'T WORRY, KIDS... I WAS JUST KIDDING. I'M NOT HERE TO SCOLD YOU!
I'VE DECIDED YOU ARE READY TO RECEIVE YOUR ARMORS!

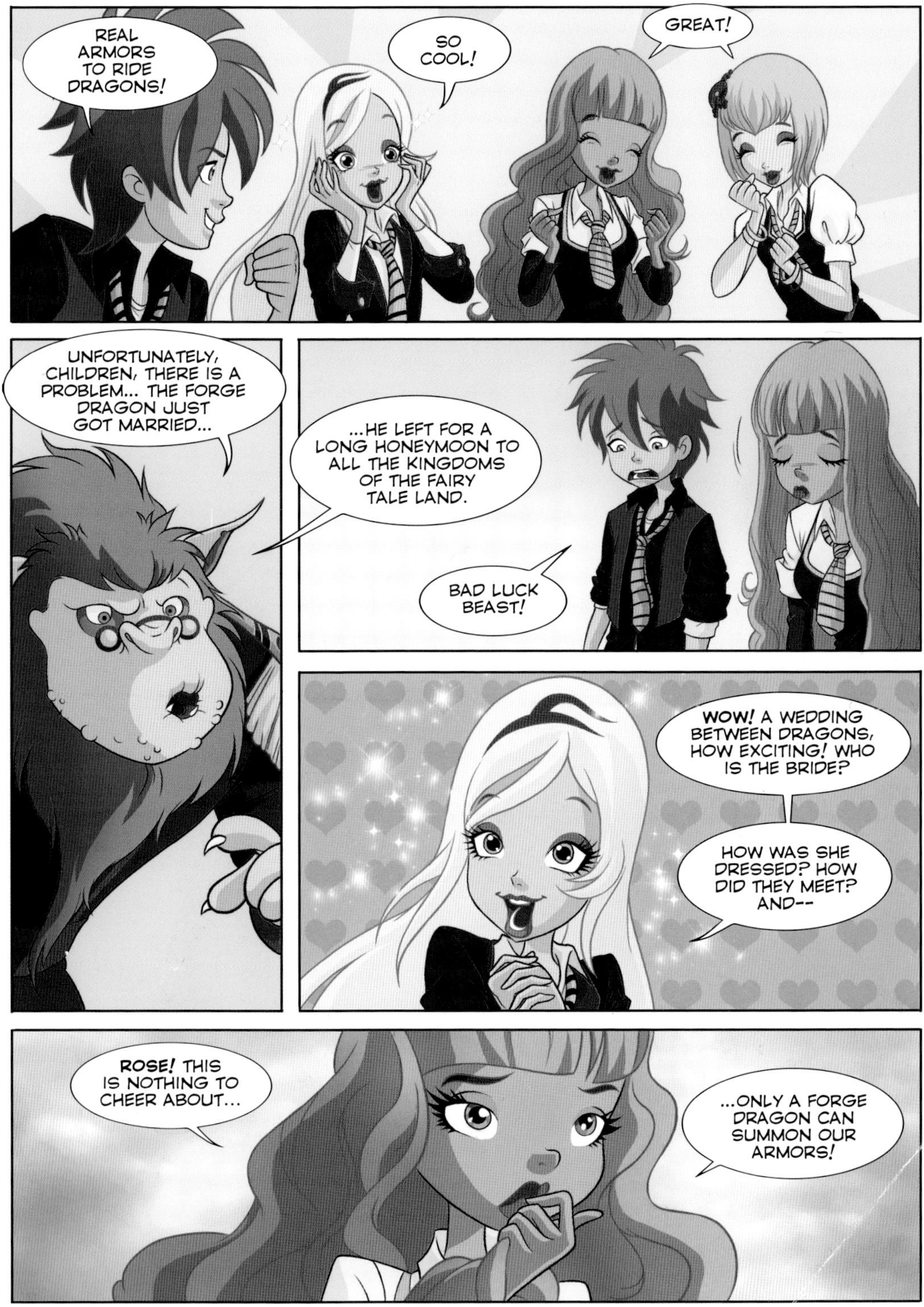
REAL ARMORS TO RIDE DRAGONS!
SO COOL!
GREAT!
UNFORTUNATELY, CHILDREN, THERE IS A PROBLEM... THE FORGE DRAGON JUST GOT MARRIED...
...HE LEFT FOR A LONG HONEYMOON TO ALL THE KINGDOMS OF THE FAIRY TALE LAND.
BAD LUCK BEAST!
WOW! A WEDDING BETWEEN DRAGONS, HOW EXCITING! WHO IS THE BRIDE?
HOW WAS SHE DRESSED? HOW DID THEY MEET? AND--
ROSE! THIS IS NOTHING TO CHEER ABOUT...
...ONLY A FORGE DRAGON CAN SUMMON OUR ARMORS!

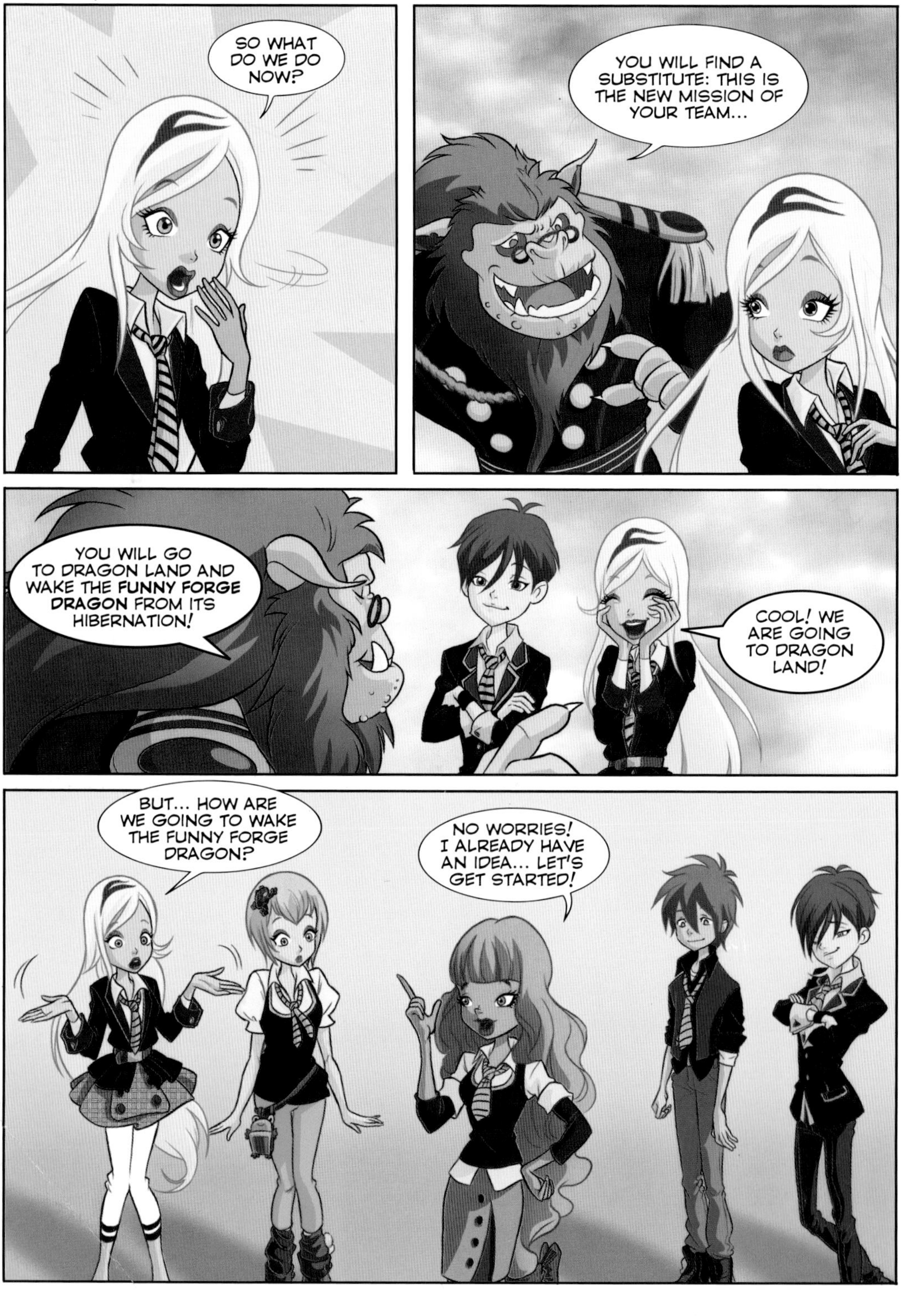
SO WHAT DO WE DO NOW?
YOU WILL FIND A SUBSTITUTE: THIS IS THE NEW MISSION OF YOUR TEAM...
YOU WILL GO TO DRAGON LAND AND WAKE THE **FUNNY FORGE DRAGON** FROM ITS HIBERNATION!
COOL! WE ARE GOING TO DRAGON LAND!
BUT... HOW ARE WE GOING TO WAKE THE FUNNY FORGE DRAGON?
NO WORRIES! I ALREADY HAVE AN IDEA... LET'S GET STARTED!

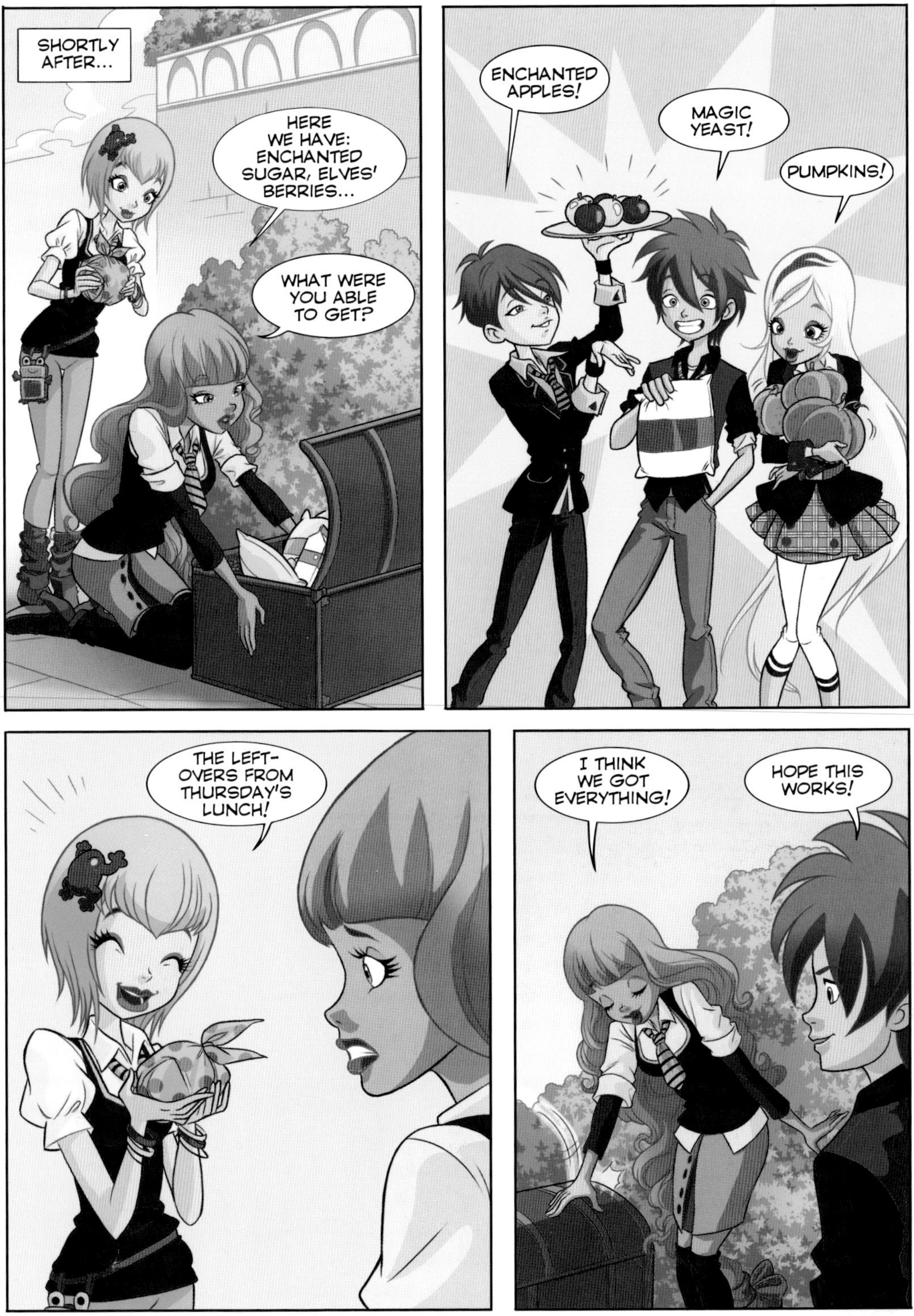
SHORTLY AFTER...
HERE WE HAVE: ENCHANTED SUGAR, ELVES' BERRIES...
WHAT WERE YOU ABLE TO GET?
ENCHANTED APPLES!
MAGIC YEAST!
PUMPKINS!
THE LEFT-OVERS FROM THURSDAY'S LUNCH!
I THINK WE GOT EVERYTHING!
HOPE THIS WORKS!

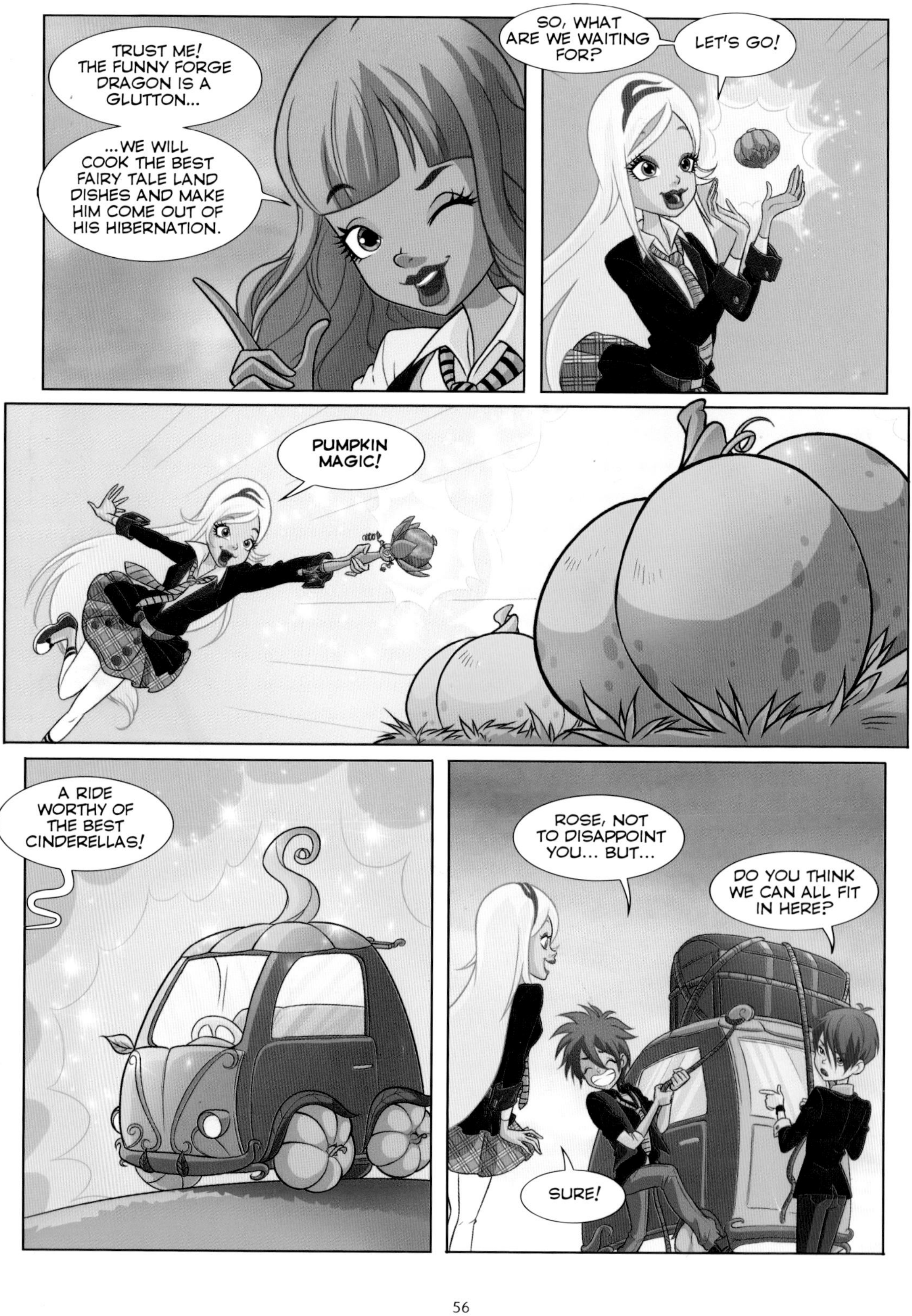
TRUST ME! THE FUNNY FORGE DRAGON IS A GLUTTON...
...WE WILL COOK THE BEST FAIRY TALE LAND DISHES AND MAKE HIM COME OUT OF HIS HIBERNATION.
SO, WHAT ARE WE WAITING FOR?
LET'S GO!
PUMPKIN MAGIC!
A RIDE WORTHY OF THE BEST CINDERELLAS!
ROSE, NOT TO DISAPPOINT YOU... BUT...
DO YOU THINK WE CAN ALL FIT IN HERE?
SURE!

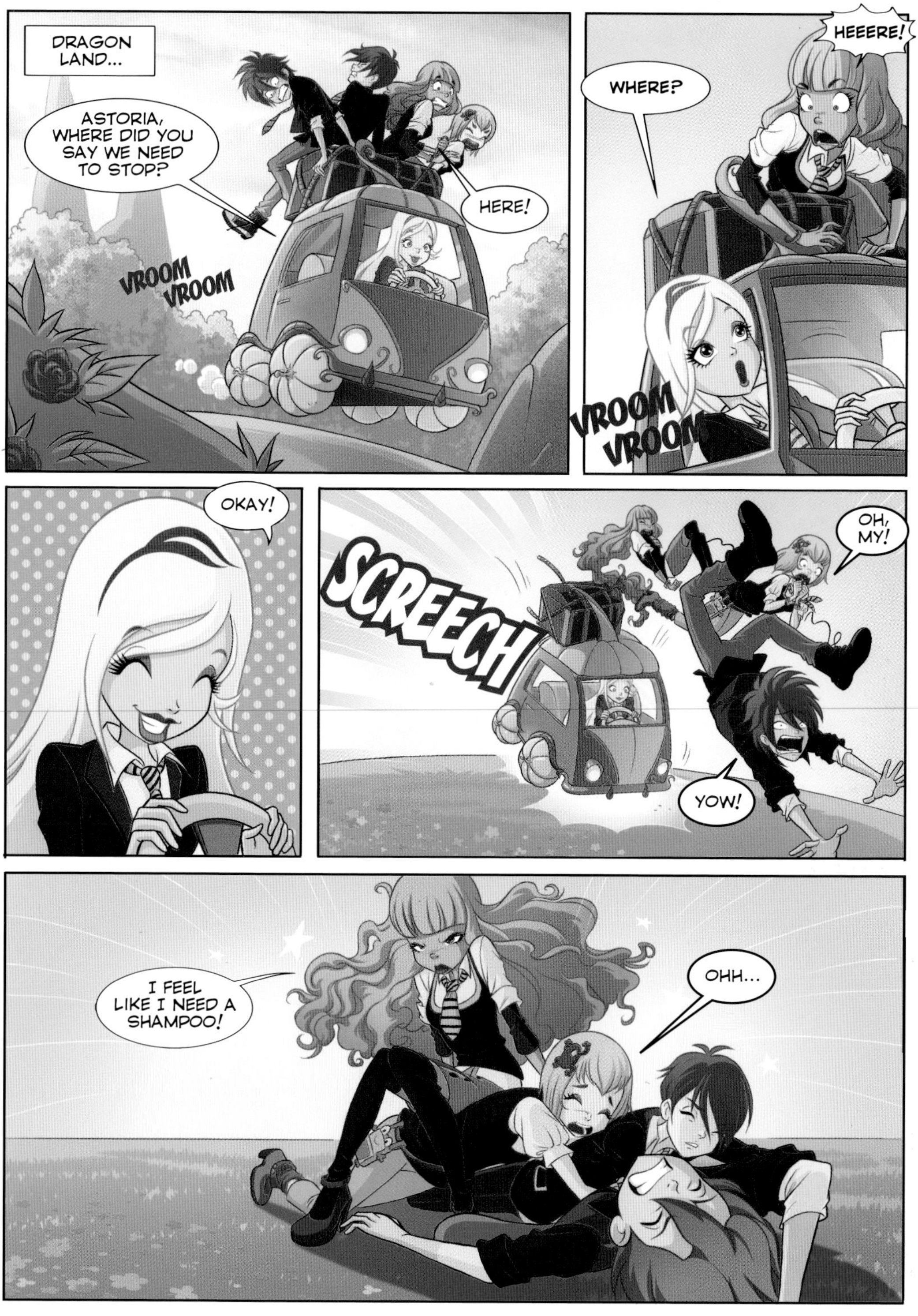
DRAGON LAND...
ASTORIA, WHERE DID YOU SAY WE NEED TO STOP?
HERE!
VROOM VROOM
WHERE?
HEEERE!
VROOM VROOM
OKAY!
SCREECH
OH, MY!
YOW!
I FEEL LIKE I NEED A SHAMPOO!
OHH...

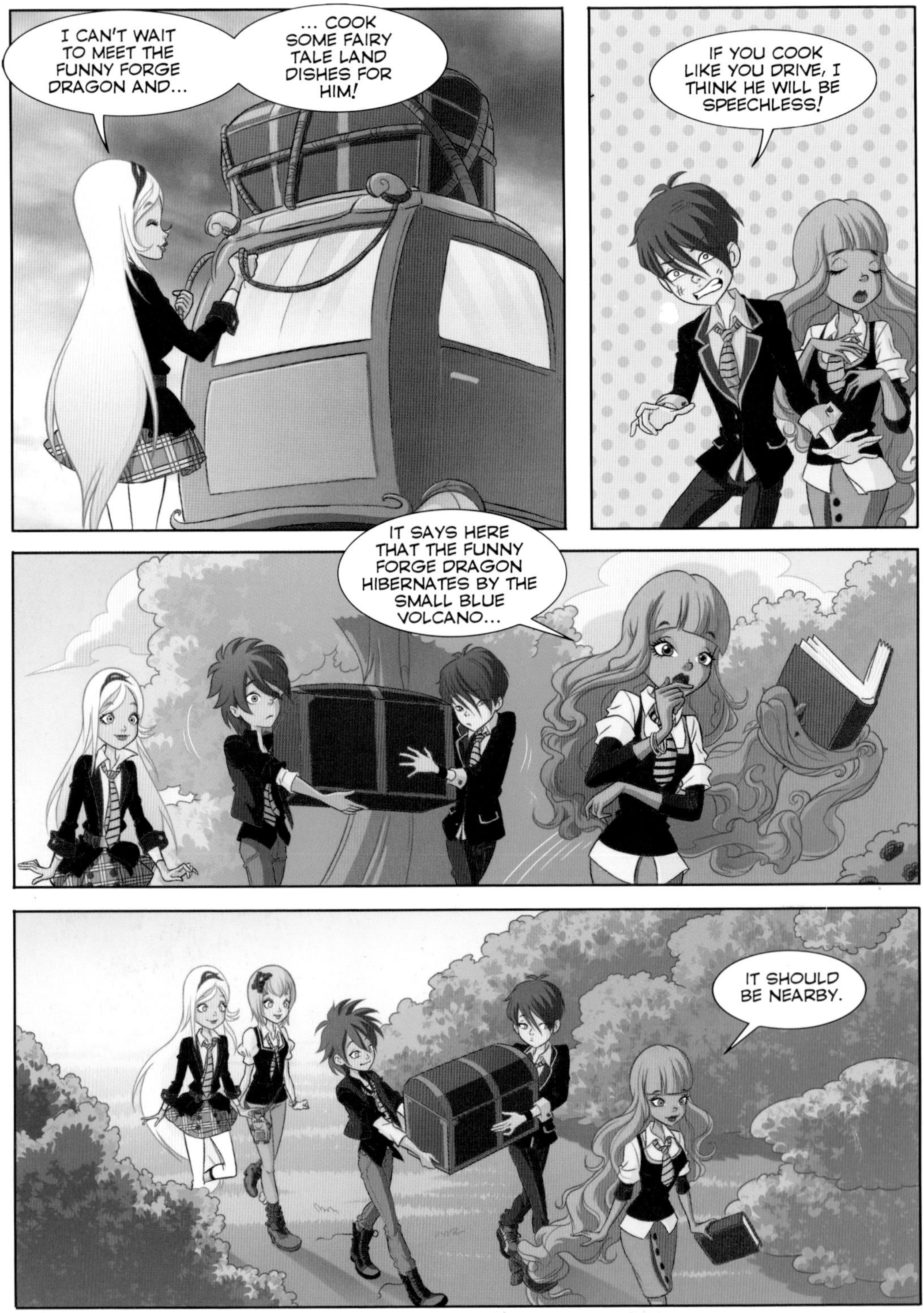
I CAN'T WAIT TO MEET THE FUNNY FORGE DRAGON AND...
... COOK SOME FAIRY TALE LAND DISHES FOR HIM!
IF YOU COOK LIKE YOU DRIVE, I THINK HE WILL BE SPEECHLESS!
IT SAYS HERE THAT THE FUNNY FORGE DRAGON HIBERNATES BY THE SMALL BLUE VOLCANO...
IT SHOULD BE NEARBY.

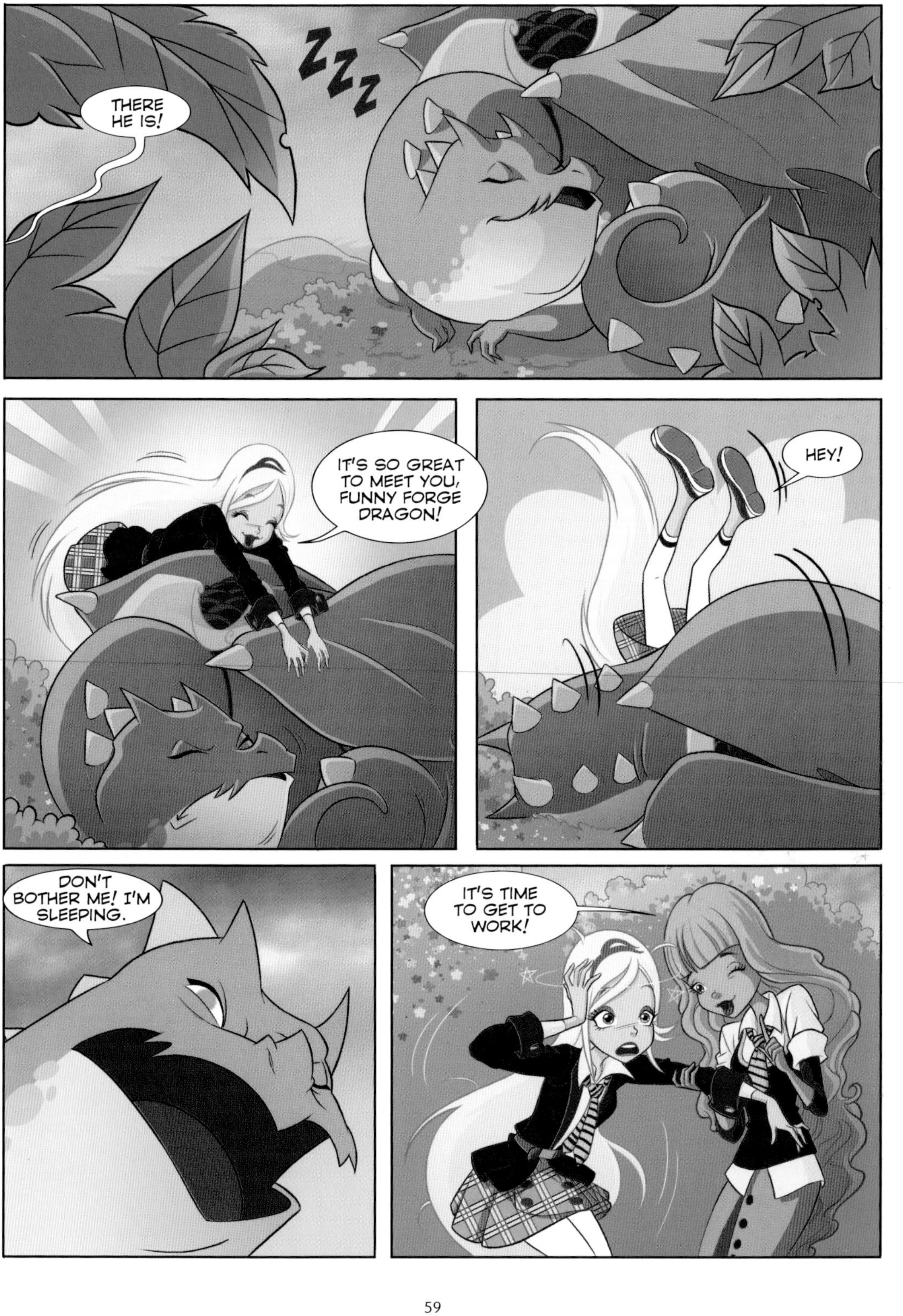
ZZZ
THERE HE IS!
IT'S SO GREAT TO MEET YOU, FUNNY FORGE DRAGON!
HEY!
DON'T BOTHER ME! I'M SLEEPING.
IT'S TIME TO GET TO WORK!

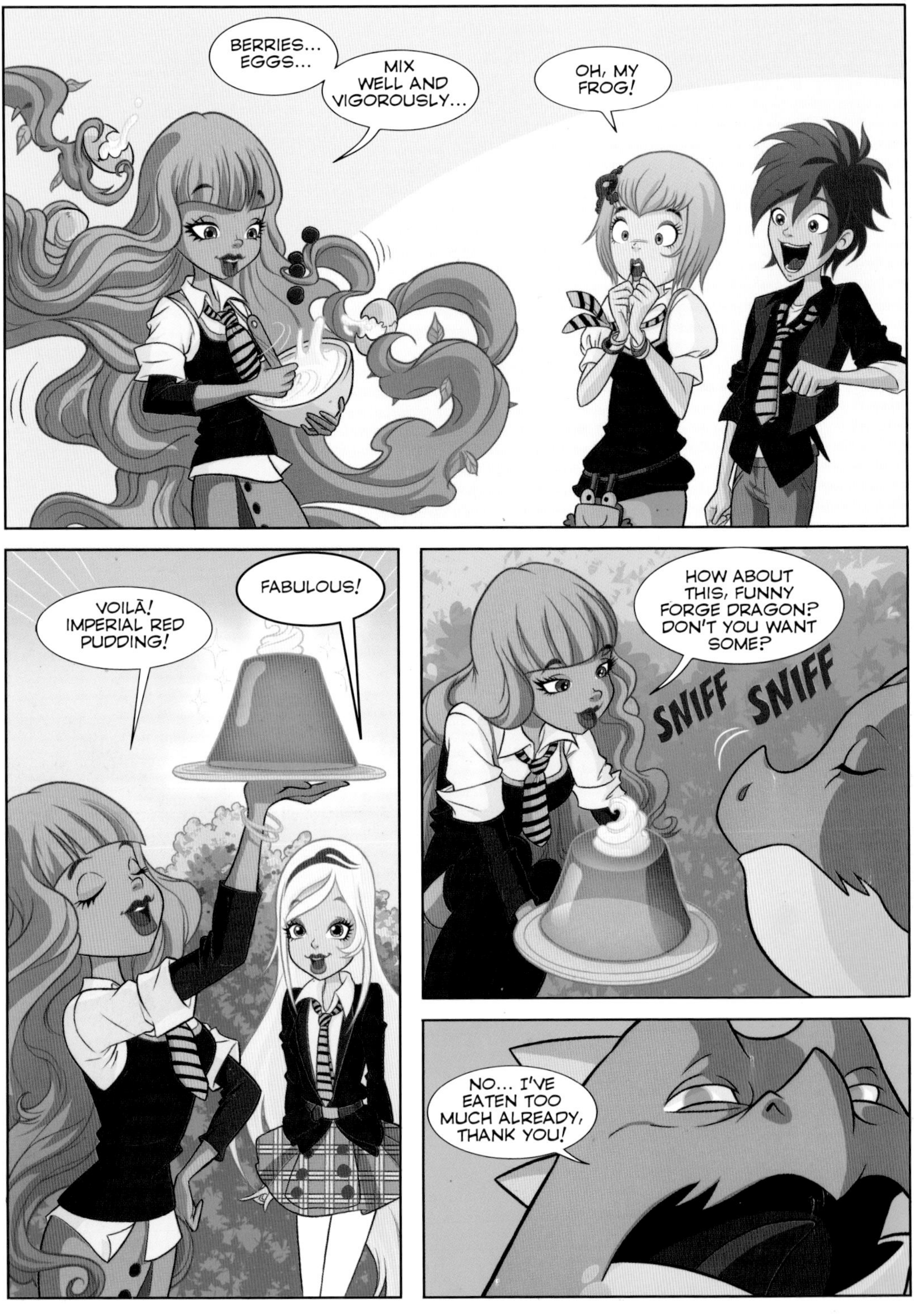
BERRIES... EGGS...
MIX WELL AND VIGOROUSLY...
OH, MY FROG!
VOILÃ! IMPERIAL RED PUDDING!
FABULOUS!
HOW ABOUT THIS, FUNNY FORGE DRAGON? DON'T YOU WANT SOME?
SNIFF SNIFF
NO... I'VE EATEN TOO MUCH ALREADY, THANK YOU!

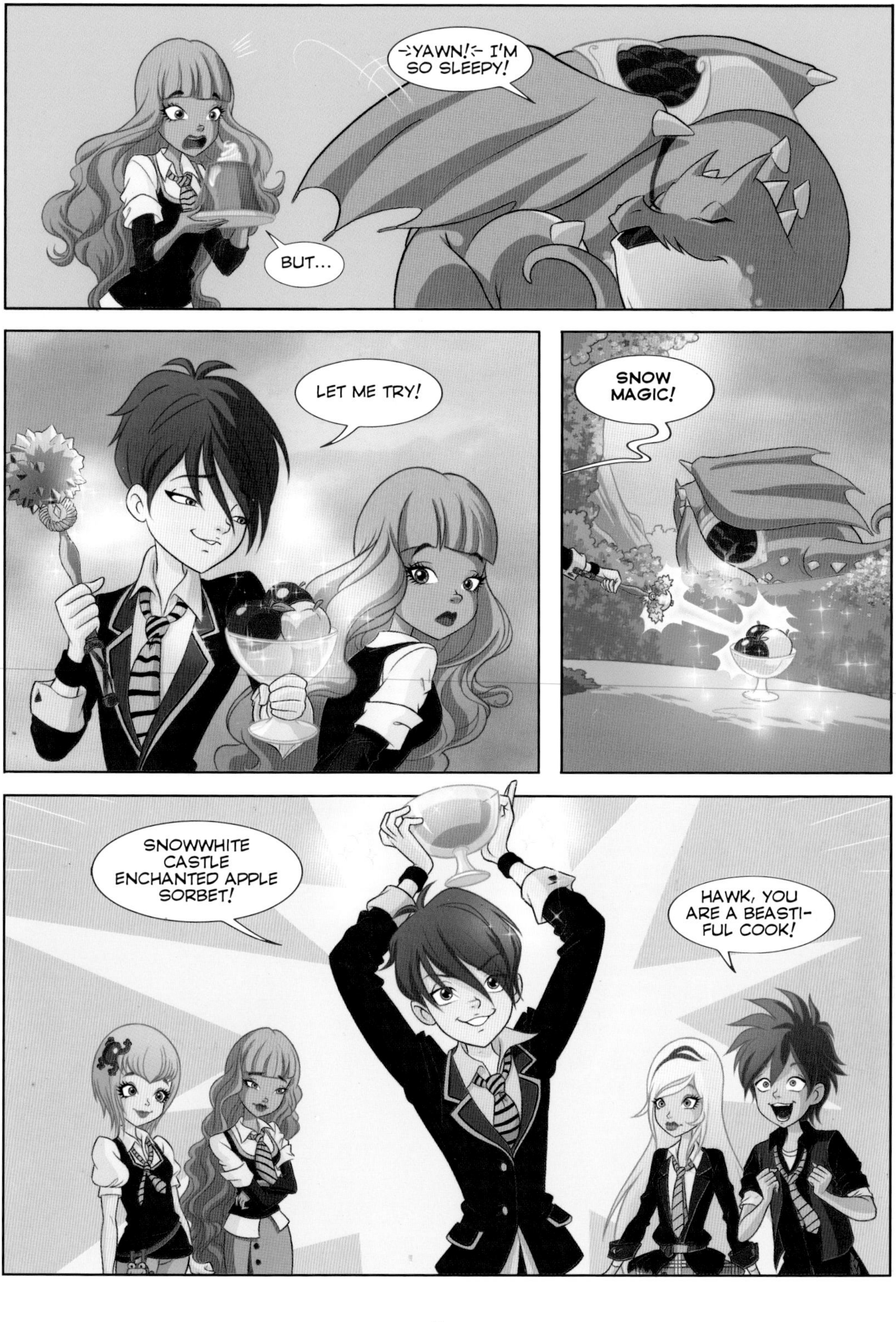
-YAWN!- I'M SO SLEEPY!
BUT...
LET ME TRY!
SNOW MAGIC!
SNOWWHITE CASTLE ENCHANTED APPLE SORBET!
HAWK, YOU ARE A BEASTI-FUL COOK!

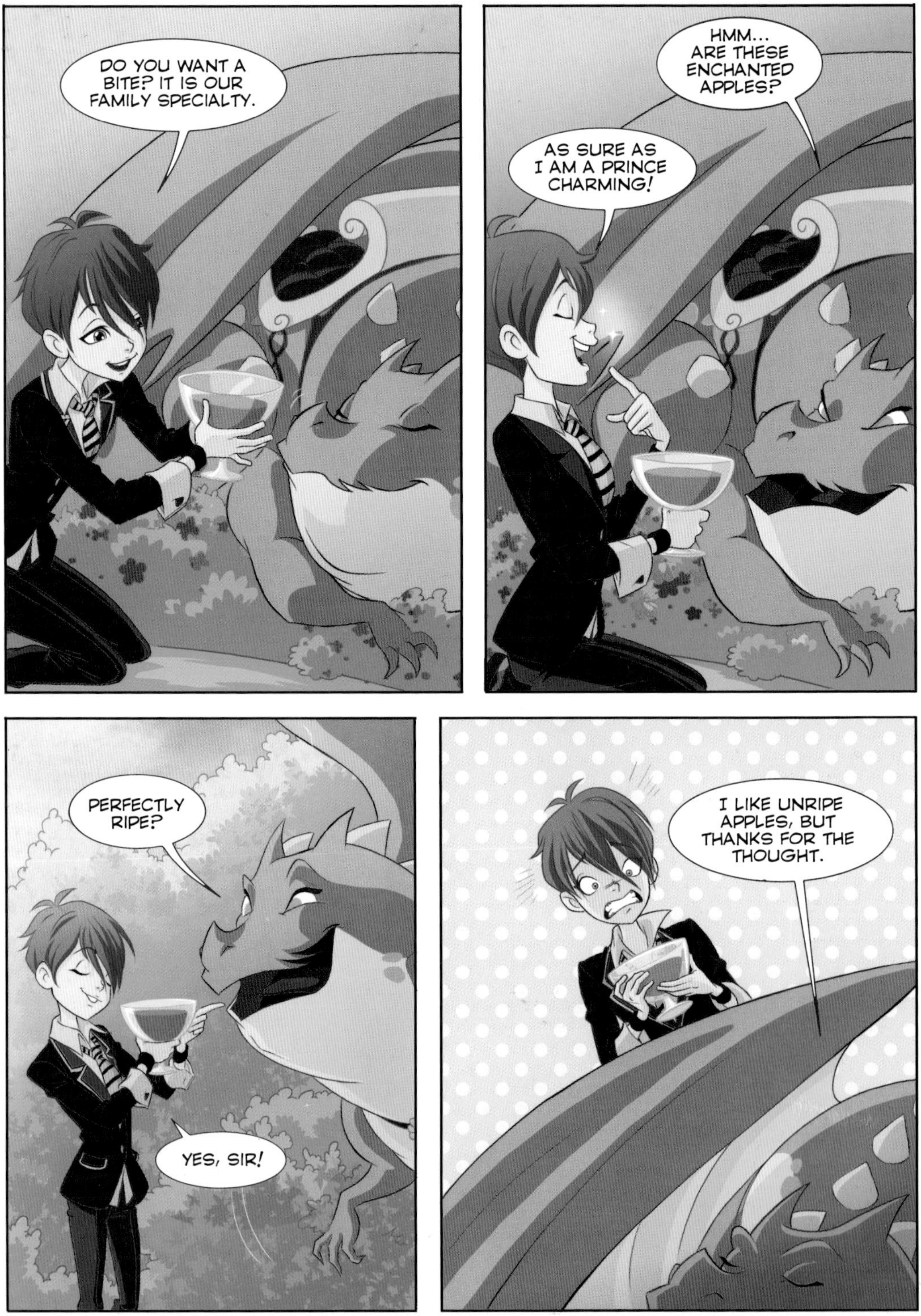
DO YOU WANT A BITE? IT IS OUR FAMILY SPECIALTY.
HMM... ARE THESE ENCHANTED APPLES?
AS SURE AS I AM A PRINCE CHARMING!
PERFECTLY RIPE?
YES, SIR!
I LIKE UNRIPE APPLES, BUT THANKS FOR THE THOUGHT.

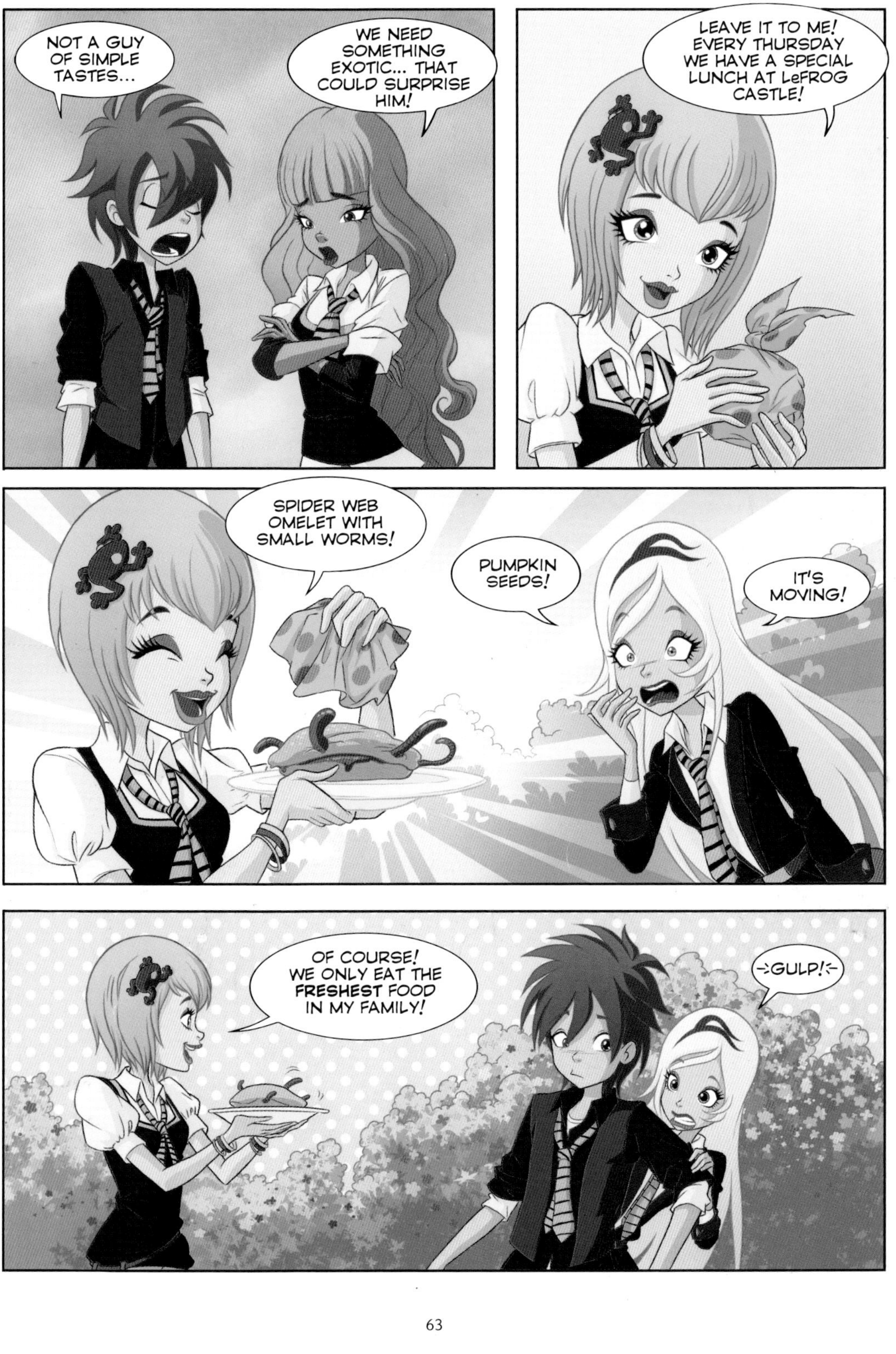
NOT A GUY OF SIMPLE TASTES...
WE NEED SOMETHING EXOTIC... THAT COULD SURPRISE HIM!
LEAVE IT TO ME! EVERY THURSDAY WE HAVE A SPECIAL LUNCH AT LeFROG CASTLE!
SPIDER WEB OMELET WITH SMALL WORMS!
PUMPKIN SEEDS!
IT'S MOVING!
OF COURSE! WE ONLY EAT THE FRESHEST FOOD IN MY FAMILY!
GULP!

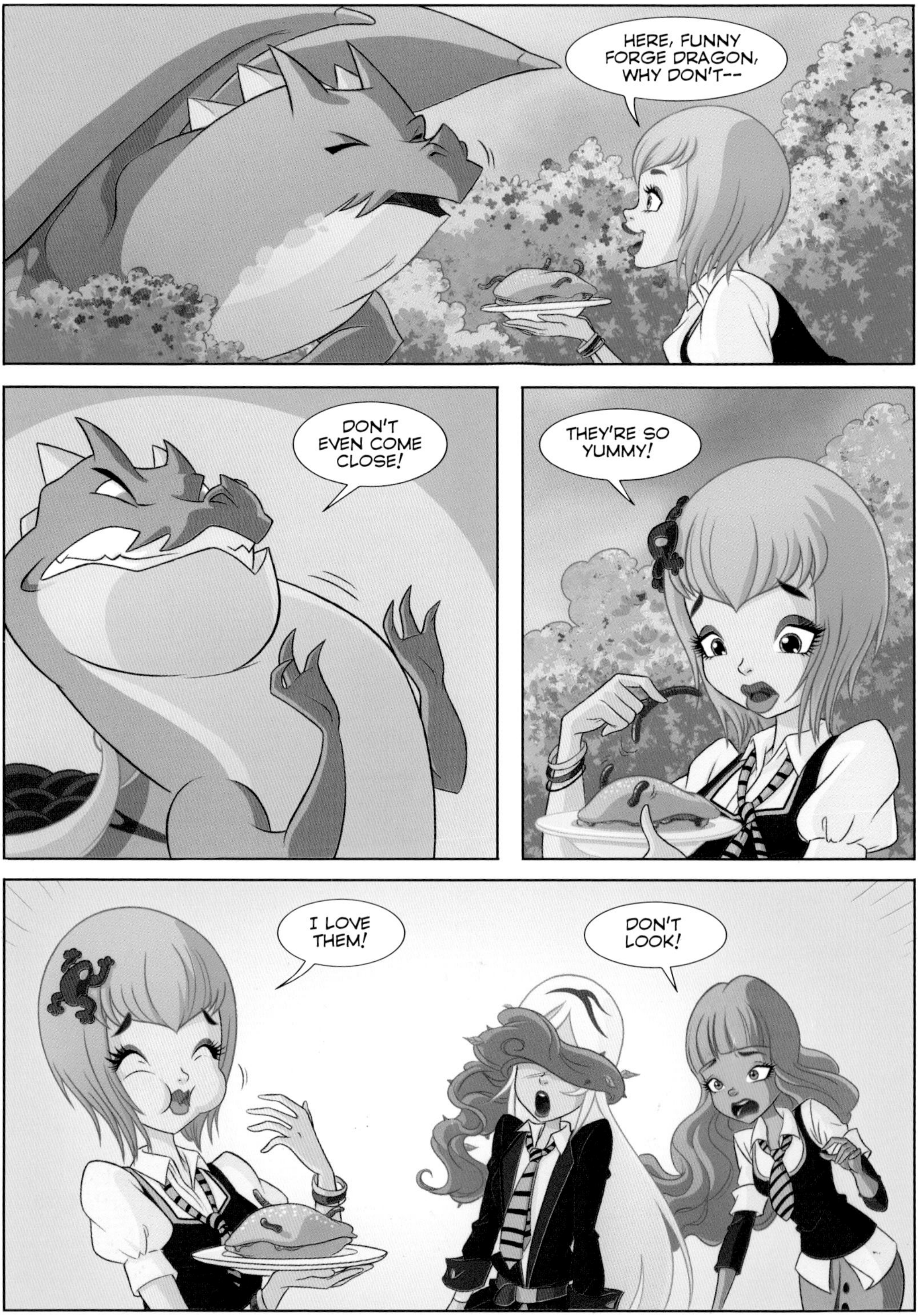
HERE, FUNNY FORGE DRAGON, WHY DON'T--
DON'T EVEN COME CLOSE!
THEY'RE SO YUMMY!
I LOVE THEM!
DON'T LOOK!

THERE'S NOT MUCH LEFT!

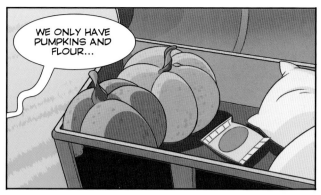

WE ONLY HAVE PUMPKINS AND FLOUR...

THERE IS ALSO A PACKET OF YEAST!

AND WITH YEAST, SOME FLOUR AND...

SOME PUMPKINS...

WE CAN TOTALLY PREPARE A...

PUMPKIN PIZZA!

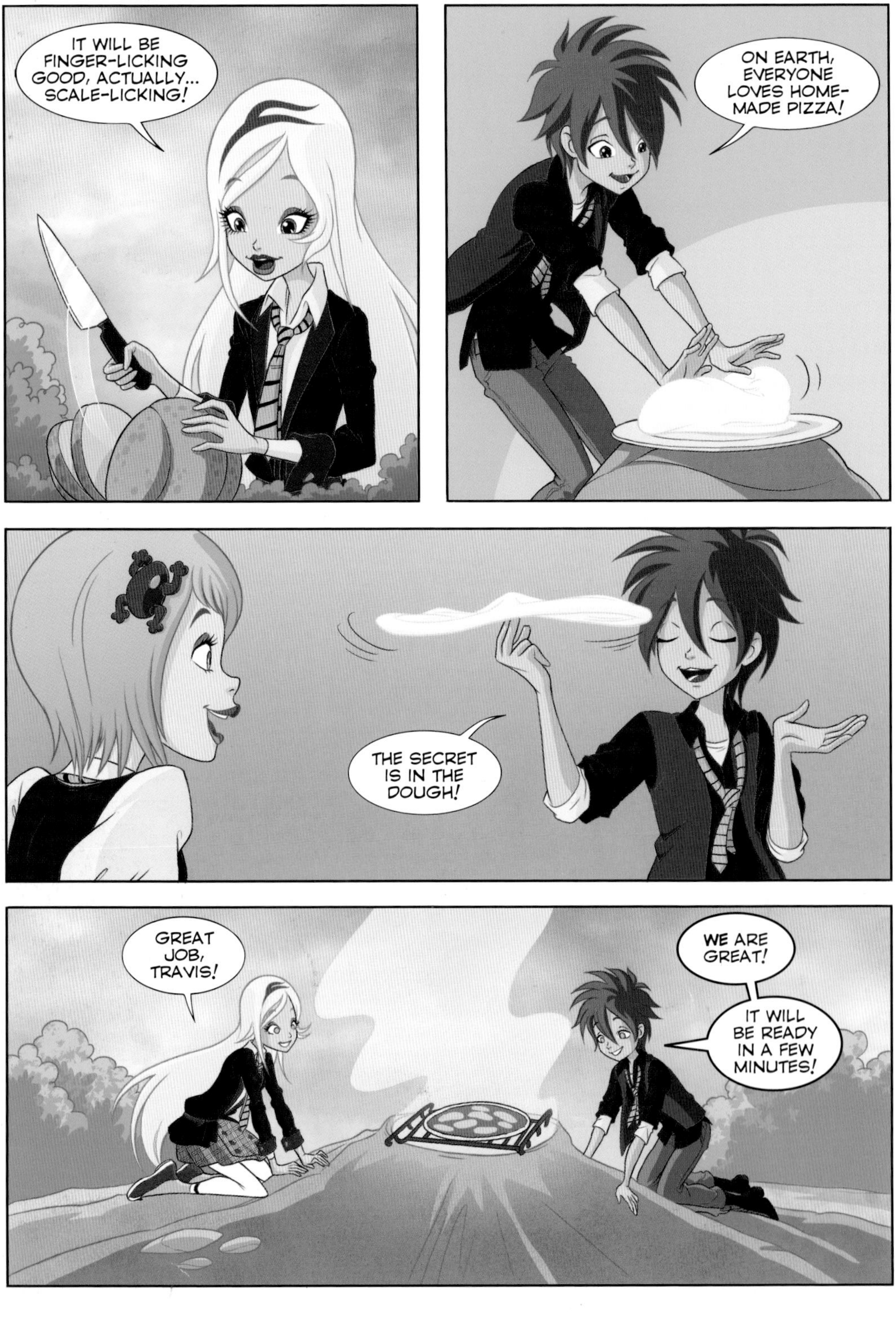
IT WILL BE FINGER-LICKING GOOD, ACTUALLY... SCALE-LICKING!
ON EARTH, EVERYONE LOVES HOME-MADE PIZZA!
THE SECRET IS IN THE DOUGH!
GREAT JOB, TRAVIS!
WE ARE GREAT!
IT WILL BE READY IN A FEW MINUTES!

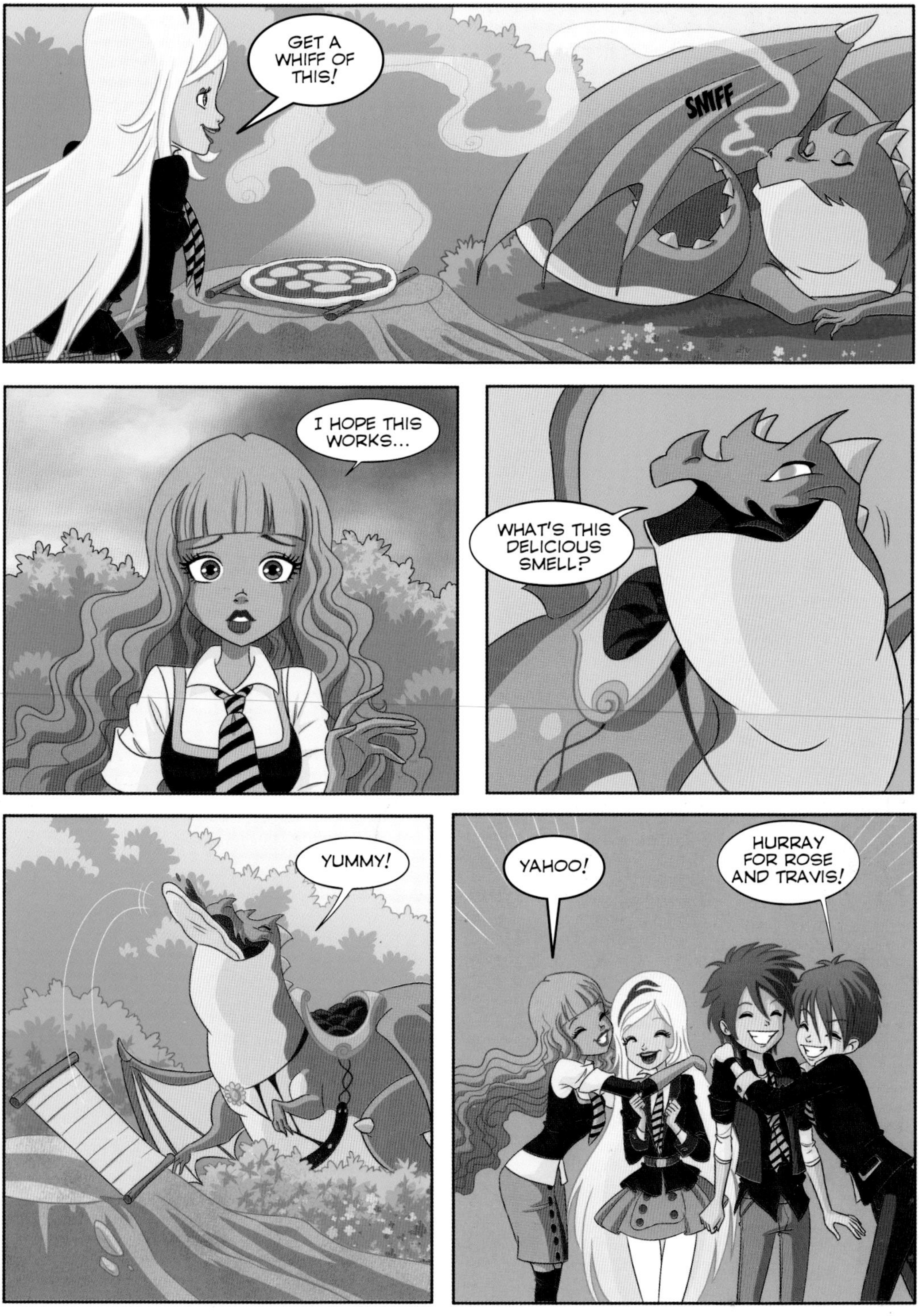
GET A WHIFF OF THIS!
SNIFF
I HOPE THIS WORKS...
WHAT'S THIS DELICIOUS SMELL?
YUMMY!
YAHOO!
HURRAY FOR ROSE AND TRAVIS!

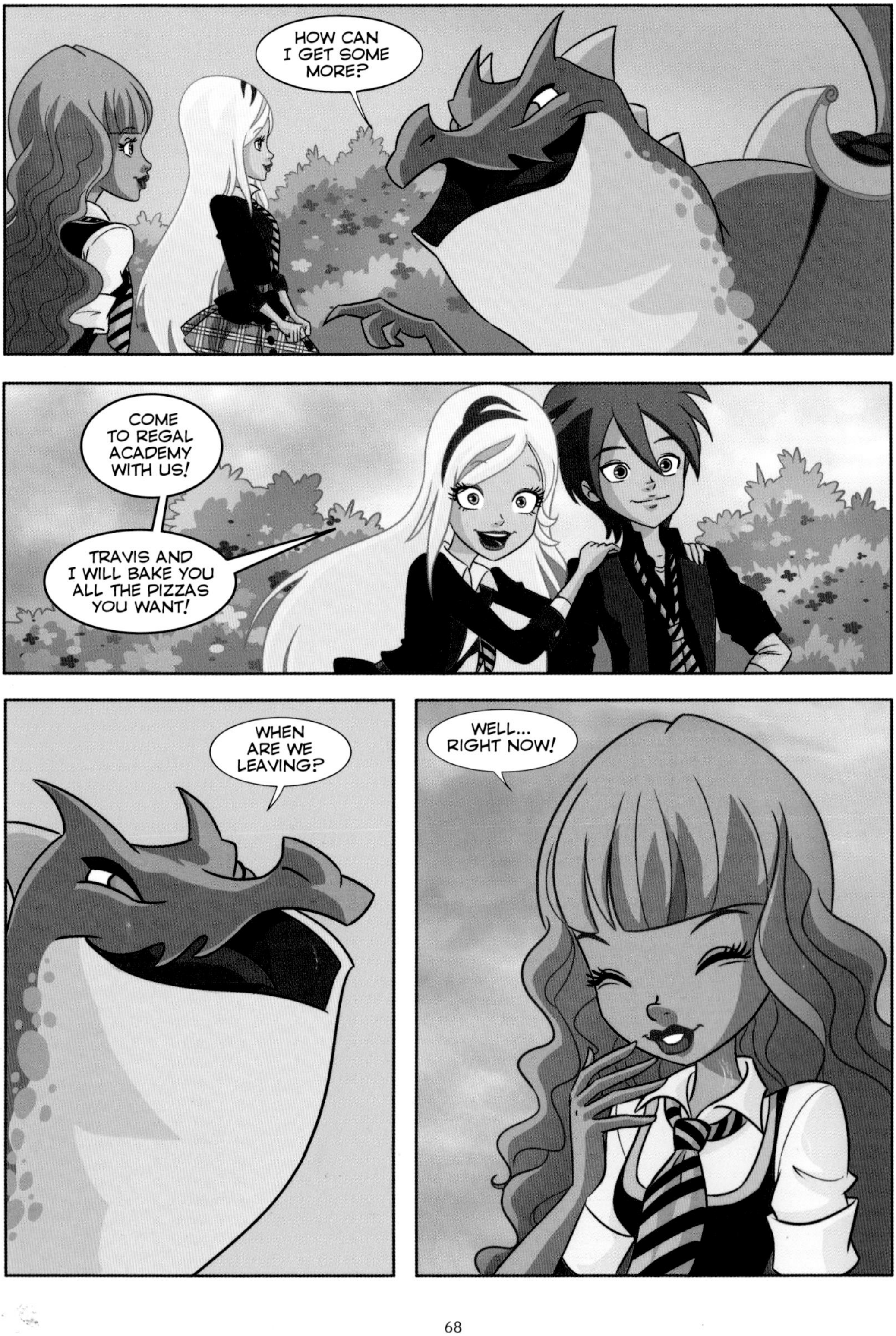
HOW CAN I GET SOME MORE?
COME TO REGAL ACADEMY WITH US!
TRAVIS AND I WILL BAKE YOU ALL THE PIZZAS YOU WANT!
WHEN ARE WE LEAVING?
WELL... RIGHT NOW!

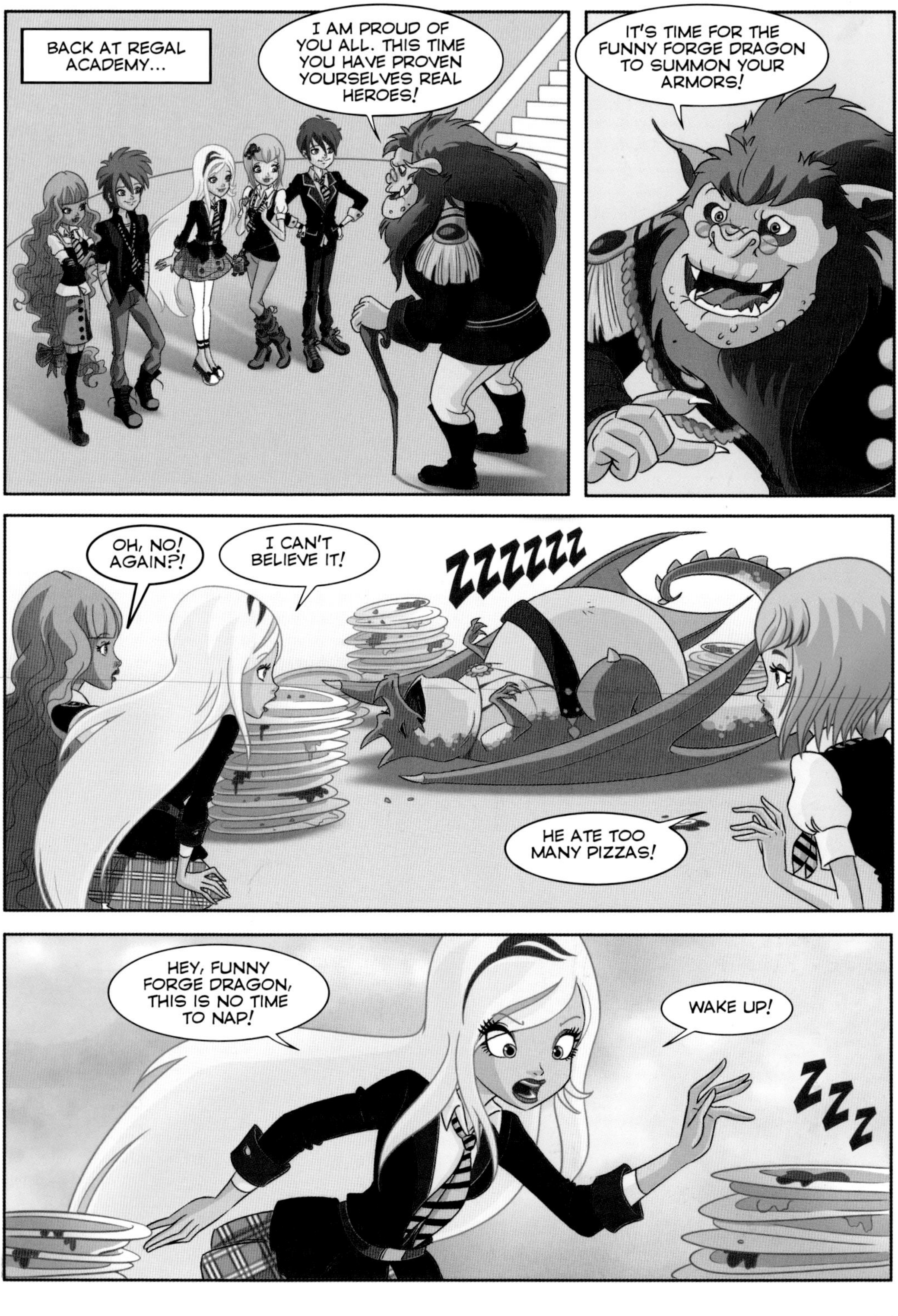
BACK AT REGAL ACADEMY...
I AM PROUD OF YOU ALL. THIS TIME YOU HAVE PROVEN YOURSELVES REAL HEROES!
IT'S TIME FOR THE FUNNY FORGE DRAGON TO SUMMON YOUR ARMORS!
OH, NO! AGAIN?!
I CAN'T BELIEVE IT!
ZZZZZZ
HE ATE TOO MANY PIZZAS!
HEY, FUNNY FORGE DRAGON, THIS IS NO TIME TO NAP!
WAKE UP!
ZZZ

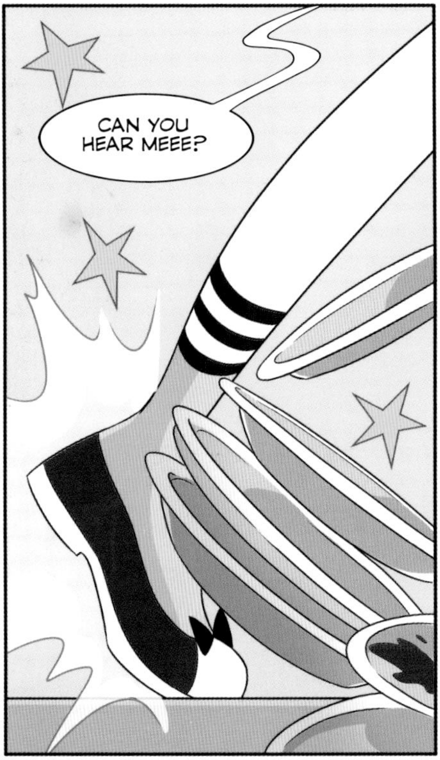
CAN YOU HEAR MEEE?

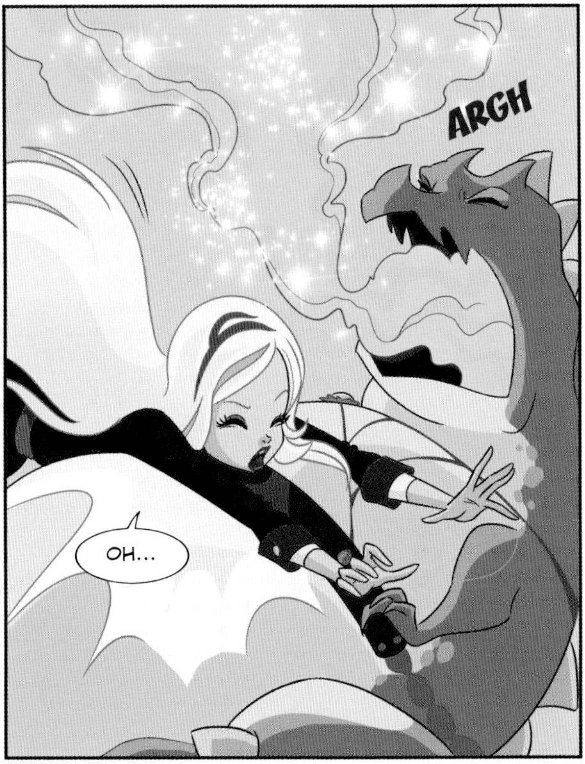
ARGH
OH...

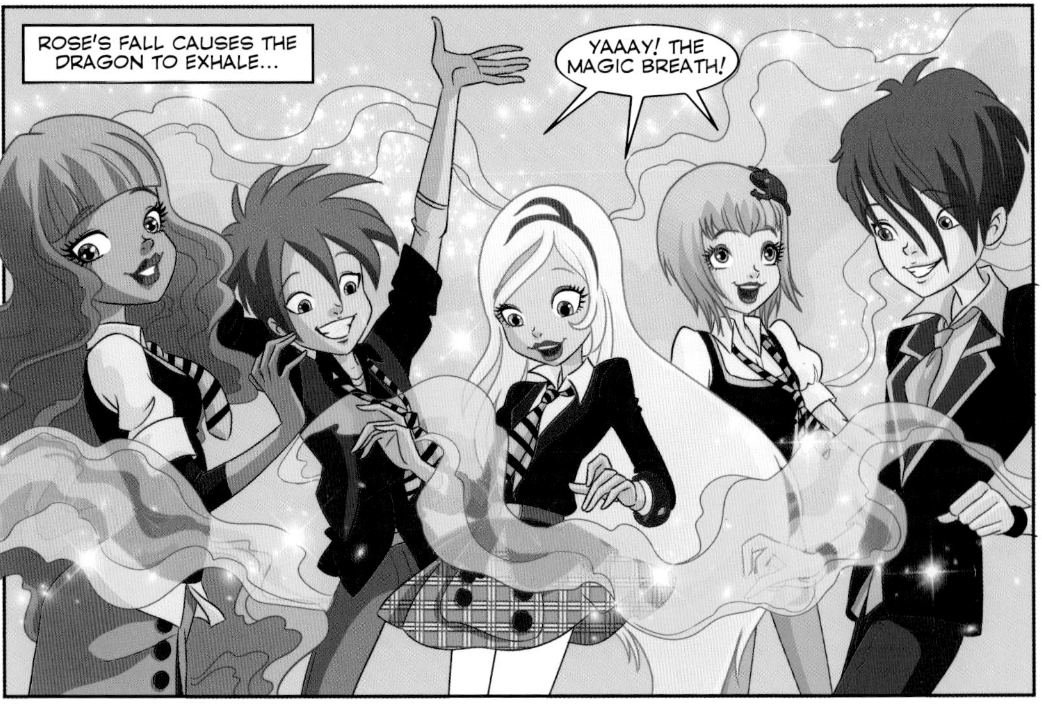
ROSE'S FALL CAUSES THE DRAGON TO EXHALE...
YAAAY! THE MAGIC BREATH!

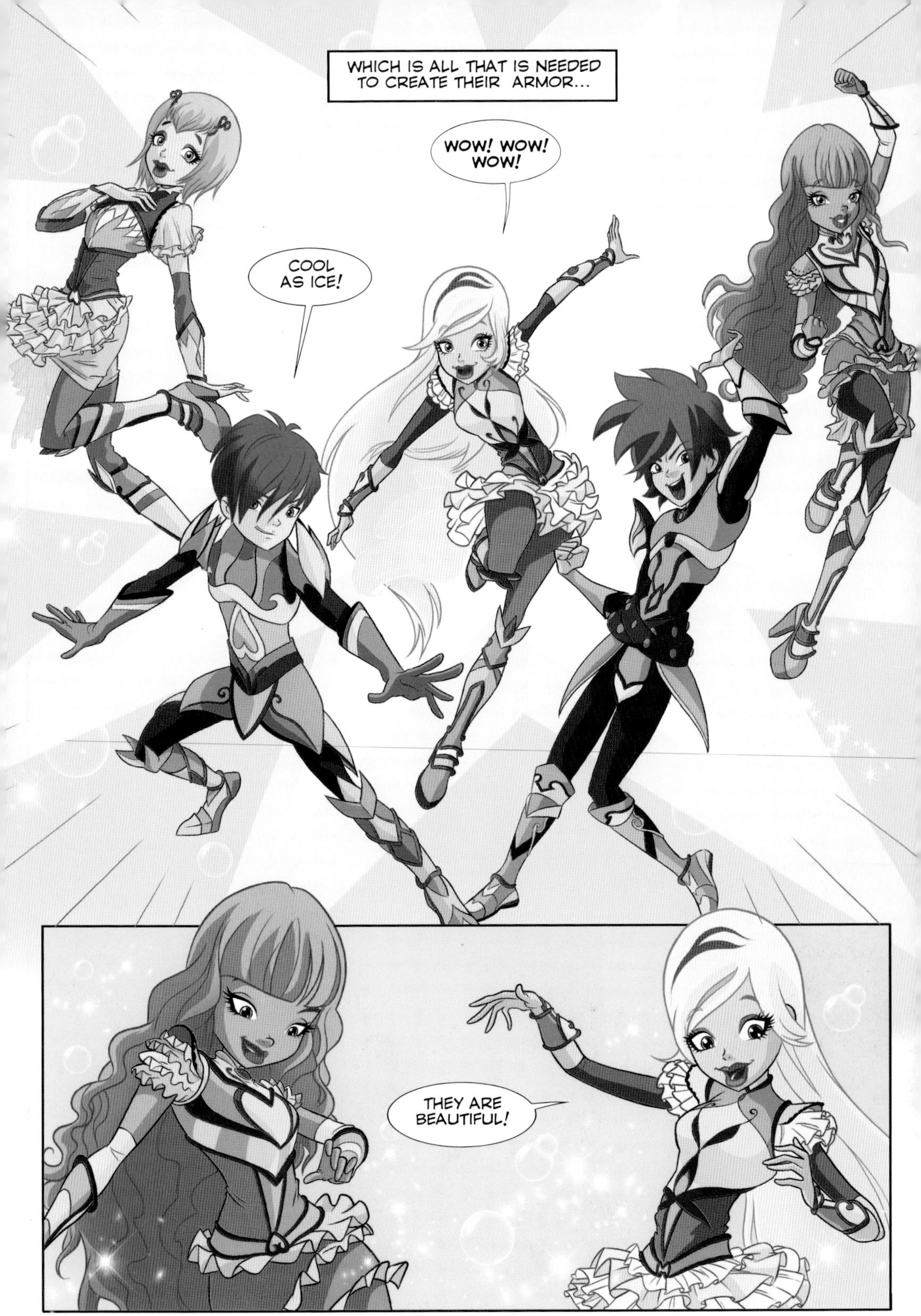
WHICH IS ALL THAT IS NEEDED TO CREATE THEIR ARMOR...
COOL AS ICE!
WOW! WOW! WOW!
THEY ARE BEAUTIFUL!

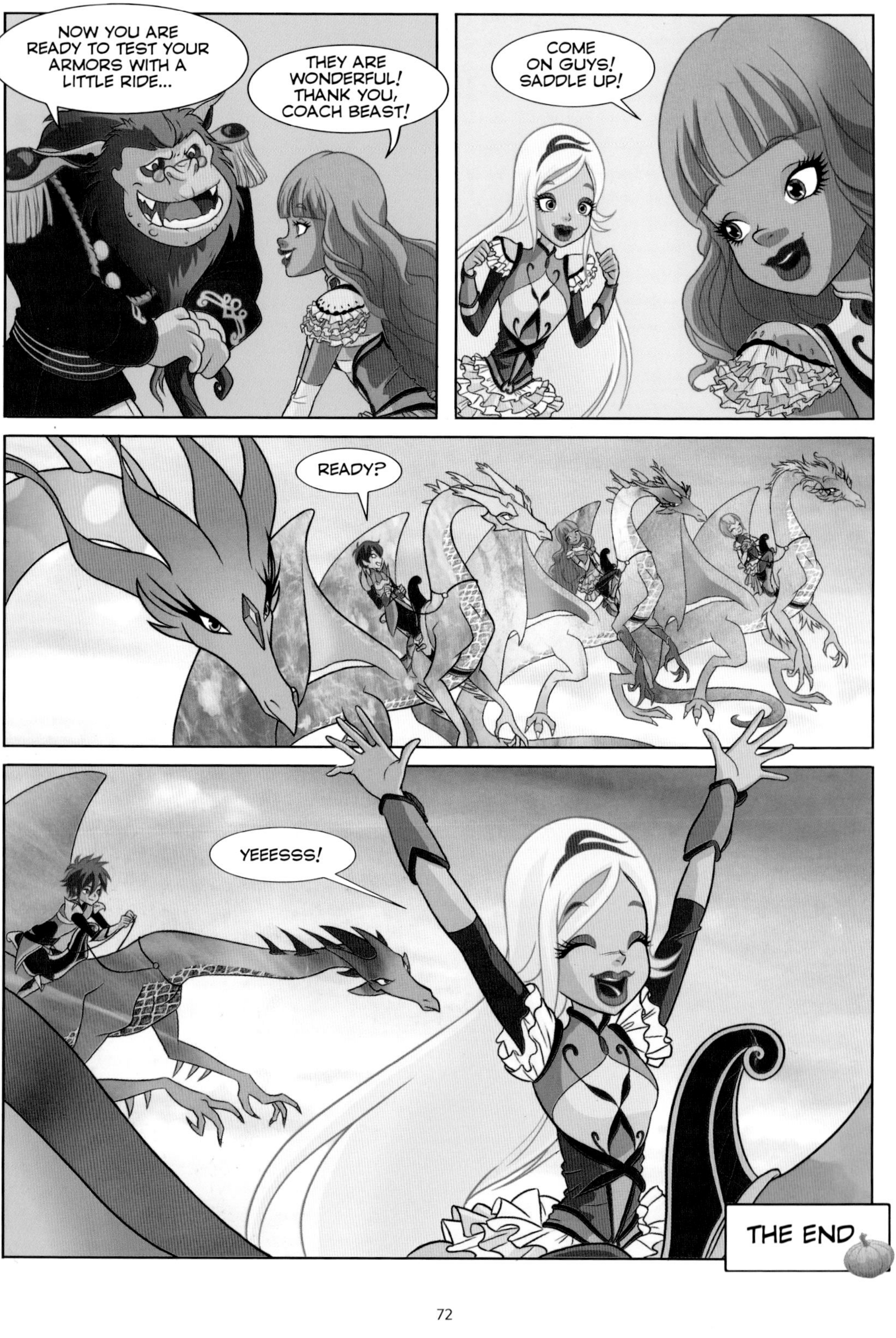
NOW YOU ARE READY TO TEST YOUR ARMORS WITH A LITTLE RIDE...
THEY ARE WONDERFUL! THANK YOU, COACH BEAST!
COME ON GUYS! SADDLE UP!
READY?
YEEESSS!
THE END

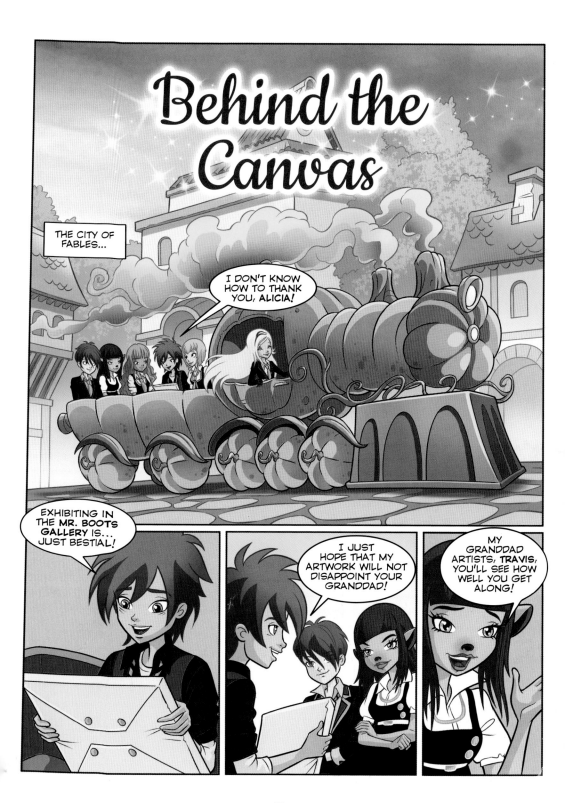

Behind the Canvas

THE CITY OF FABLES...

I DON'T KNOW HOW TO THANK YOU, ALICIA!

EXHIBITING IN THE **MR. BOOTS** GALLERY IS... JUST BESTIAL!

I JUST HOPE THAT MY ARTWORK WILL NOT DISAPPOINT YOUR GRANDDAD!

MY GRANDDAD ARTISTS, **TRAVIS**, YOU'LL SEE HOW WELL YOU GET ALONG!

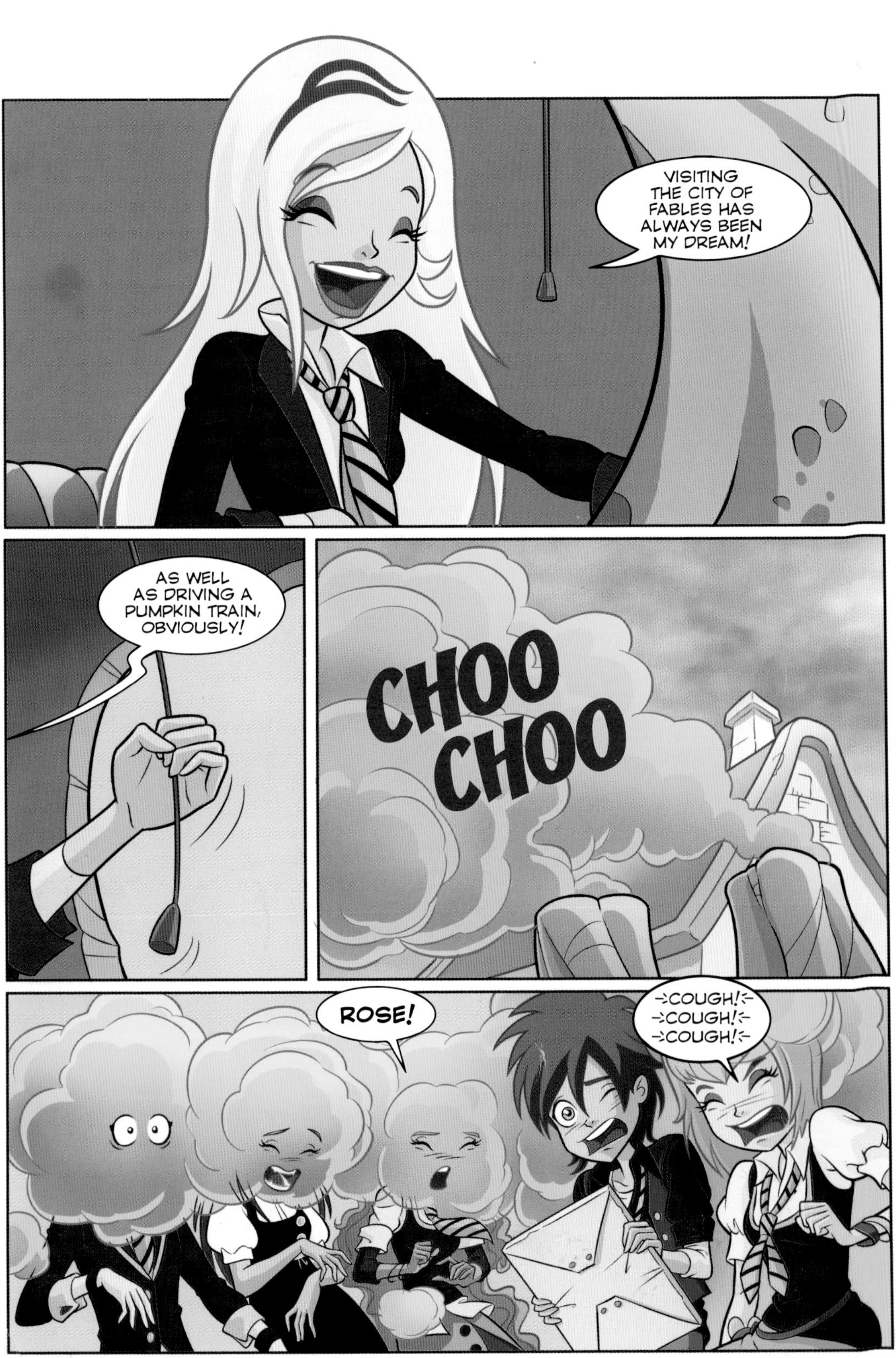

VISITING THE CITY OF FABLES HAS ALWAYS BEEN MY DREAM!
AS WELL AS DRIVING A PUMPKIN TRAIN, OBVIOUSLY!
CHOO CHOO
ROSE!
COUGH! COUGH! COUGH!

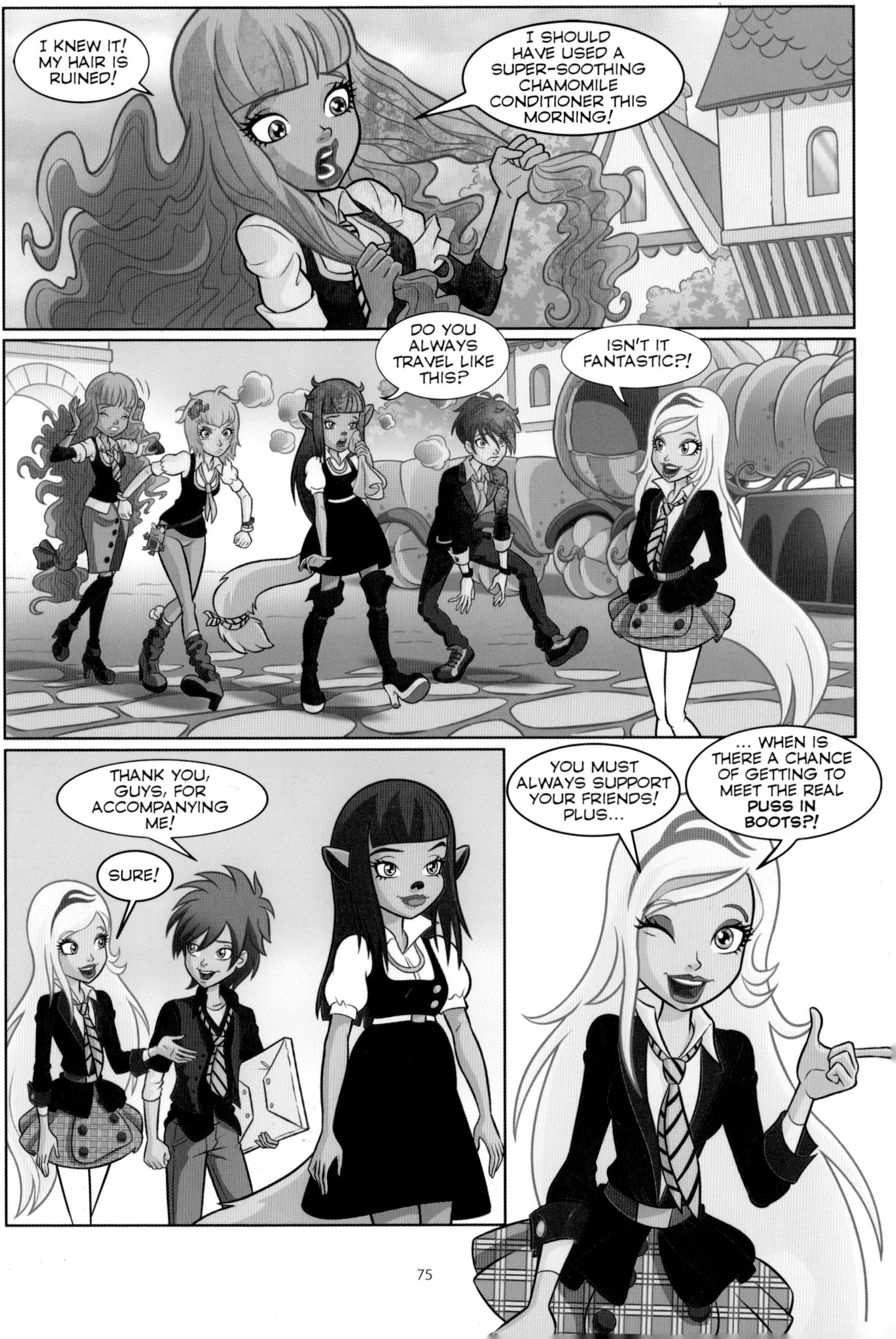
I KNEW IT! MY HAIR IS RUINED!
I SHOULD HAVE USED A SUPER-SOOTHING CHAMOMILE CONDITIONER THIS MORNING!
DO YOU ALWAYS TRAVEL LIKE THIS?
ISN'T IT FANTASTIC?!
THANK YOU, GUYS, FOR ACCOMPANYING ME!
SURE!
YOU MUST ALWAYS SUPPORT YOUR FRIENDS! PLUS...
... WHEN IS THERE A CHANCE OF GETTING TO MEET THE REAL **PUSS IN BOOTS**?!

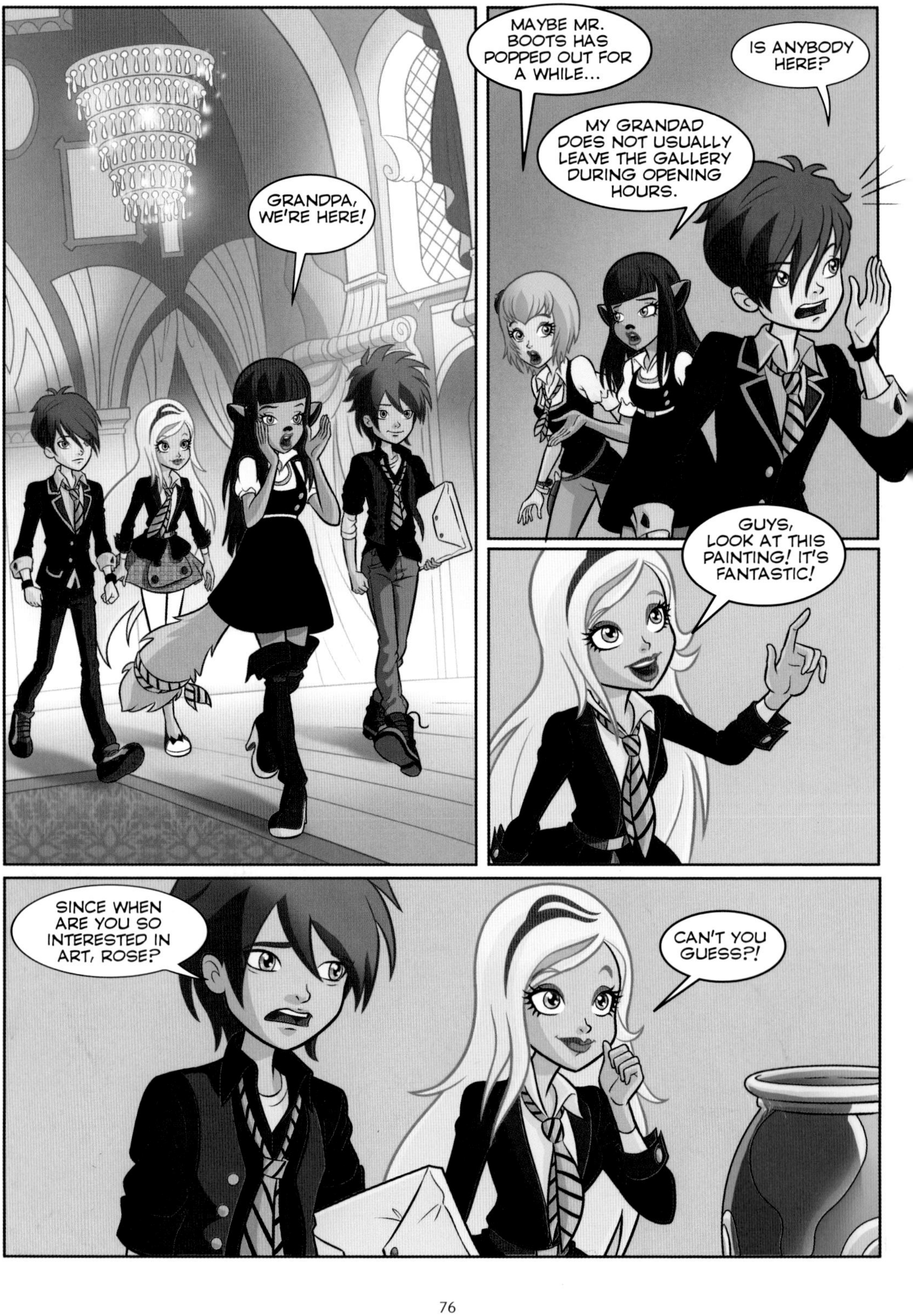
GRANDPA, WE'RE HERE!
MAYBE MR. BOOTS HAS POPPED OUT FOR A WHILE...
IS ANYBODY HERE?
MY GRANDAD DOES NOT USUALLY LEAVE THE GALLERY DURING OPENING HOURS.
GUYS, LOOK AT THIS PAINTING! IT'S FANTASTIC!
SINCE WHEN ARE YOU SO INTERESTED IN ART, ROSE?
CAN'T YOU GUESS?!

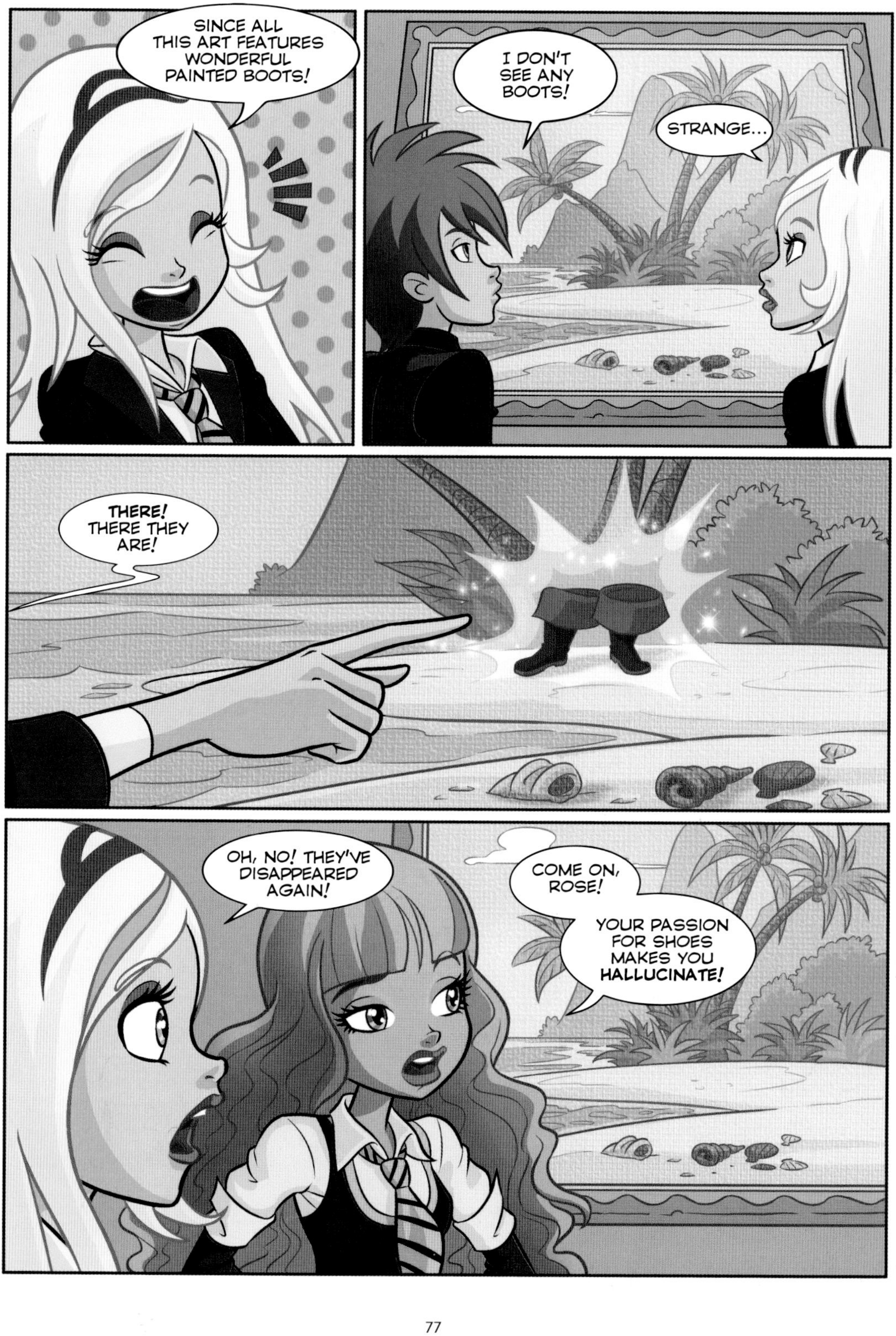
SINCE ALL THIS ART FEATURES WONDERFUL PAINTED BOOTS!
I DON'T SEE ANY BOOTS!
STRANGE...
THERE! THERE THEY ARE!
OH, NO! THEY'VE DISAPPEARED AGAIN!
COME ON, ROSE!
YOUR PASSION FOR SHOES MAKES YOU HALLUCINATE!

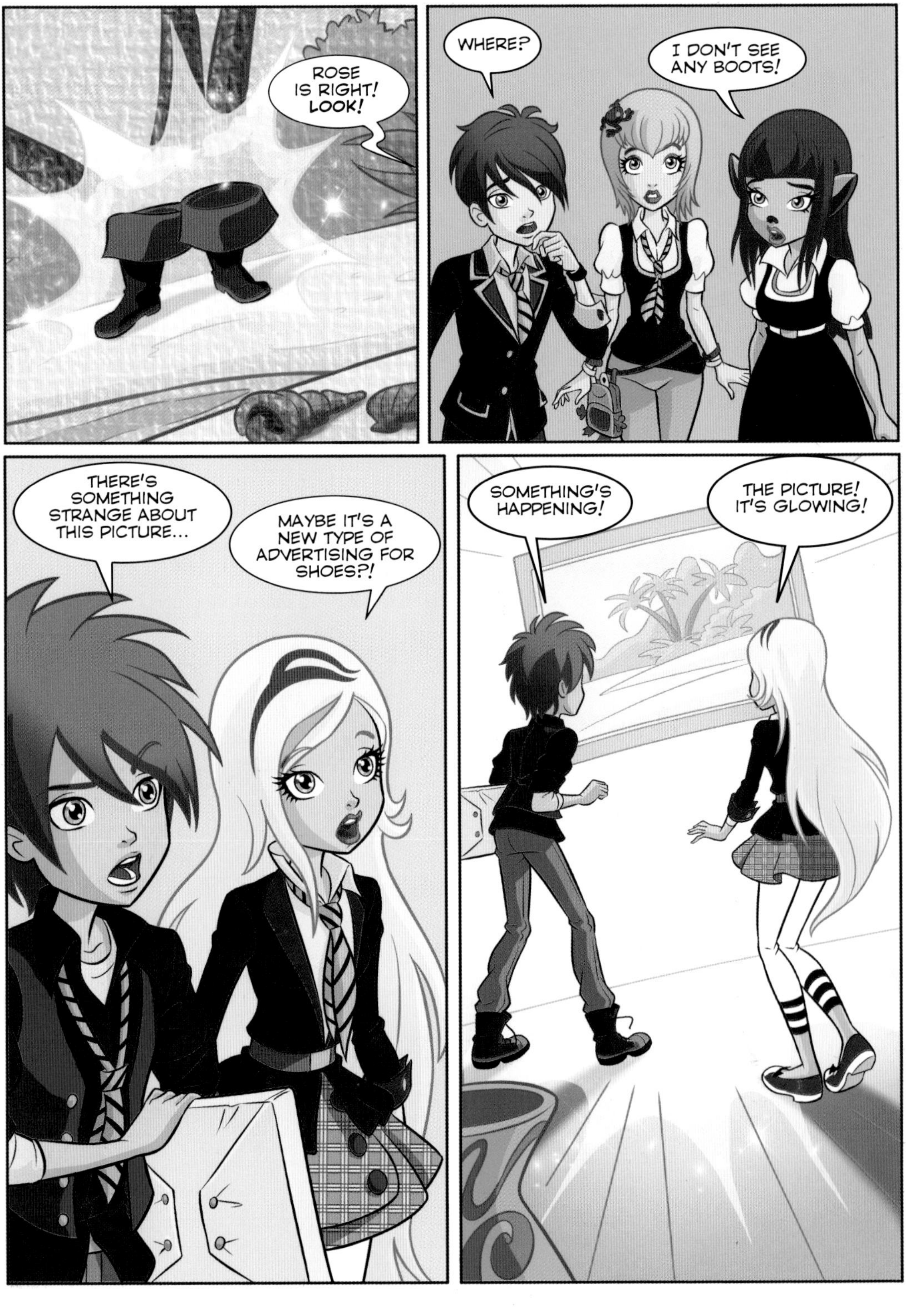
ROSE IS RIGHT! LOOK!
WHERE?
I DON'T SEE ANY BOOTS!
THERE'S SOMETHING STRANGE ABOUT THIS PICTURE...
MAYBE IT'S A NEW TYPE OF ADVERTISING FOR SHOES?!
SOMETHING'S HAPPENING!
THE PICTURE! IT'S GLOWING!

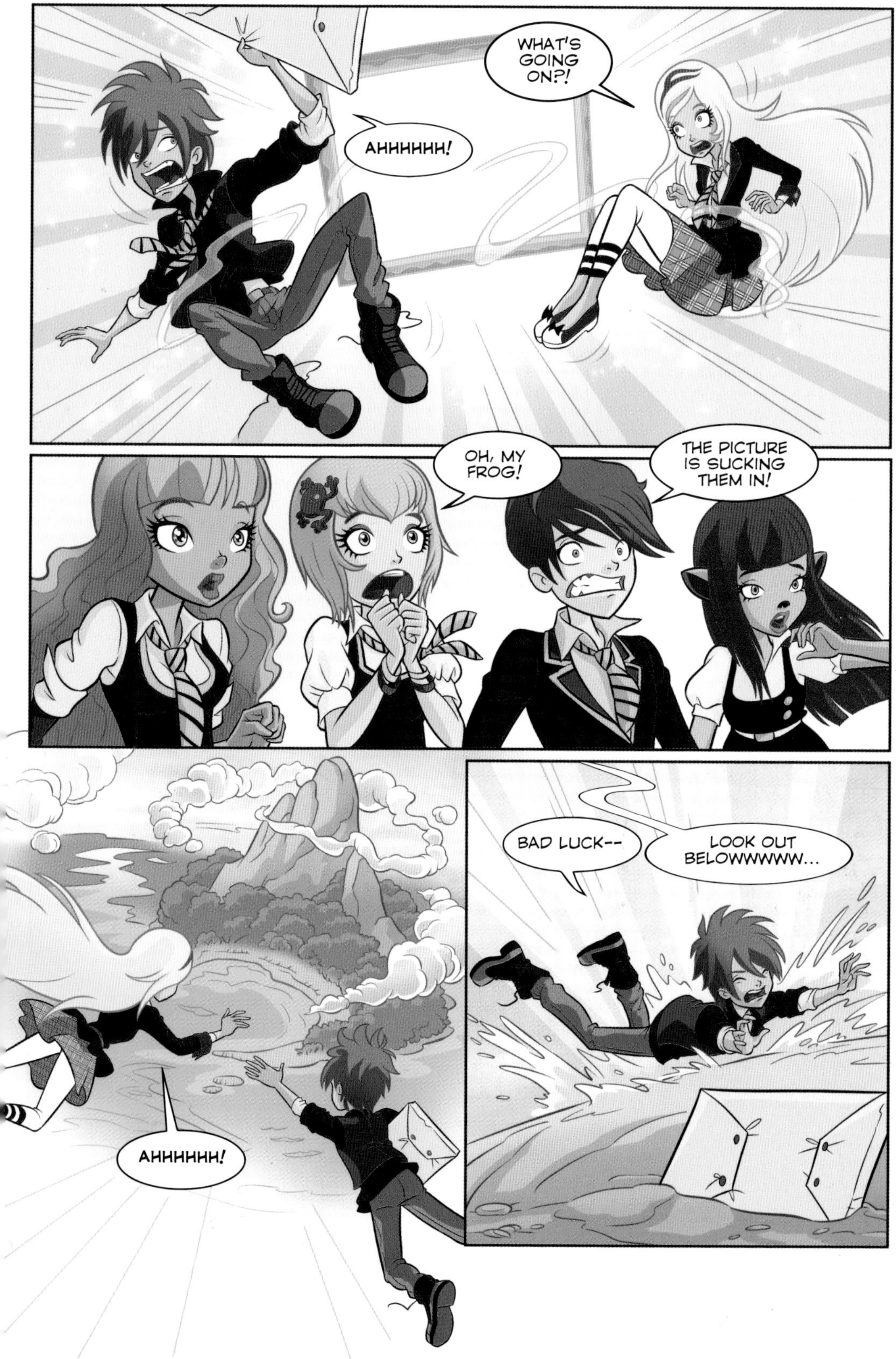
WHAT'S GOING ON?!
AHHHHHH!
OH, MY FROG!
THE PICTURE IS SUCKING THEM IN!
AHHHHHH!
BAD LUCK--
LOOK OUT BELOWWWWW...

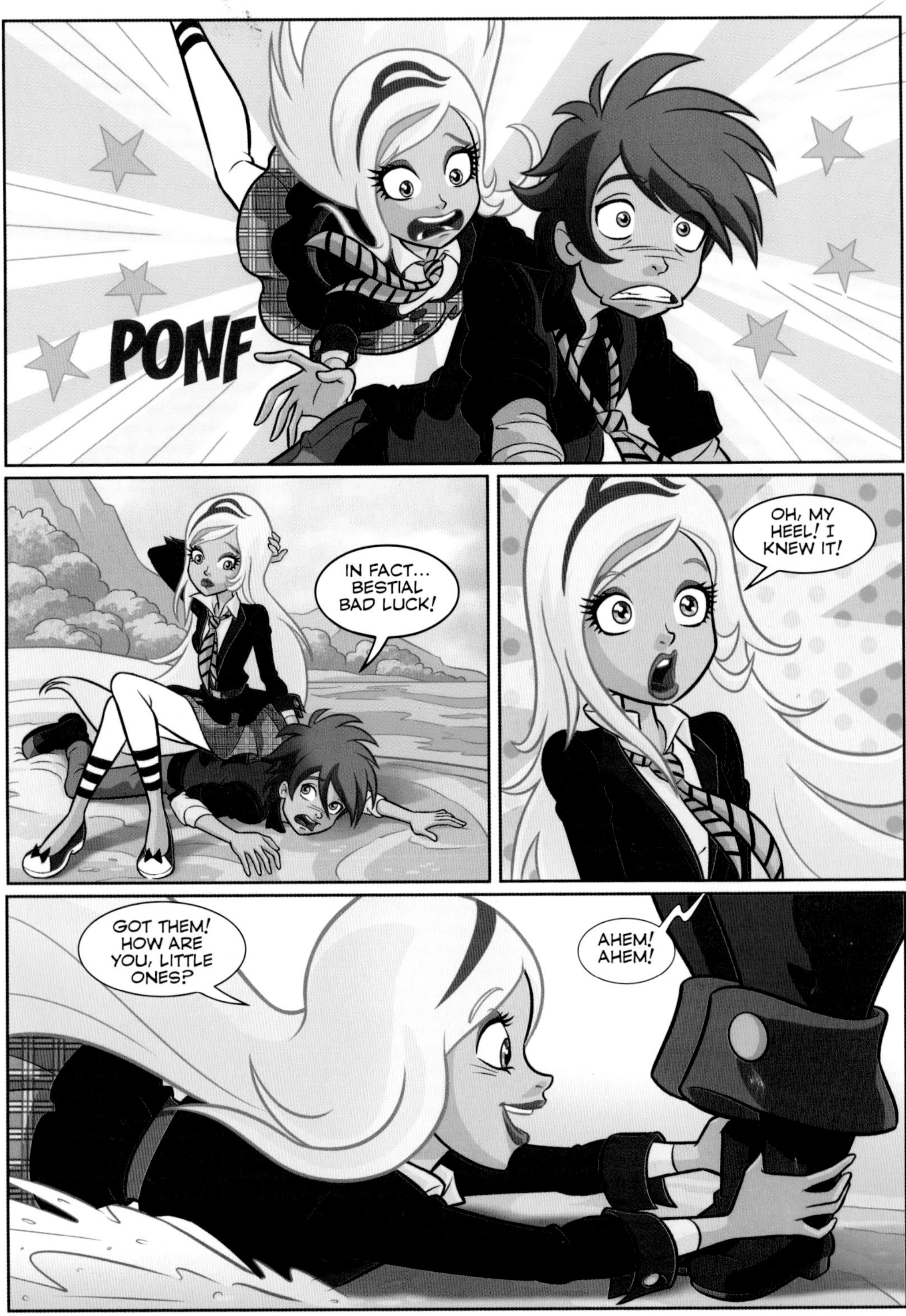
PONF
IN FACT... BESTIAL BAD LUCK!
OH, MY HEEL! I KNEW IT!
GOT THEM! HOW ARE YOU, LITTLE ONES?
AHEM! AHEM!

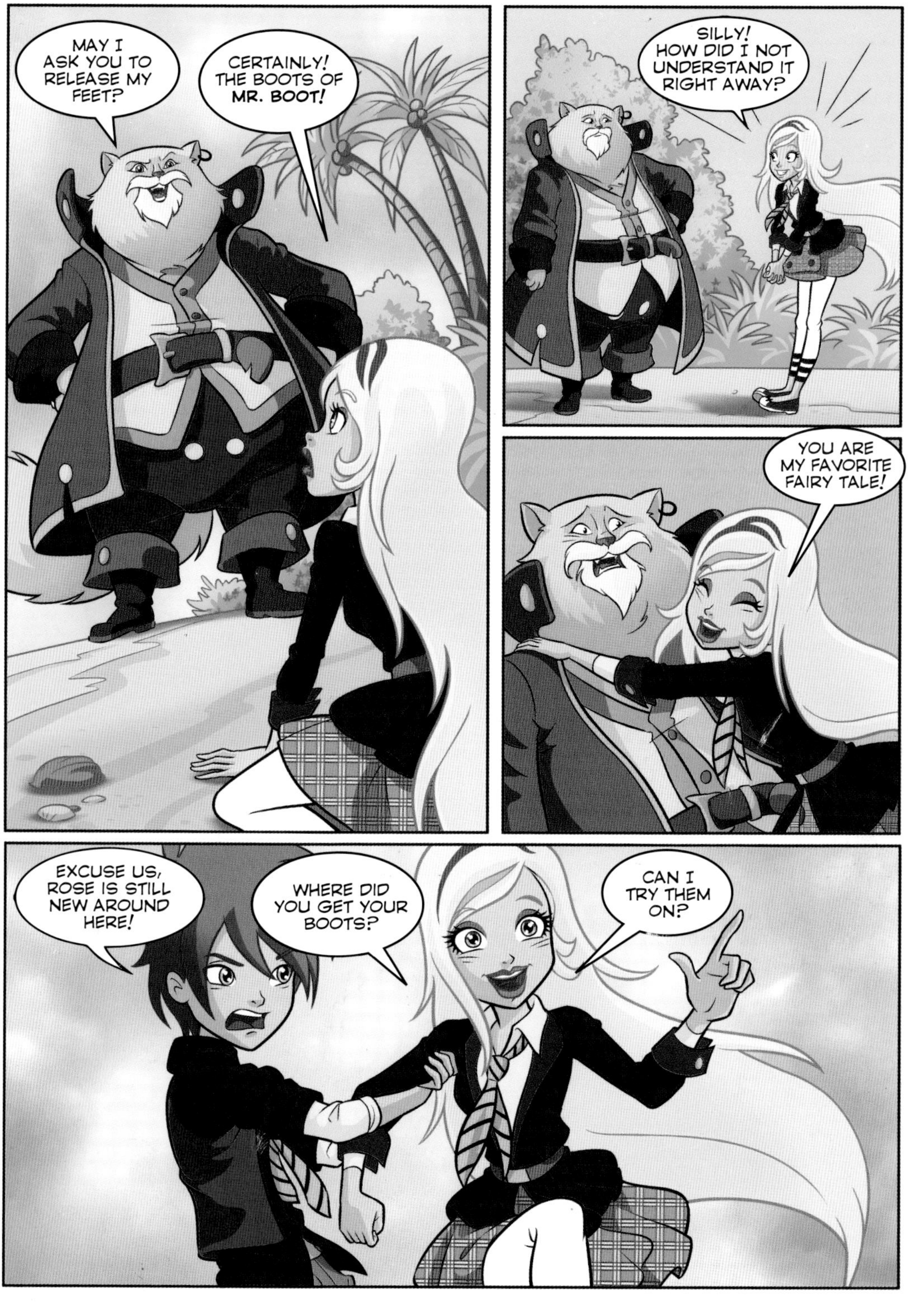
MAY I ASK YOU TO RELEASE MY FEET?
CERTAINLY! THE BOOTS OF MR. BOOT!
SILLY! HOW DID I NOT UNDERSTAND IT RIGHT AWAY?
YOU ARE MY FAVORITE FAIRY TALE!
EXCUSE US, ROSE IS STILL NEW AROUND HERE!
WHERE DID YOU GET YOUR BOOTS?
CAN I TRY THEM ON?

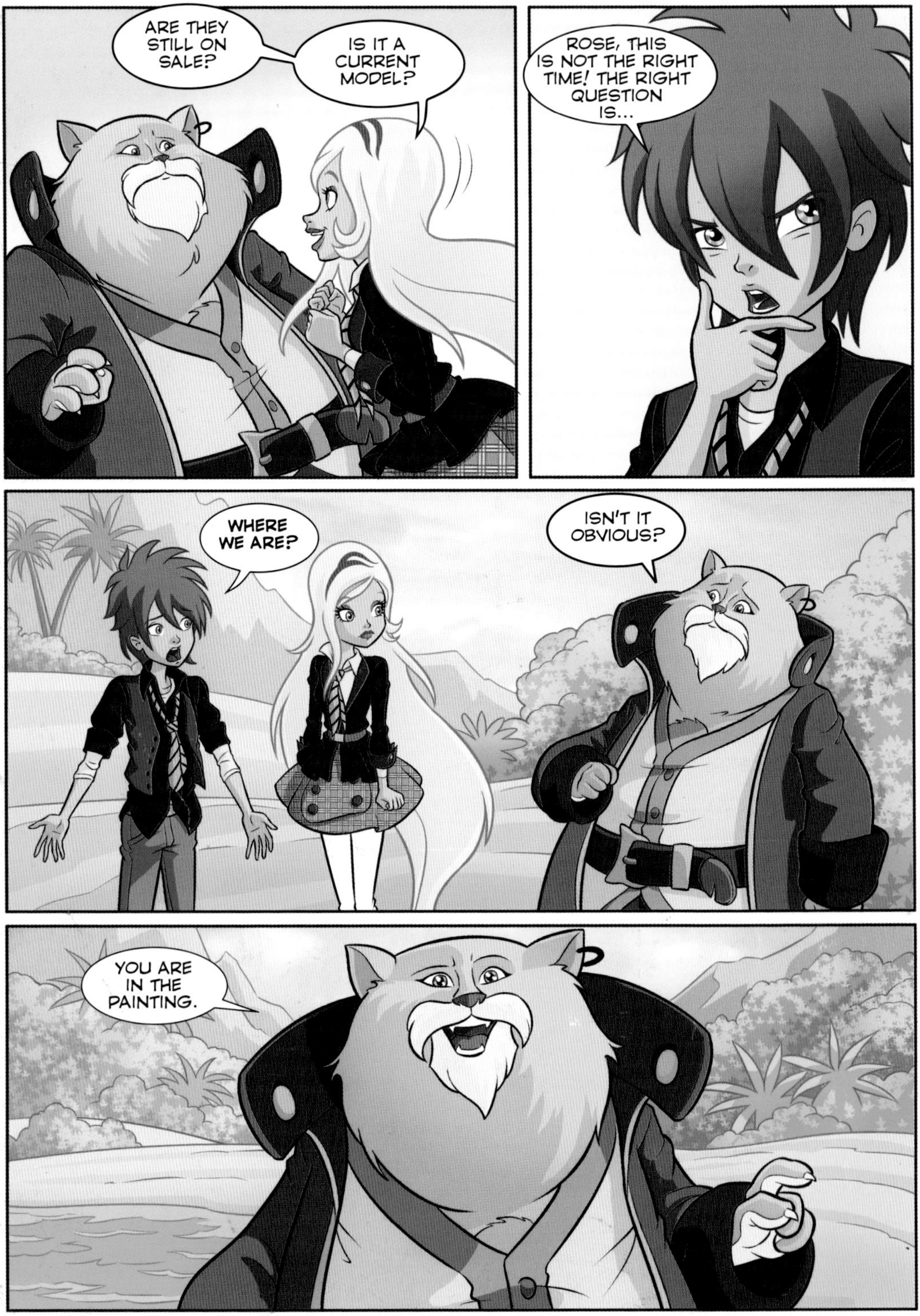
ARE THEY STILL ON SALE?
IS IT A CURRENT MODEL?
ROSE, THIS IS NOT THE RIGHT TIME! THE RIGHT QUESTION IS...
WHERE WE ARE?
ISN'T IT OBVIOUS?
YOU ARE IN THE PAINTING.

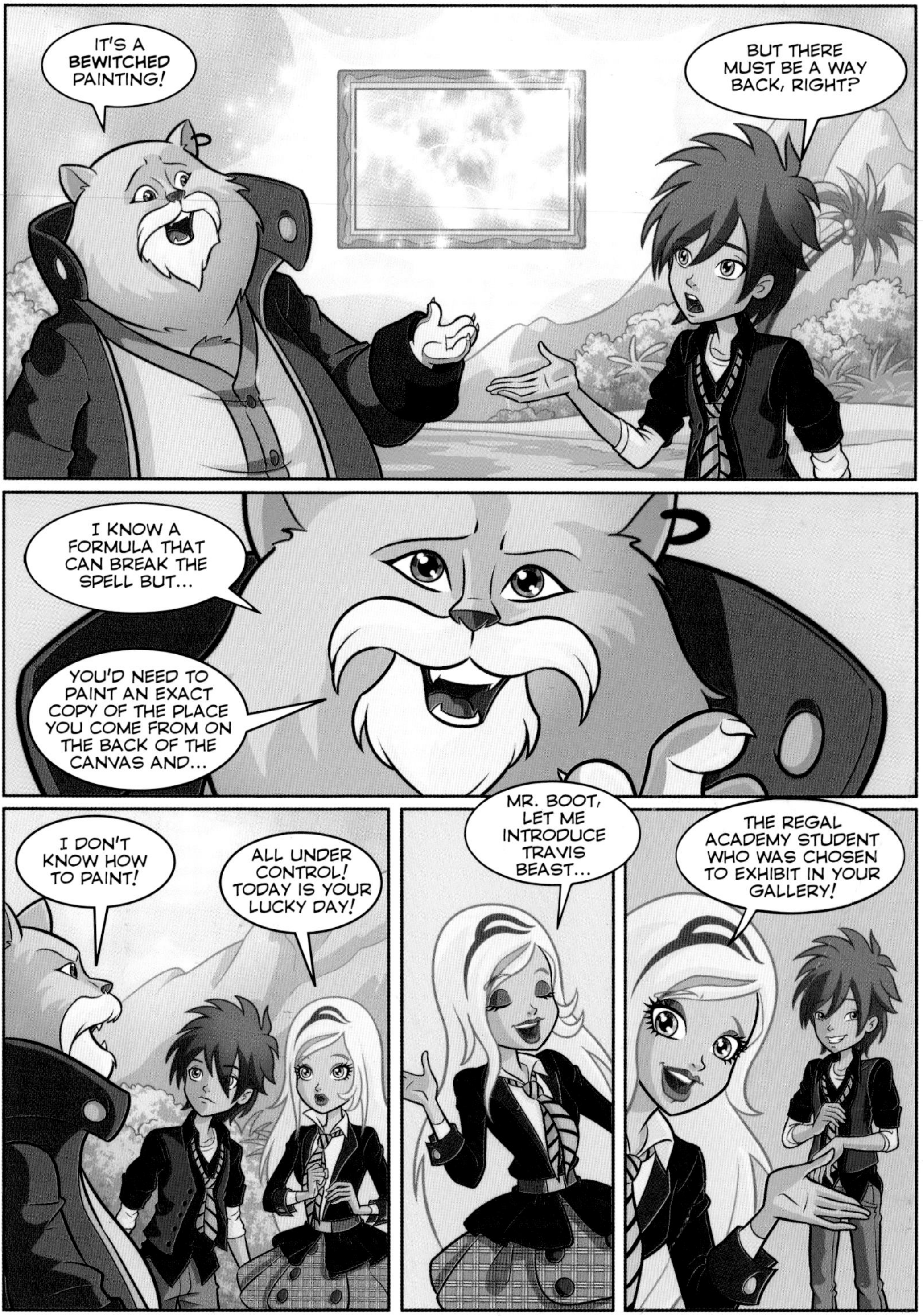
IT'S A BEWITCHED PAINTING!
BUT THERE MUST BE A WAY BACK, RIGHT?
I KNOW A FORMULA THAT CAN BREAK THE SPELL BUT...
YOU'D NEED TO PAINT AN EXACT COPY OF THE PLACE YOU COME FROM ON THE BACK OF THE CANVAS AND...
I DON'T KNOW HOW TO PAINT!
ALL UNDER CONTROL! TODAY IS YOUR LUCKY DAY!
MR. BOOT, LET ME INTRODUCE TRAVIS BEAST...
THE REGAL ACADEMY STUDENT WHO WAS CHOSEN TO EXHIBIT IN YOUR GALLERY!

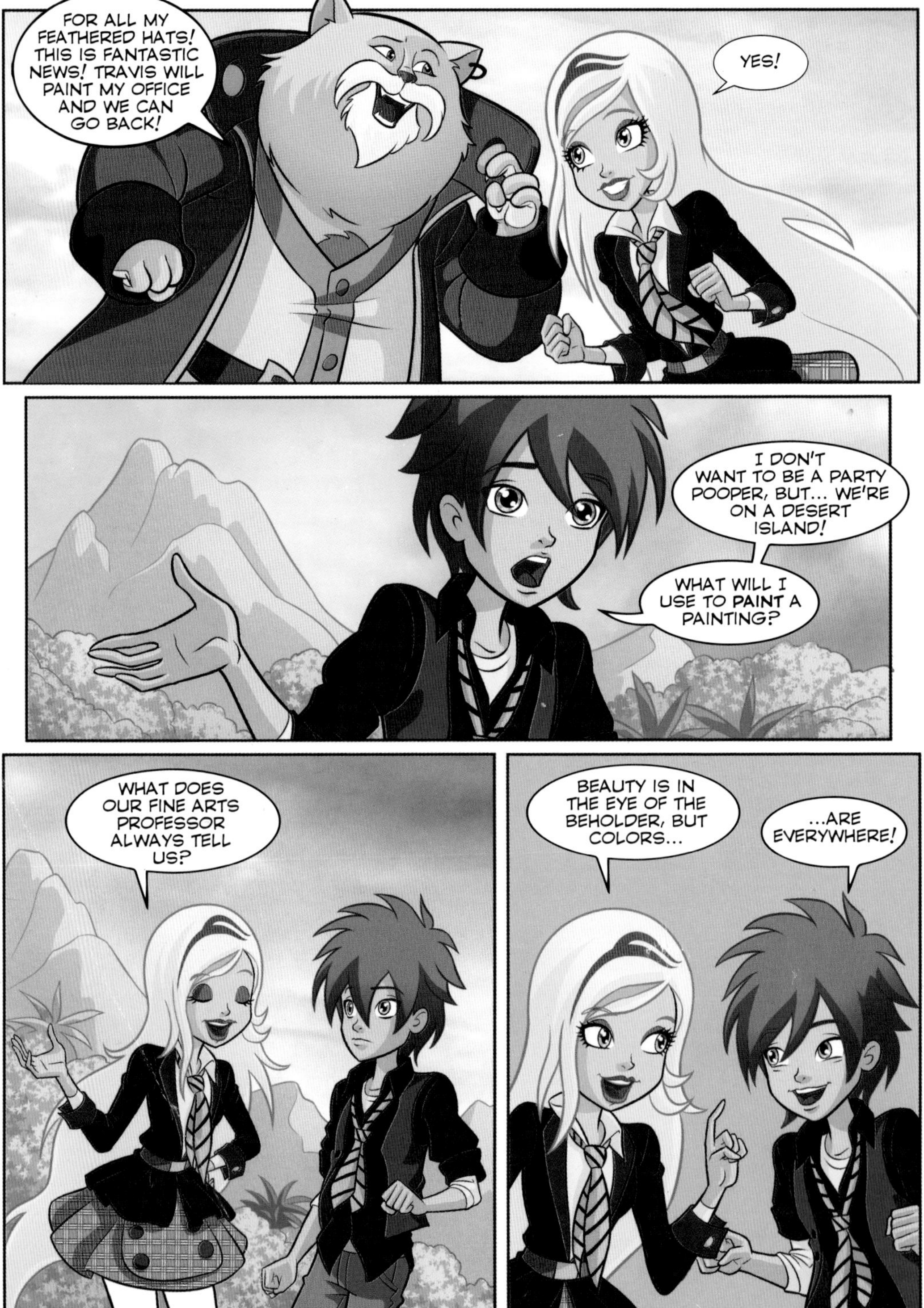
FOR ALL MY FEATHERED HATS! THIS IS FANTASTIC NEWS! TRAVIS WILL PAINT MY OFFICE AND WE CAN GO BACK!
YES!
I DON'T WANT TO BE A PARTY POOPER, BUT... WE'RE ON A DESERT ISLAND!
WHAT WILL I USE TO PAINT A PAINTING?
WHAT DOES OUR FINE ARTS PROFESSOR ALWAYS TELL US?
BEAUTY IS IN THE EYE OF THE BEHOLDER, BUT COLORS...
...ARE EVERYWHERE!

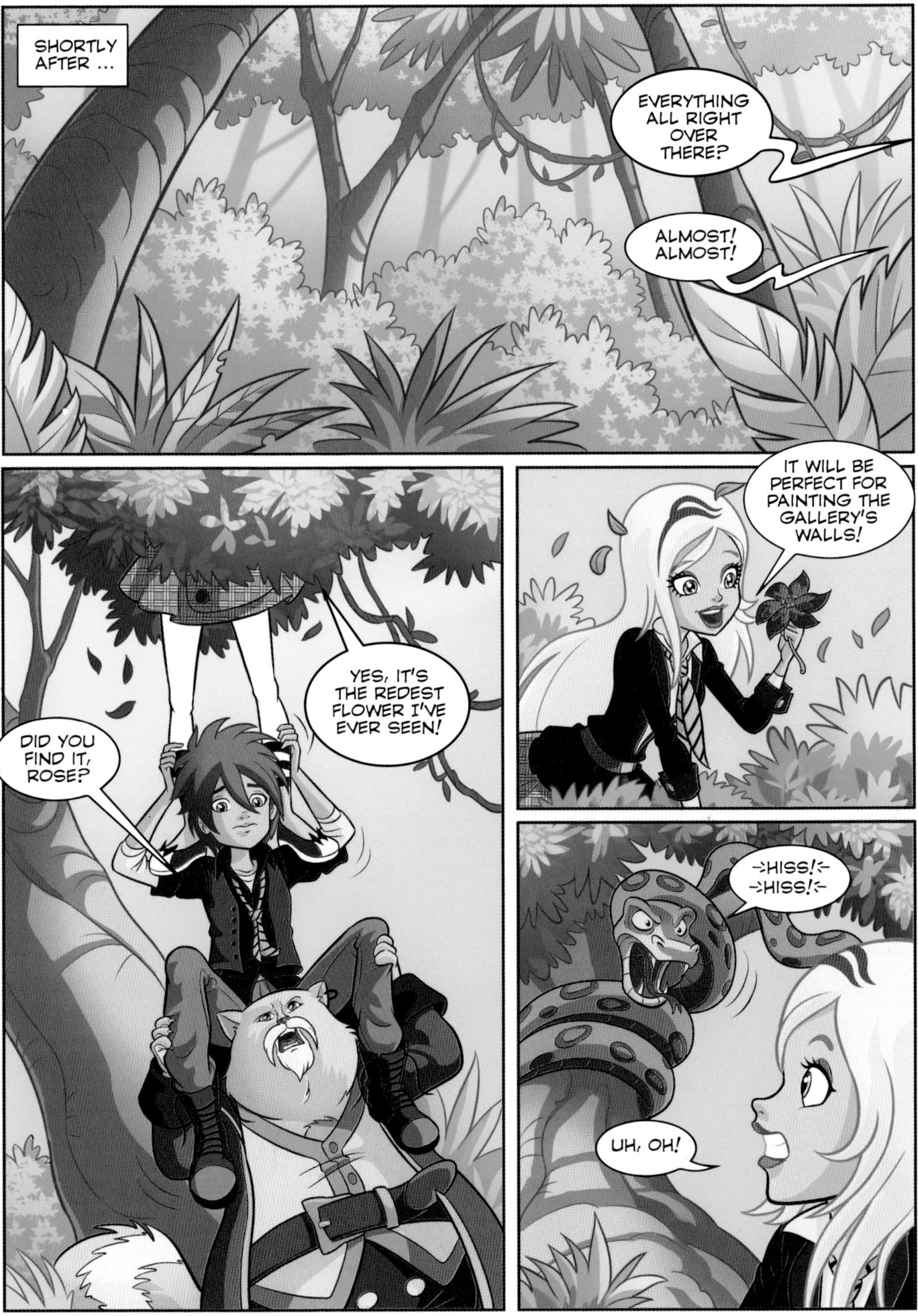
SHORTLY AFTER ...
EVERYTHING ALL RIGHT OVER THERE?
ALMOST! ALMOST!
DID YOU FIND IT, ROSE?
YES, IT'S THE REDEST FLOWER I'VE EVER SEEN!
IT WILL BE PERFECT FOR PAINTING THE GALLERY'S WALLS!
HISS! HISS!
UH, OH!

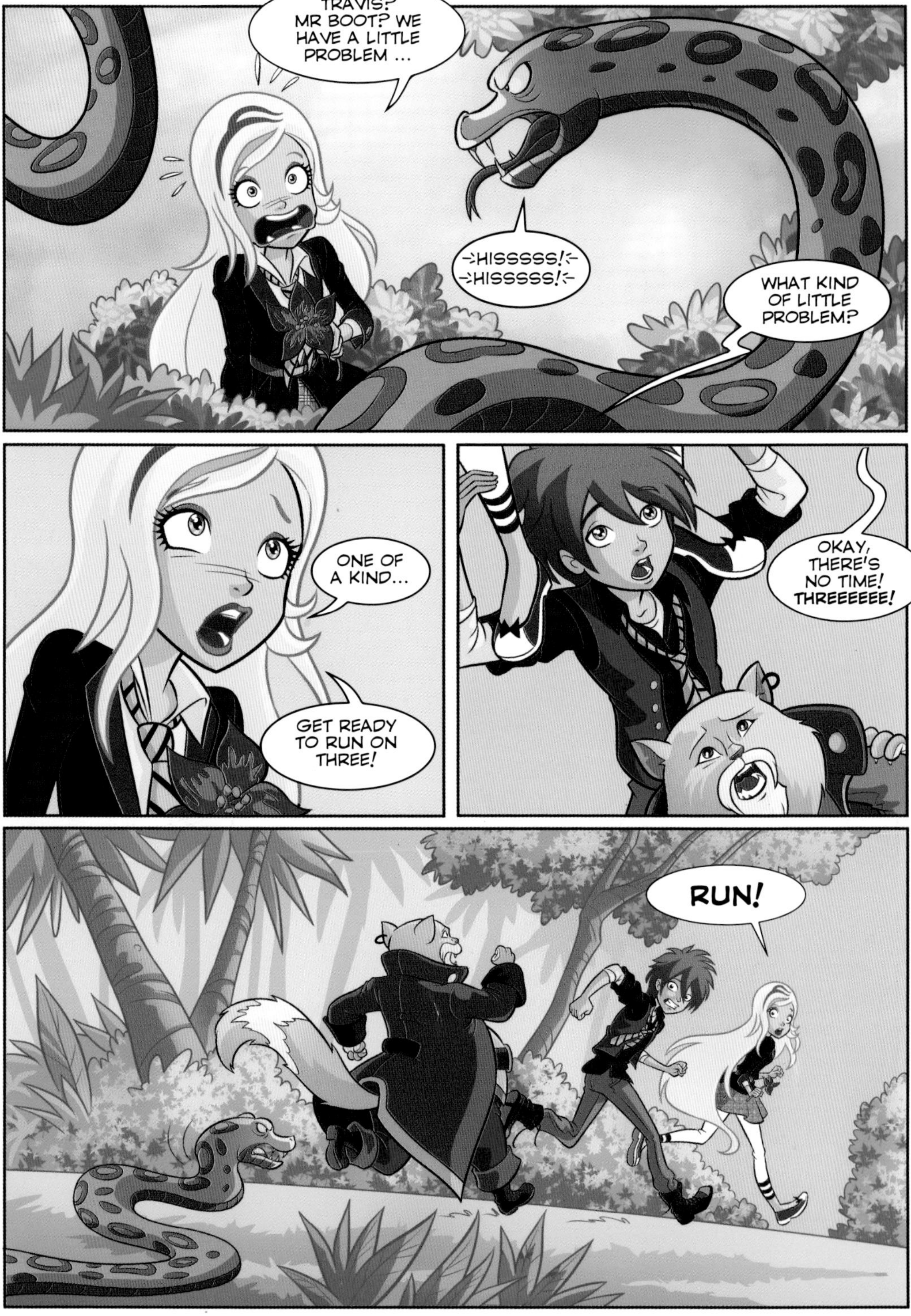
TRAVIS? MR BOOT? WE HAVE A LITTLE PROBLEM ...
HISSSSS! HISSSSS!
WHAT KIND OF LITTLE PROBLEM?
ONE OF A KIND...
GET READY TO RUN ON THREE!
OKAY, THERE'S NO TIME! THREEEEEE!
RUN!

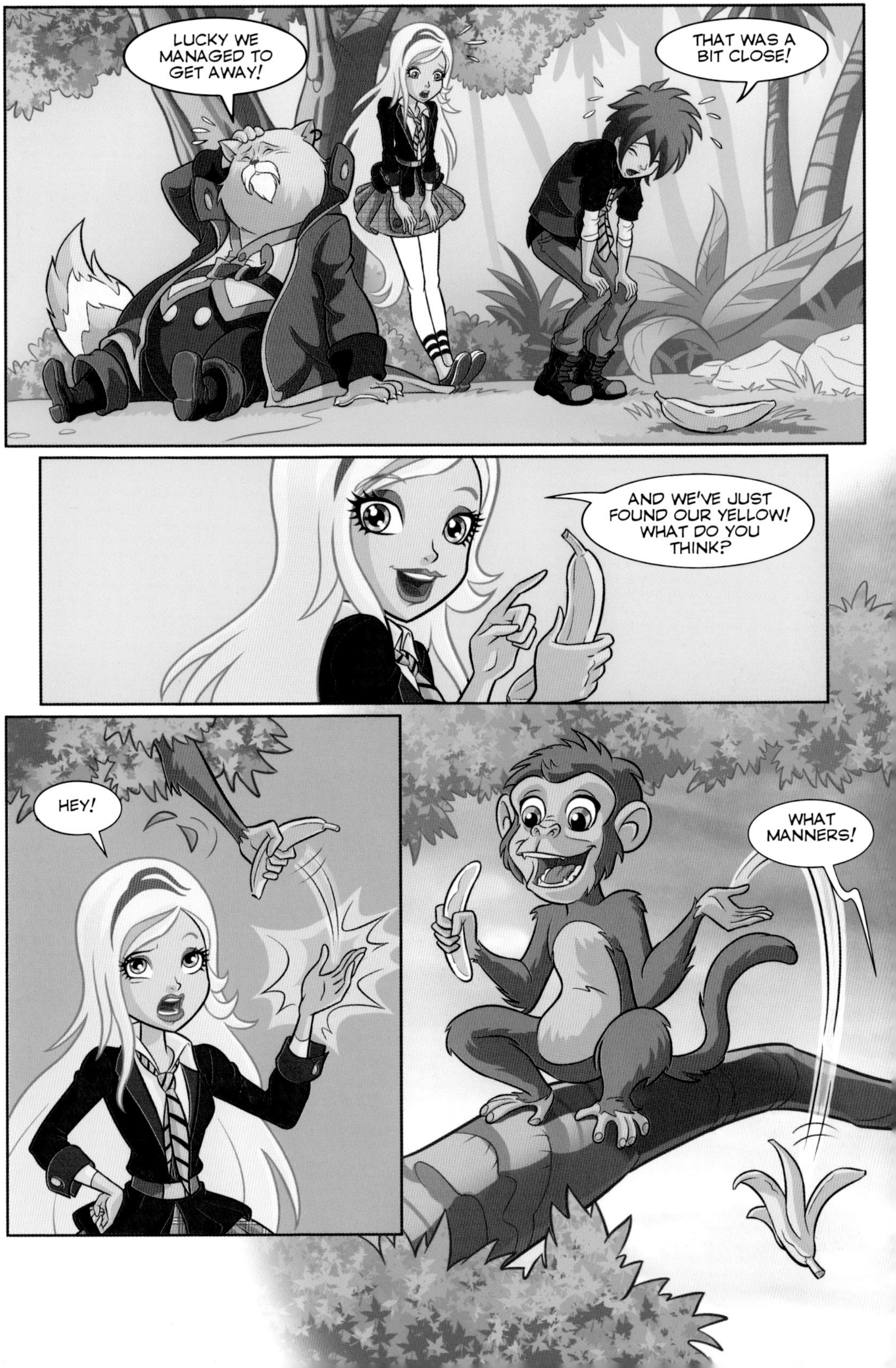
LUCKY WE MANAGED TO GET AWAY!
THAT WAS A BIT CLOSE!
AND WE'VE JUST FOUND OUR YELLOW! WHAT DO YOU THINK?
HEY!
WHAT MANNERS!

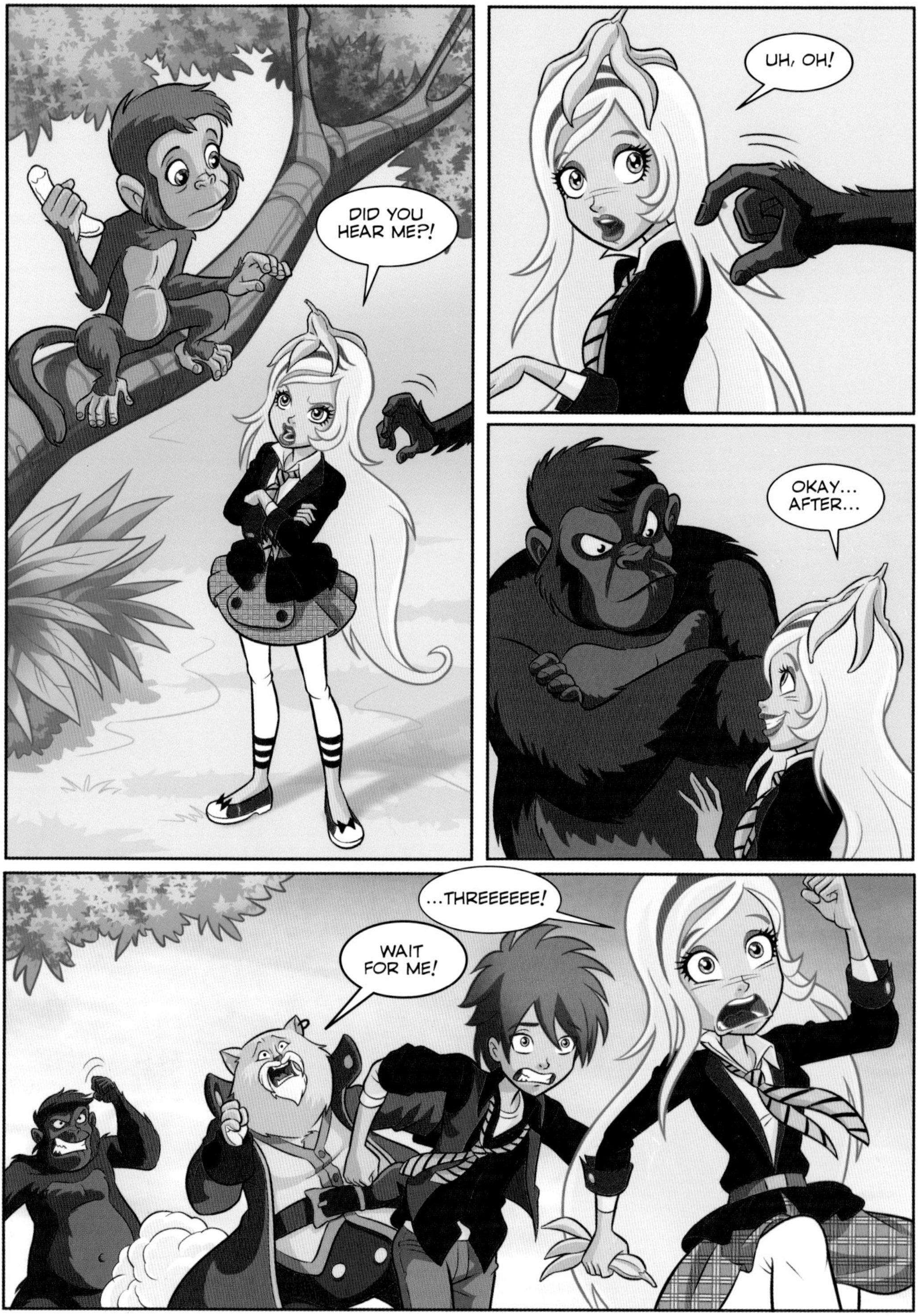
DID YOU HEAR ME?!
UH, OH!
OKAY... AFTER...
...THREEEEEE!
WAIT FOR ME!

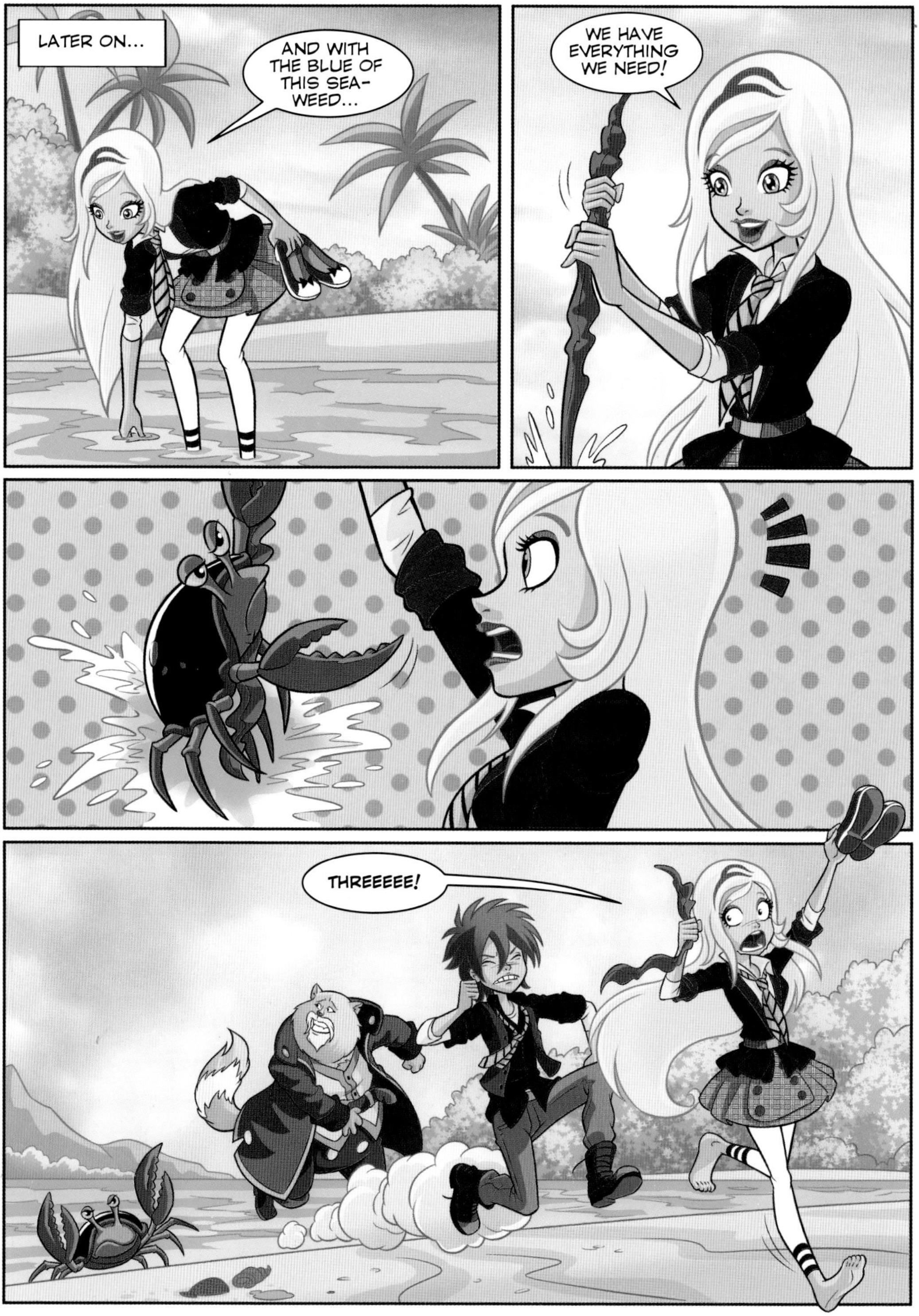
LATER ON...
AND WITH THE BLUE OF THIS SEA-WEED...
WE HAVE EVERYTHING WE NEED!
THREEEEE!

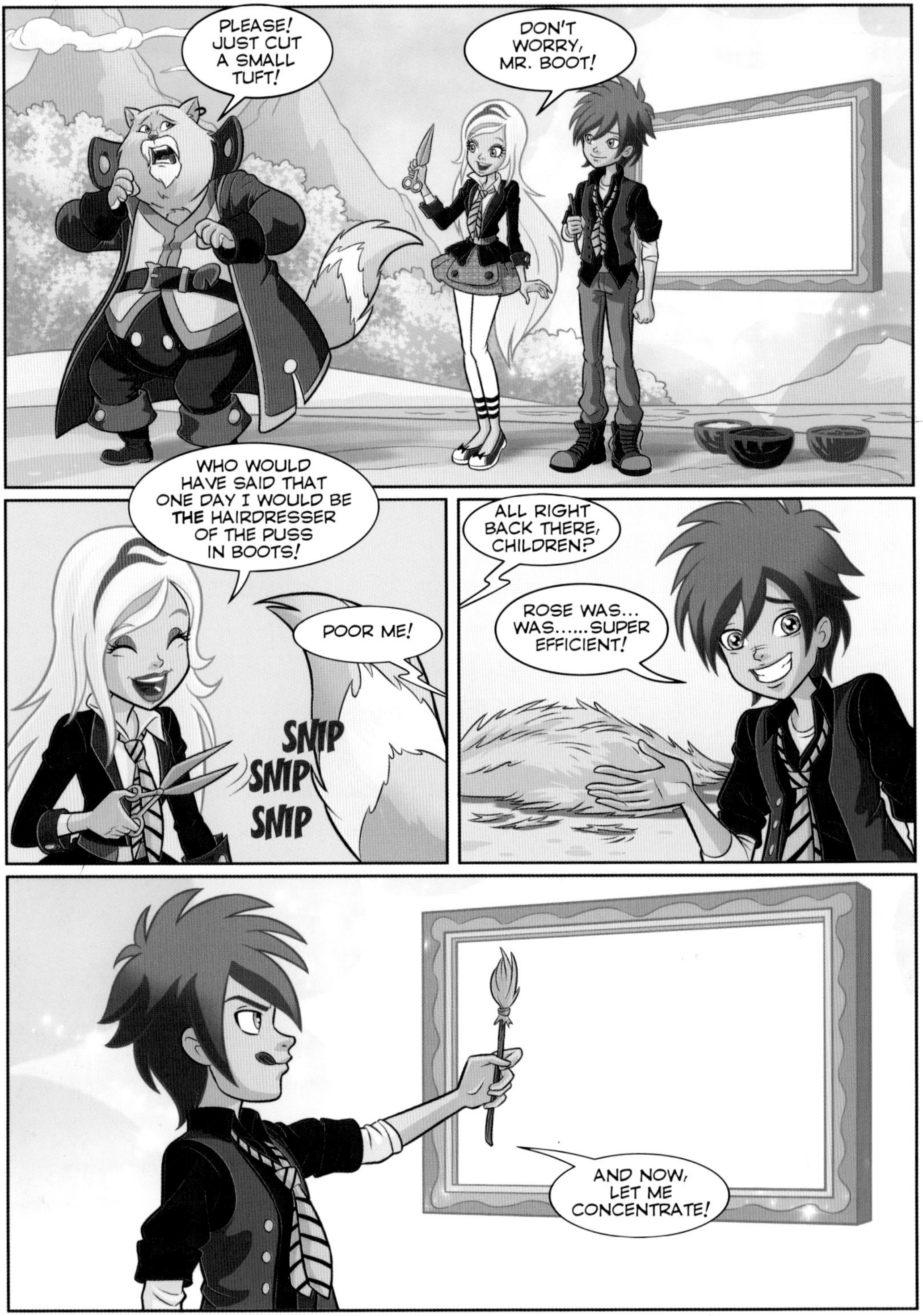
PLEASE! JUST CUT A SMALL TUFT!
DON'T WORRY, MR. BOOT!
WHO WOULD HAVE SAID THAT ONE DAY I WOULD BE THE HAIRDRESSER OF THE PUSS IN BOOTS!
POOR ME!
SNIP
SNIP
SNIP
ALL RIGHT BACK THERE, CHILDREN?
ROSE WAS... WAS...... SUPER EFFICIENT!
AND NOW, LET ME CONCENTRATE!

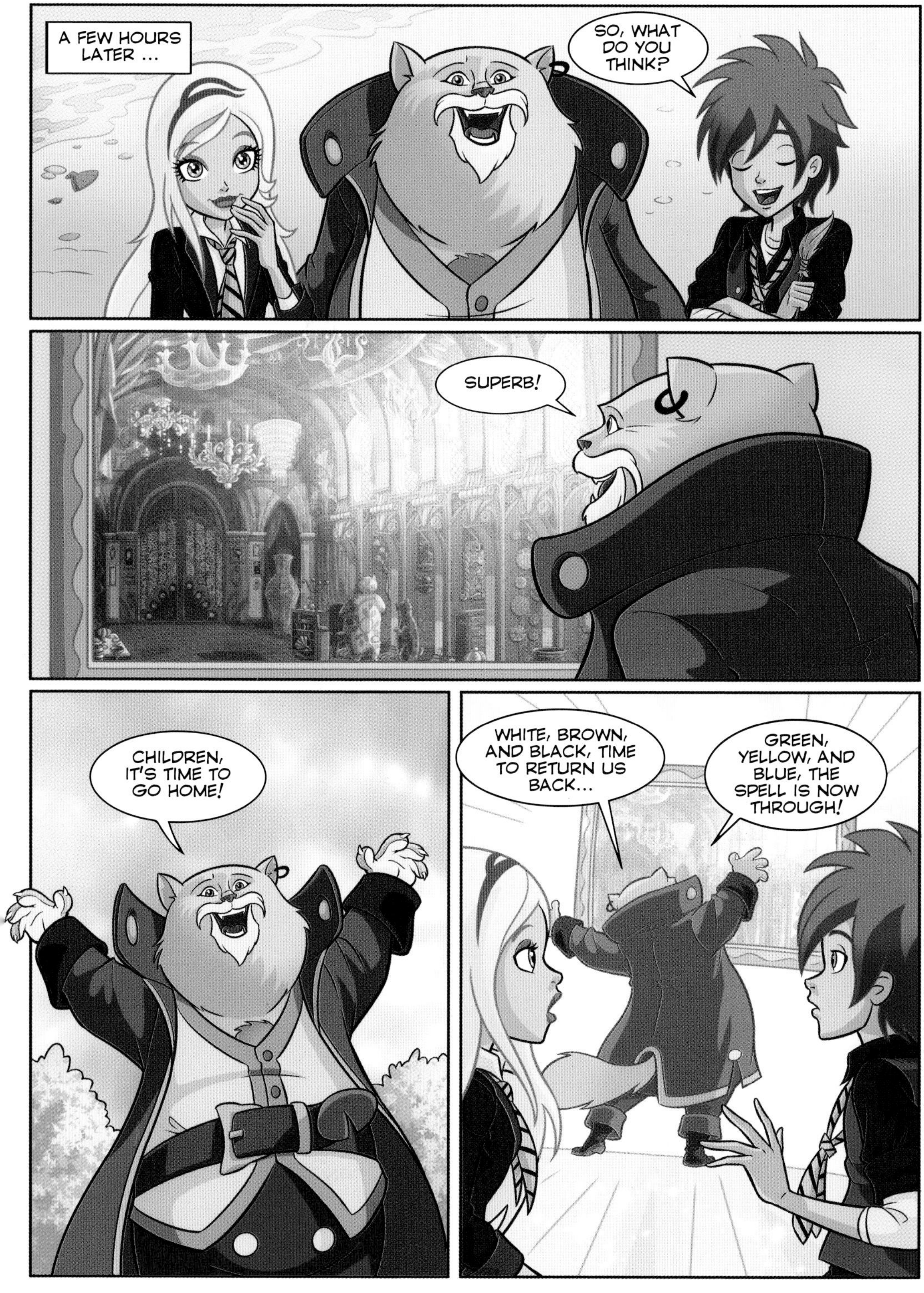
A FEW HOURS LATER ...
SO, WHAT DO YOU THINK?
SUPERB!
CHILDREN, IT'S TIME TO GO HOME!
WHITE, BROWN, AND BLACK, TIME TO RETURN US BACK...
GREEN, YELLOW, AND BLUE, THE SPELL IS NOW THROUGH!

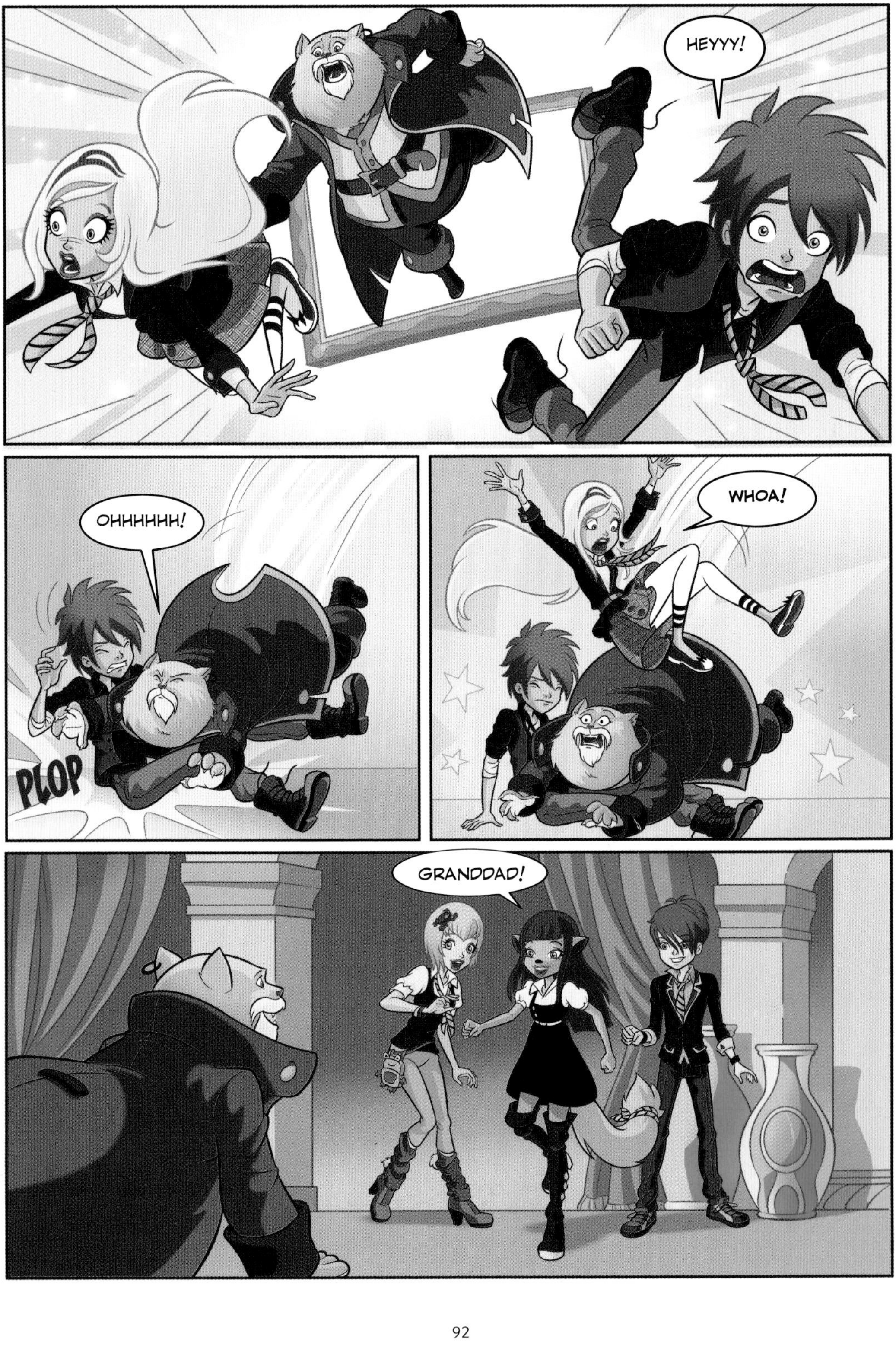
HEYYY!
OHHHHHH!
PLOP
WHOA!
GRANDDAD!

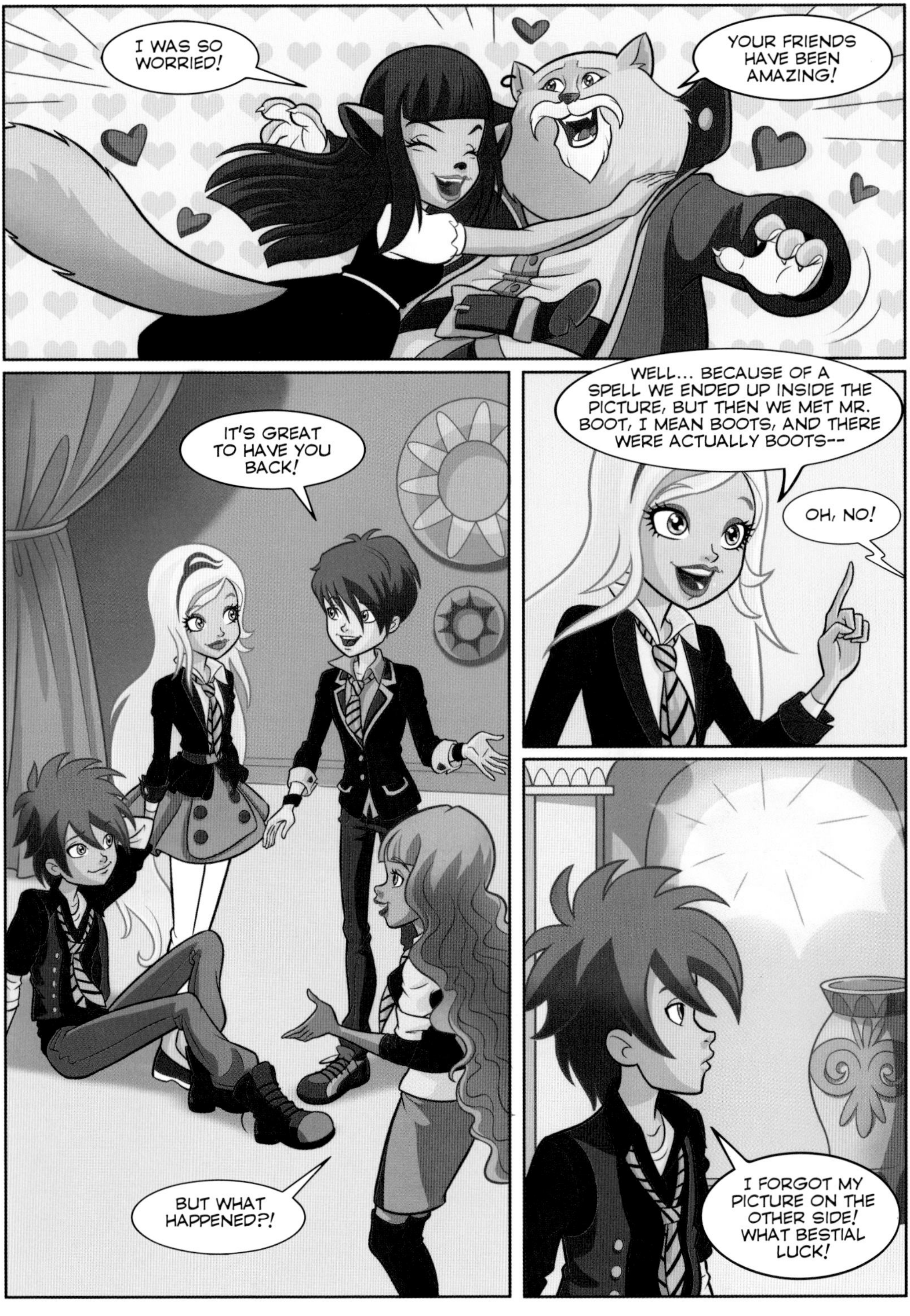
I WAS SO WORRIED!
YOUR FRIENDS HAVE BEEN AMAZING!
IT'S GREAT TO HAVE YOU BACK!
BUT WHAT HAPPENED?!
WELL... BECAUSE OF A SPELL WE ENDED UP INSIDE THE PICTURE, BUT THEN WE MET MR. BOOT, I MEAN BOOTS, AND THERE WERE ACTUALLY BOOTS--
OH, NO!
I FORGOT MY PICTURE ON THE OTHER SIDE! WHAT BESTIAL LUCK!

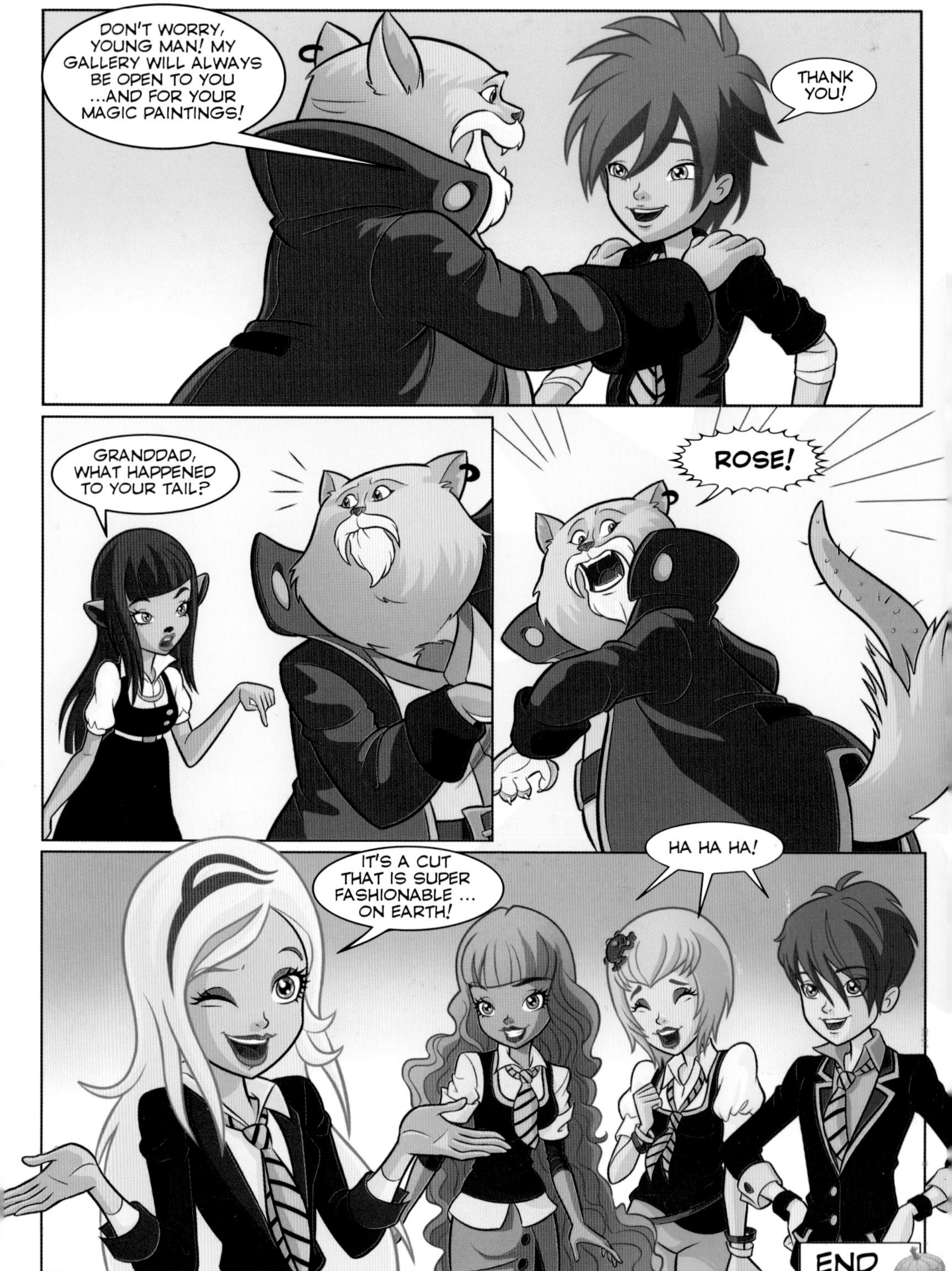
DON'T WORRY, YOUNG MAN! MY GALLERY WILL ALWAYS BE OPEN TO YOU ...AND FOR YOUR MAGIC PAINTINGS!
THANK YOU!
GRANDDAD, WHAT HAPPENED TO YOUR TAIL?
ROSE!
IT'S A CUT THAT IS SUPER FASHIONABLE ... ON EARTH!
HA HA HA!
END

WATCH OUT FOR PAPERCUTZ

Welcome to the second sorcery-laden REGAL ACADEMY graphic novel from Papercutz—those Hogwarts dropouts that are dedicated to publishing great graphic novels for all ages. I'm Professor Jim Salicrup, the Editor-in-Chief and your official magical guide in the land of Papercutz.

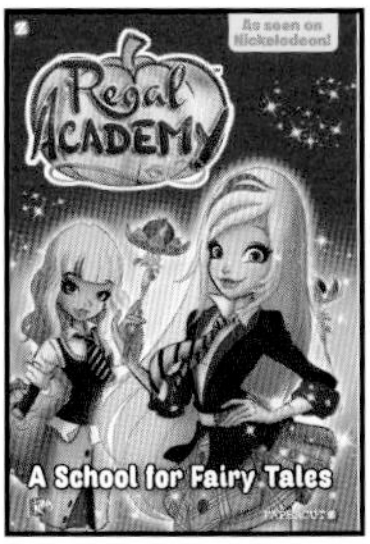
As seen on Nickelodeon!
Regal Academy
A School for Fairy Tales
PAPERCUTZ

In REGAL ACADEMY #1, I told you the true-life fairy tale of how Papercutz came to be. I happily told the wondrous tale of how Terry Nantier dreamed of a special graphic novel publisher that exclusively created awesome graphic novels for kids of all ages. I was fortunate enough to join Terry when he made his dream come true by starting Papercutz. And here's the best part, things just keep getting better and better, because now we're able to bring you the REGAL ACADEMY graphic novels.

Over the years we've been able to bring you all sorts of amazing magical graphic novels such as...

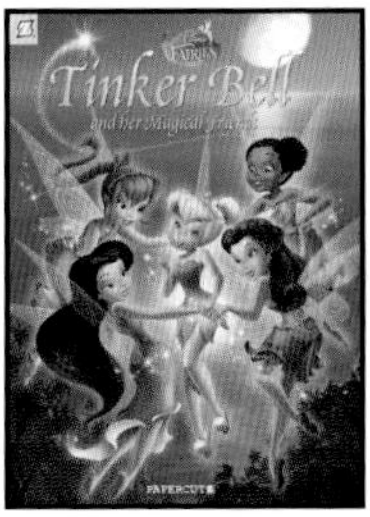
Tinker Bell
PAPERCUTZ

DISNEY FAIRIES featuring TINKER BELL—While on rare occasions Tink visited the world of humans, most of these stories feature everyone's favorite fairy in Never Land, with her fairy friends. There have even been a few sightings of Captain Hook and Peter Pan!

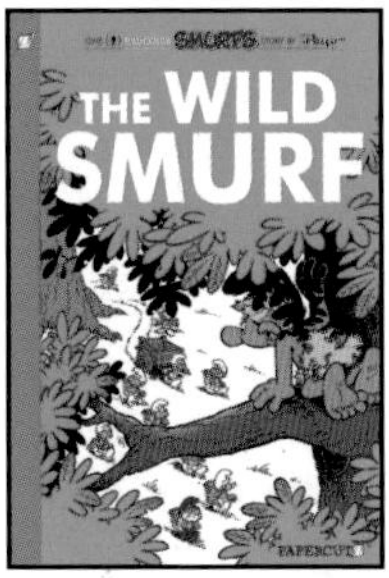
SMURFS
THE WILD SMURF
PAPERCUTZ

THE SMURFS—Far, far away in the Cursed Lands there's a tiny little village filled little happy little blue elves known as THE SMURFS! They've had their hands full dealing with the wicked wizard Gargamel, not to mention a Purple Smurf, a Howlibird, and much, much more.

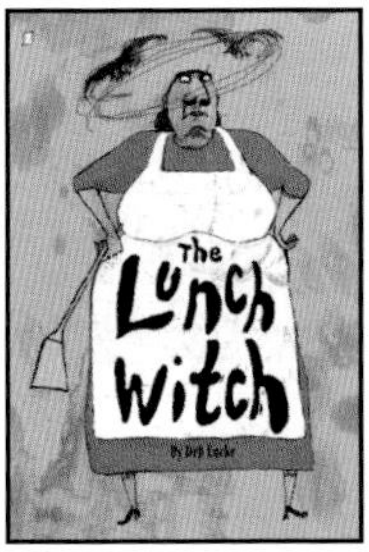
The Lunch Witch

THE LUNCH WITCH—Is the story of Grunhilda the Blackheart, a witch who is down on her luck because no one believes in witches anymore. Desperate, she looks for a job and winds up as the Lunch Lady at an elementary school.

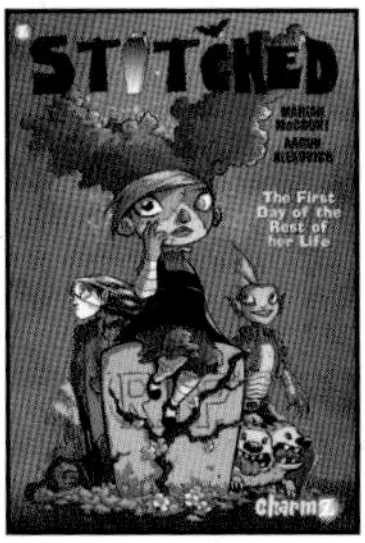
STITCHED
The First Day of the Rest of her Life
charmz

And there's even a special line of books called Charmz, that features STITCHED, the story of Crimson Volania Mulch, who wakes up in the weirdest spot—a cemetery! She doesn't know anything but her name, and her first few nights "alive" are a spooky whirlwind of ghosts, werewolves, witches, and more.

So, Papercutz is where the magic is! Just visit us at Papercutz.com for more information, and don't forget to pick up REGAL ACADEMY #3 for even more magical enlightenment!

Class Dismissed!

Thanks,

Jim

STAY IN TOUCH!

EMAIL:	salicrup@papercutz.com
WEB:	papercutz.com
TWITTER:	@papercutzgn
INSTAGRAM:	@papercutzgn
FACEBOOK:	PAPERCUTZGRAPHICNOVELS
FAN MAIL:	Papercutz, 160 Broadway, Suite 700, East Wing, New York, NY 10038

MORE GREAT GRAPHIC NOVEL SERIES AVAILABLE FROM PAPERCUTZ

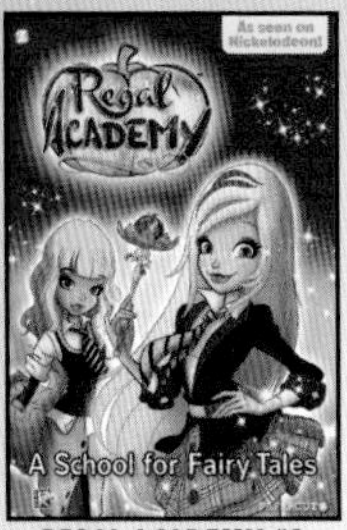
As seen on Nickelodeon!
Regal Academy
A School for Fairy Tales
REGAL ACADEMY #1

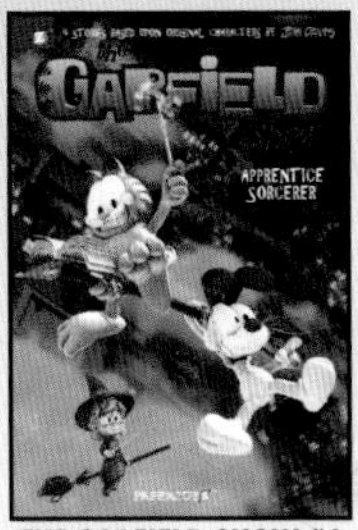
Garfield
Apprentice Sorcerer
THE GARFIELD SHOW #6

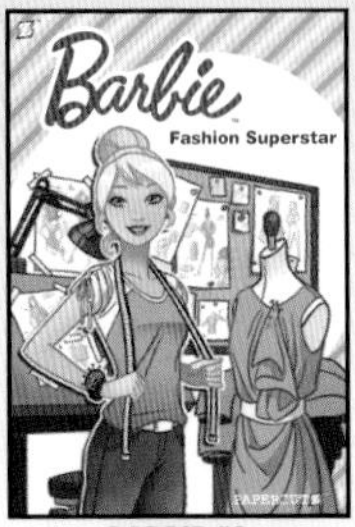
Barbie
Fashion Superstar
BARBIE #1

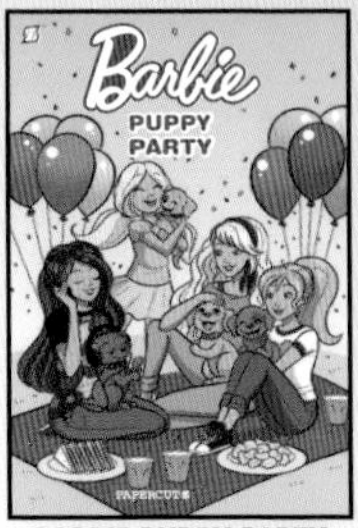
Barbie
Puppy Party
BARBIE PUPPY PARTY

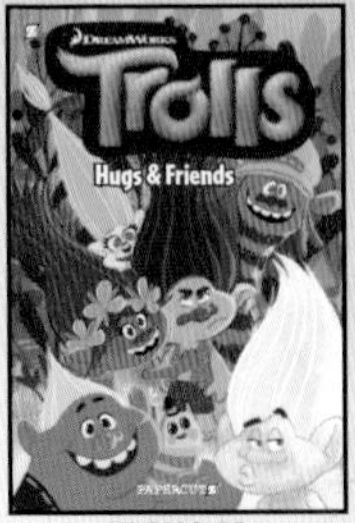
DreamWorks
Trolls
Hugs & Friends
TROLLS #1

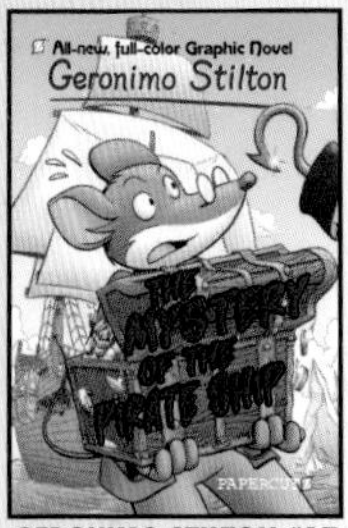
All-new, full-color Graphic Novel
Geronimo Stilton
The Mystery of the Pirate Ship
GERONIMO STILTON #17

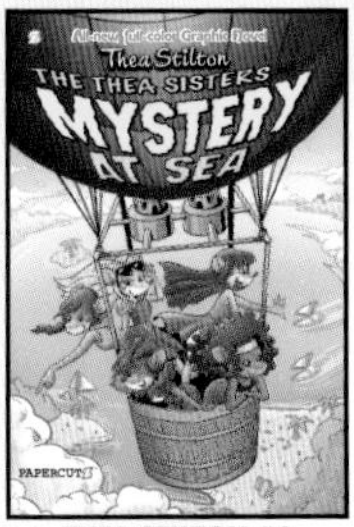
Thea Stilton
The Thea Sisters
Mystery at Sea
THEA STILTON #6

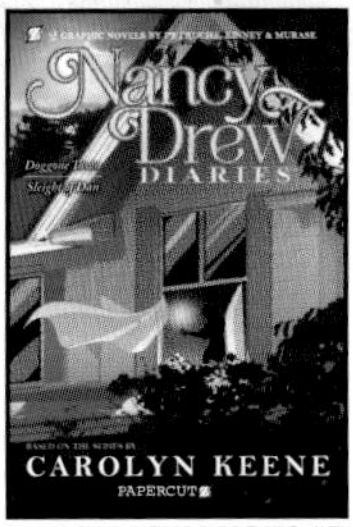
Nancy Drew Diaries
Carolyn Keene
NANCY DREW DIARIES #7

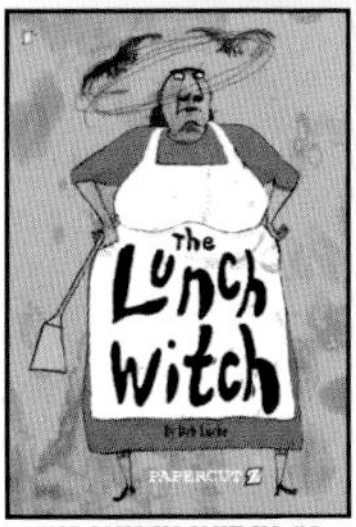
The Lunch Witch
THE LUNCH WITCH #1

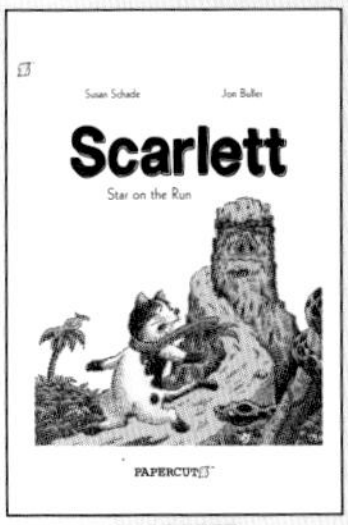
Susan Schade
Jon Buller
Scarlett
Star on the Run
SCARLETT

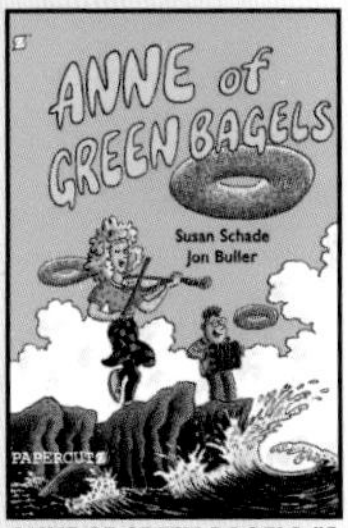
Anne of Green Bagels
Susan Schade
Jon Buller
ANNE OF GREEN BAGELS #1

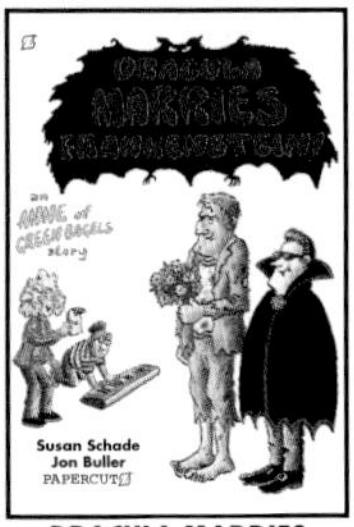
Susan Schade
Jon Buller
DRACULA MARRIES FRANKENSTEIN!

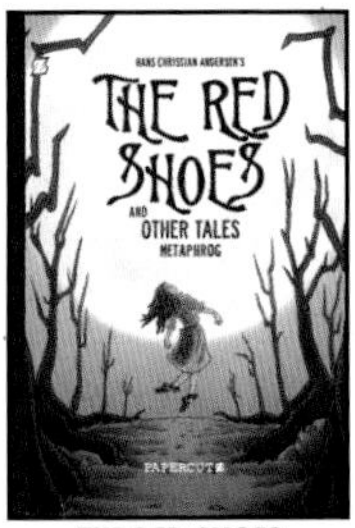
Hans Christian Andersen's
The Red Shoes
and Other Tales
Metaphrog
THE RED SHOES

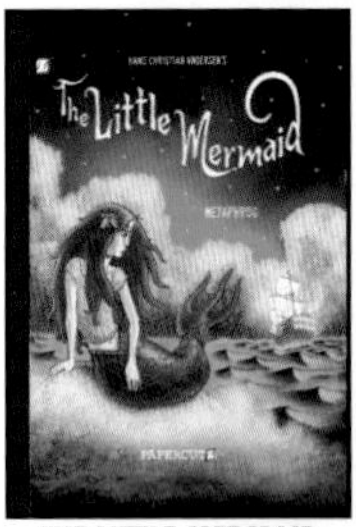
Hans Christian Andersen's
The Little Mermaid
THE LITTLE MERMAID

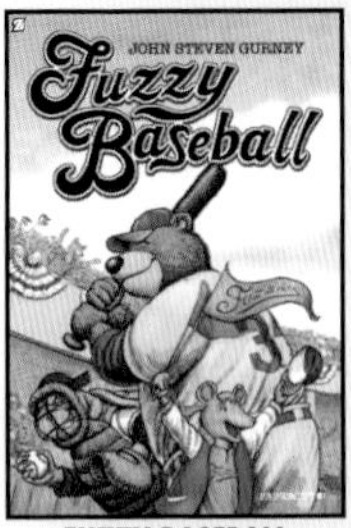
John Steven Gurney
Fuzzy Baseball
FUZZY BASEBALL

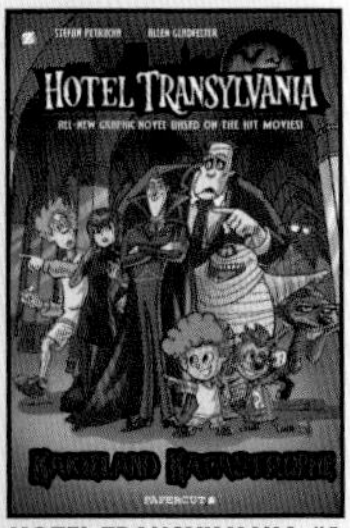
Hotel Transylvania
HOTEL TRANSYLVANIA #1

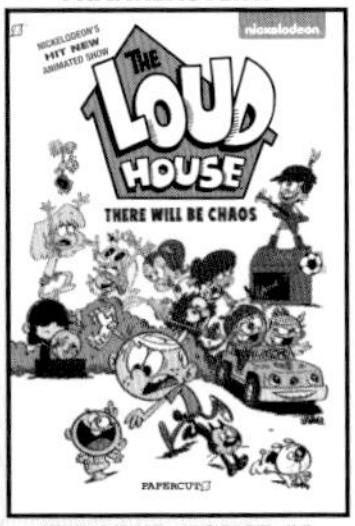
nickelodeon
The Loud House
There Will Be Chaos
THE LOUD HOUSE #1

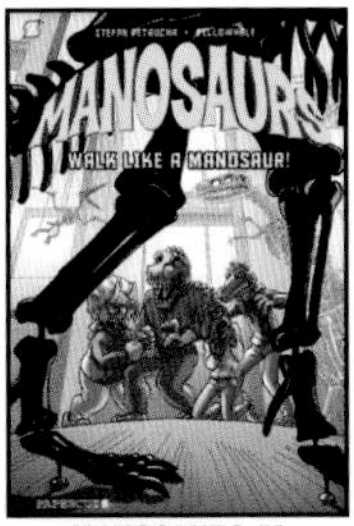
Manosaurs
Walk Like a Manosaur!
MANOSAURS #1

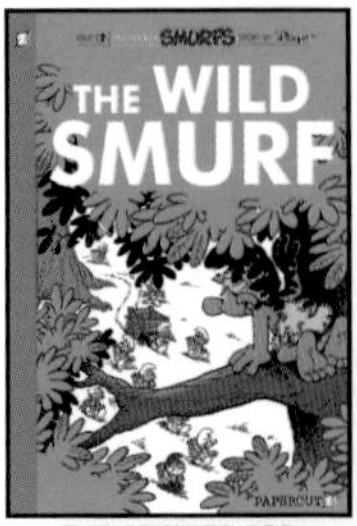
Smurfs
The Wild Smurf
THE SMURFS #21

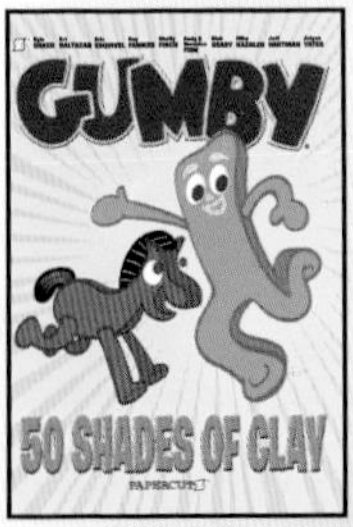
Gumby
50 Shades of Clay
GUMBY #1

THE SMURFS, THE GARFIELD SHOW, BARBIE, HOTEL TRANSYLVANIA, MANOSAURS, THE LOUD HOUSE and TROLLS graphic novels are available for $7.99 in paperback, and $12.99 in hardcover. THE ONLY LIVING BOY and GUMBY graphic novels are available for $8.99 in paperback, and $13.99 in hardcover. GERONIMO STILTON and THEA STILTON graphic novels are available for $9.99 in hardcover only. FUZZY BASEBALL graphic novels are available for $9.99 in paperback only. THE LUNCH WITCH, SCARLETT, and ANNE OF GREEN BAGELS graphic novels are available for $14.99 in paperback only. THE RED SHOES and THE LITTLE MERMAID graphic novels are available for $12.99 in hardcover only. DRACULA MARRIES FRANKENSTEIN graphic novels are available for $12.99 in paperback only.

Available from booksellers everywhere. You can also order online from www.papercutz.com. Or call 1-800-886-1223, Monday through Friday, 9–5 EST. MC, Visa, and AmEx accepted. To order by mail, please add $5.00 for postage and handling for first book ordered, $1.00 for each additional book and make check payable to NBM Publishing. Send to: Papercutz, 160 Broadway, Suite 700, East Wing, New York, NY 10038.

THE SMURFS, GUMBY, THE GARFIELD SHOW, THE LOUD HOUSE, THE ONLY LIVING BOY, BARBIE, TROLLS, GERONIMO STILTON, THEA STILTON, FUZZY BASEBALL, THE LUNCH WITCH, THE LITTLE MERMAID, HOTEL TRANSYLVANIA, MANOSAURS, THE RED SHOES, ANNE OF GREEN BAGELS, and SCARLETT graphic novels are also available wherever e-books are sold.

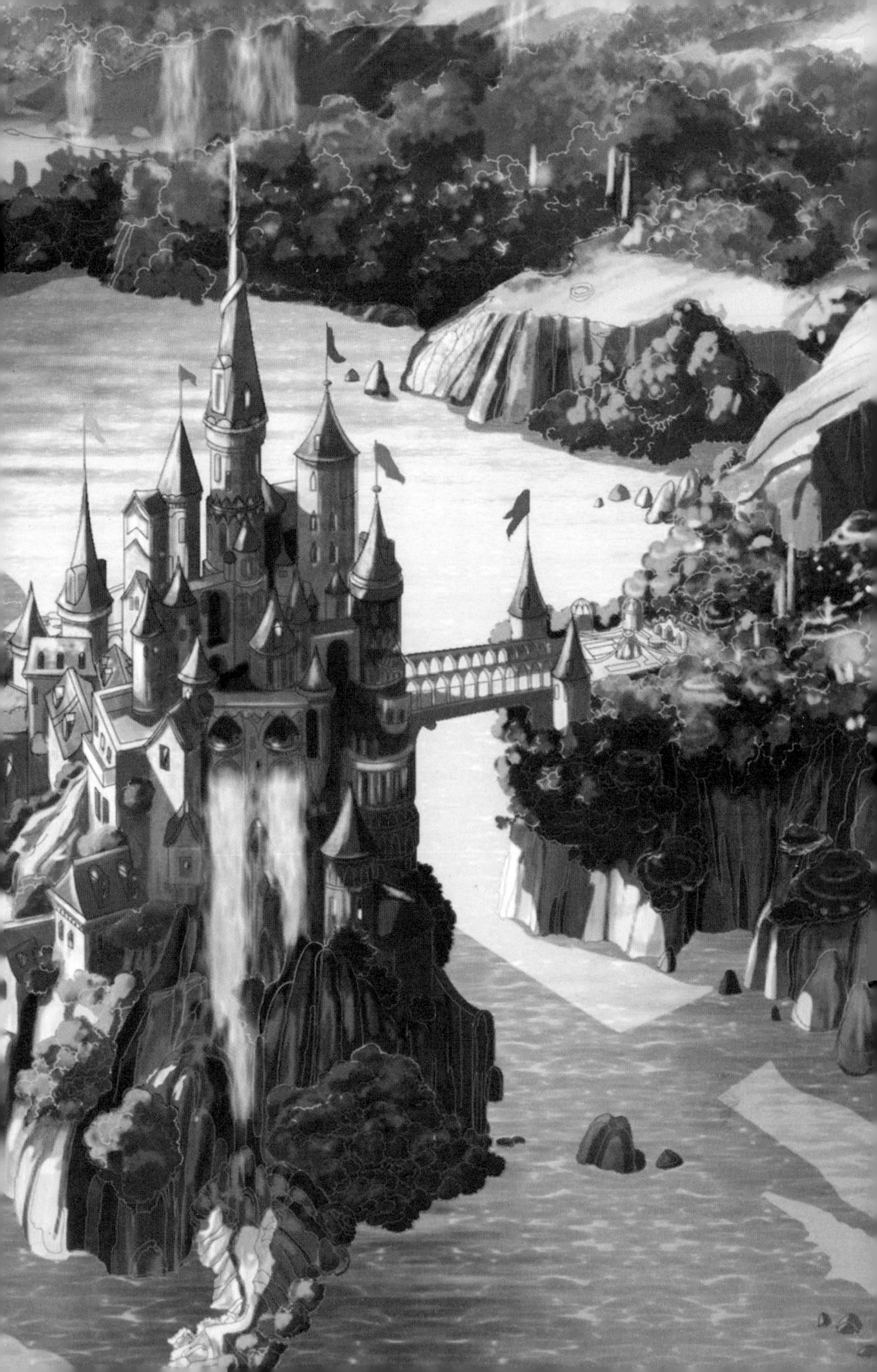